"I have been meaning to call on your father."

Ranson smiled at her. "I would like to make myself known to him, but circumstances have kept me away."

Lavinia did not want her father to come to know Lord Weston, for he would most likely judge him a perfect match for her. "Do not worry, my lord. My father is still weak from his illness and keeps to his rooms much of the time."

"Then I will wait until his health is better," Ransom replied before changing the subject. "Have you ridden in Hyde Park yet?"

"I haven't had the time."

"You should do so," he urged. "It is at its loveliest, nearly untouched by the crowd that will soon fill it so that even the flowers will go unseen."

"I will make a point to go soon."

"Then come ride with me," he cajoled. "Let me bring the mare I mentioned, for she is exactly suited to you."

"Do you always know what is best for a person?" asked Lavinia, irked by his self-confidence.

Ranson tightened his grip on her hand just enough to make her look up at him. "For you I do," he said.

She could not mistake his meaning, and her desire was to push him away and walk off the dance floor. But if she wished to avenge her sister she needed to put aside her personal desires and allow him to think he was winning her over.

"My lord," she murmured, lowering her lashes and feigning confusion, "you put me to the blush."

BOOK YOUR PLACE ON OUR WEBSITE AND MAKE THE READING CONNECTION!

We've created a customized website just for our very special readers, where you can get the inside scoop on everything that's going on with Zebra, Pinnacle and Kensington books.

When you come online, you'll have the exciting opportunity to:

- View covers of upcoming books

- Read sample chapters

- Learn about our future publishing schedule (listed by publication month *and author*)

- Find out when your favorite authors will be visiting a city near you

- Search for and order backlist books from our online catalog

- Check out author bios and background information

- Send e-mail to your favorite authors

- Meet the Kensington staff online

- Join us in weekly chats with authors, readers and other guests

- Get writing guidelines

- AND MUCH MORE!

Visit our website at
http://www.kensingtonbooks.com

THE MISTRESS THIEF

ALANA CLAYTON

ZEBRA BOOKS
Kensington Publishing Corp.
http://www.kensingtonbooks.com

10302628

For a great nephew,
Todd Breaden
and for the greatest great nephew,
Evan Alexander Breaden

ONE

Ranson Baldwin, Lord Weston, was at breakfast when he found he had lost another mistress. His surprise was not as profound as when it had occurred the first time, nor even the second; however, a third missing mistress was a nuisance that put a severe crimp in Ranson's plans.

He looked again at the note that had just been placed in his hand by the butler, but he had not misread; it remained the same. "Damnation!" he snapped, tossing the missive onto the mahogany table.

"Trouble?" asked Andrew, Viscount Stanford, who was seated across the table from Ranson. The two men had taken an early morning ride and had returned to the town house for breakfast.

Ranson propped his elbow on the table, resting his chin on his half-closed hand, a breach of manners which revealed the depth of his absorption in whatever matter had been brought to his attention. His expression was dark, and for a moment Drew doubted that he had even heard his inquiry. But before he could repeat his question, Ranson spoke.

"Another's gone missing," he complained irritably, without lifting his gaze from his plate.

Drew had no idea what his friend meant by his terse answer, and wondered whether he should interrupt his brown study to pursue the topic. He waited a moment to allow Ranson time to continue on his own. When he didn't, Drew took matters into his own hands.

"Another what?" he queried, hoping to elicit a comprehensible reply.

Ranson removed his elbow from the table and leaned back in his chair. "Another mistress," he replied shortly, disgust filling his voice.

Drew was aware that several fashionable impures had occupied Ranson's other house in London since the beginning of the Season. The current resident was a small blond woman whom he had seen only once at the theater a sennight ago. He quickly searched his memory until he recalled her name. "Felicity?" he asked, hoping he had remembered correctly.

Ranson nodded.

"Lovely woman," commented Drew.

"I thought so," said Ranson. "For all of the two weeks she occupied my house."

"Does she say why she left?"

"This isn't from Felicity," said Ranson, motioning toward the letter lying on the table between them. "It's from Jones. He and his wife are the permanent staff at the house. He only tells me she is gone, but I am assuming her disappearance is no different from the others."

Ranson hesitated, then glanced across the table at his friend. "I've attempted to keep this secret because I don't relish becoming the butt of countless jokes, but Felicity is the third mistress who has left my protection since the beginning of the Season. Joylene was the first," he said.

Drew frowned, attempting to conjure up a mental image of Joylene. Giving up, he remarked, "Don't remember the lady."

"No reason you should; she had come and gone before you arrived in Town," explained Ranson. "I arrived in London in January for Parliament. There was an unusual fog that was so thick people were forced to keep to their homes because they couldn't see to travel. A freeze immediately followed and the Thames froze over as solid as rock."

"Heard it was the worst anyone could remember," said Drew.

Ranson nodded in agreement. "It was; but it also spawned what has become known as the greatest frost fair in memory. I met Joylene on what was called the City Road, a walk running from Black Friars Bridge on the Thames. She was alone and having a difficult time negotiating her way over the slippery ice. I offered her my arm, and before a sennight had passed, I offered her my protection."

"She was passing fair, I assume," Drew commented, aware that Ranson's demireps would be judged diamonds-of-the-first water if they were members of the *haut ton*.

"Exceedingly," acknowledged Ranson. "She was small and delicate, with a cap of reddish-colored curls and whiskey-brown eyes that glittered like the topaz and diamonds I gave her."

"Always generous with the barks of frailty," observed Drew.

"Perhaps too generous, too soon," Ranson remarked. "Three days after I presented the jewels to her she disappeared."

"Without leaving a message?" inquired Drew.

"Not a word to either me or my staff," confirmed Ranson.

"Odd," mused Drew.

"It grows even more bizarre," said Ranson. "Not long after, I met Lilly one evening at Amy Wilson's. Lilly was far different from Joylene. She was tall and slim and elegant in manner. Her long, dark brown hair could cover her like a cape, and her eyes were as dark as chocolate.

"Lilly didn't last long after I set her up in my house," confided Ranson. "Just as before there was no indication as to why or how she left."

"Give her any jewels?" asked Drew.

Ranson gave a bark of laughter in appreciation of his friend's jest. "Didn't have the time," he replied. "I suppose I should be grateful for that."

"Then there was Felicity," prompted Drew.

"I met her a fortnight ago. She was young, new to the life, and surprisingly innocent. I had great hopes for our liaison," revealed Ranson. "Now she has followed the first two into oblivion.

"Dammit! But it's infuriating," burst out Ranson, slapping his hand on the table. "They were simply there one day and gone the next. There was no indication of foul play, nor of another man luring them away. They departed while the staff was out so there was no one who observed their leave-taking."

"Knew you had changed mistresses, but thought you were merely growing bored more quickly."

"If that were only true," said Ranson. "I've allowed people to think I was dissatisfied and gave them their congee. I'm fortunate to have a reputation that allows me to do so and remain believable."

"Odd that you would lose three women in a row," said Drew. "But don't suppose it's unheard of. Maybe they decided to return home and didn't want to bid you farewell."

"Perhaps," said Ranson, without any real belief.

"Don't be so quick off the mark to take another ladybird under your wing again. Look around; be selective," advised Drew.

Ranson poured himself another cup of coffee, selected an apple muffin, broke it open, and liberally spread butter over the warm center. He bit into it, chewed deliberately, and swallowed before he spoke.

"If it were up to me, my friend, I would entirely swear off women until I understood their capricious ways. However, I must have a mistress whom I can rely upon staying with me at least until the end of the Season, and I must have her quickly."

While Ranson was bemoaning his latest loss, Lavinia Peyton was rejoicing in it. She had just delivered Felicity to Hope House and was returning to London with her friend Lady Jessica Carter.

Lady Lavinia had come to Town with her father to enjoy the Season. Her aunt Hope, Lady Fitzhugh, had readily agreed to accompany her throughout the social whirl. However, once Lavinia and Jessica met they became fast friends and since Jessica was a married lady, the two young women were free to be on their own.

Lavinia was particularly pleased to have found someone whose company helped ease the pain of being parted from her sister.

"I am delighted you were able to accompany me today. I always find the trip back to Town extremely tedious," said Lavinia.

"I only hope Thomas does not find out where I have been," replied Jessica, her hands twisting nervously in her lap.

"Your husband would never expect you to have been to Hope House, even if he was aware of its existence."

"I was surprised that it was quite nice," commented Jessica. "I don't know what I expected, but certainly not such a fine house, nicely furnished and well kept."

"That is the purpose of Hope House," explained Lavinia. "We teach the women how to live in proper society. They learn how to run a household, how to dress, how to talk, and even how to read and do simple sums if they do not know."

"Your dedication is commendable," said Jessica.

"There are many others who give of their time and money to keep the house running. Most of them conceal their good deeds, knowing their husbands would not approve of their close proximity to the prostitutes; however, it merely makes them more determined to continue.

"We have had quite a few successes," continued Lavinia, her voice filled with enthusiasm. "Women have left Hope House to live among society without anyone knowing their past occupation. Some have married and raised families, others have found very good positions and we have also advanced money to several to begin small shops of their own."

"You are doing an excellent job to be certain, but aren't you afraid you'll be found out?"

"By whom?" asked Lavinia. "The women's disappearances leave barely a ripple in the Cyprian world. Most of them have no family of their own, and the men who support them think more of their horses than they do of their mistresses."

"That's a little harsh, don't you think?" asked Jessica. "I'm certain there are many gentlemen of the *ton* who care more than you claim."

"Ha!" said Lavinia.

"Take Felicity for example," said Jessica, determined to prove her point. "You convinced her to leave the protection of Lord Weston and she had nothing to say against him. Indeed, she seemed almost sad to be leaving him, particularly without so much as a note of explanation."

"The man does not deserve any consideration. You may take it from me that he is particularly heartless toward young women and has no regard for their feelings."

"You must have special knowledge of Lord Weston."

"I do," agreed Lavinia, "and none of it good."

"Is that why you encouraged Felicity to enter Hope House?" Jessica asked.

"Not only Felicity, but also Joylene and Lilly," Lavinia bragged proudly.

Jessica frowned in puzzlement. "Who are Joylene and Lilly?" she asked.

"Two other mistresses of Lord Weston. I was able to convince Joylene to leave his protection at the end of February, and Lilly in March."

Jessica's eyebrows rose. "He certainly wastes no time in replacing them," she observed.

"That should prove the truth of my accusation," said Lavinia.

"I do not doubt what you say, only that it surprises me," replied Jessica. "I wonder whether he knows of Felicity's defection yet?"

"You can be certain that his staff has already advised him she is gone, which will allow him to begin searching London this evening for a proper replacement. And as soon as he does, I'll be there to greet her."

Lavinia's lips curved into a satisfied smile. She had once again left Lord Weston with an empty love nest, and only regretted that her sister, Barbara, did not know what she had done to him. Perhaps if she did, she would return home.

Ranson, Lord Weston, was not a vain man, although he had every right to be. Ladies often spoke of him as the perfect gentleman in appearance and manner. His hair gleamed with a dozen different shades of blond and curled slightly over the collar of his always impeccably tailored coat. His blue eyes were not the pale, cold shade that caused a person to turn away with a shiver, but were a deep blue that could hold a woman pleasantly captivated until he chose to release her.

His cheekbones were high and his nose free from any unsightly bumps obtained in childhood fights. His hands were large but—as many women could attest to—they were gentle.

He was every inch the gentleman in dress, due, in part, to an excellent valet who kept his wardrobe in order and his Hessians shined to perfection. All in all, Lord Weston was the epitome of the man of every woman's dream, yet it seemed he could not keep a Bird of Paradise under his roof any longer than a fortnight.

Ranson's lips twisted in a cynical smile as he settled into Drew's town coach. "Where do you think we should begin the search for my next mistress?" he asked, turning his attention to his friend as the coach pulled away from the town house and rolled over the cobblestones.

"Theater sounds like an excellent starting place," said Drew in his customary curt speech. "Should be plenty of ladybirds flaunting their wares this early in the Season."

"Perhaps an actress might be of more use to me," mused Ranson.

"Heard there's several new ones who will be on stage this evening." Drew had not yet questioned Ranson as to why he needed a new mistress immediately and particularly one with the specific attribute of being faithful to him until the end of the Season. However, he had been drawn into the search, and he concluded there was no reason why he should refrain any longer.

"Have wondered all day why you are rushing to acquire a new mistress," said Drew. "Didn't want to ask, but find my curiosity is stronger than my good manners."

"We have known one another since we were in leading strings," replied Ranson. "There is no need to stand on ceremony with me."

Ranson glanced out the window of the coach and saw

that they would soon be at Covent Garden. "It concerns George Milford," he revealed.

"Lord Hayley? Ugly customer," commented Drew.

"As odious a blackguard as I've ever known," agreed Ranson. "And it is for that reason that I must have a mistress."

He met Drew's puzzled gaze with a wry smile. "With anyone else, I would begin with an account of Hayley's family, but I'm certain you know more about him than I do."

Drew had the reputation of being a walking depository of information on the upper ten thousand. "Last of his line," announced Drew. "Family fortune began to fail in his grandfather's time. Too fond of the green baize tables, so I've heard. Turned to less honorable ways to keep their coffers full."

"Activities which Hayley has expanded upon until the Home Office can no longer ignore him," added Ranson. "It seems he's begun to deal in stolen jewels, and gold and silver. Some say he plans and directs the robberies, and suspect that he is behind the jewel thief who is currently at work in London."

"Several large thefts have already occurred this Season," said Drew.

"Just so," agreed Ranson. "And sources have put Hayley in or around the houses before the robberies take place. Then there are the card parties he holds which go on for days with many men losing more money than they can afford; some going bankrupt in order to pay their vowels."

"Have seen it myself in my green days," attested Drew. "Good lesson, though. Never been caught by a Captain Sharp since then."

"Evidently there are many who haven't been as lucky. They've complained they were cheated, but no one's been able to catch Hayley at it so nothing can be done.

Hearsay is that he also owns a string of public houses which are never licensed," said Ranson, continuing to tick off the list of Hayley's crimes. "Then there are the rumors of a secret workshop where forgers work making counterfeit shillings."

Drew whistled lightly. "Hadn't heard that one yet," he admitted. "Must be slipping."

"I just learned about it yesterday," said Ranson. "The Home Office is attempting to keep it quiet, so that he won't be forewarned that they're investigating him."

"Won't say a word," promised Drew. "But that still doesn't explain your scramble to replace Felicity."

"Sorry. I was distracted by relating Hayley's crimes," said Ranson. "For the past several Seasons, Hayley has invited gentlemen and their mistresses for a Cyprian house party at his country estate. There the men may consort freely with the women without fear of being discovered by their wives or families.

"It has become a rather brilliant affair, so I'm told, culminating in a grand masked ball at the end of their stay. Of course, Hayley does nothing without gain, so there is a price to be paid to attend; however, invitations are readily accepted and many men have become regulars at the parties."

"Have heard of them, but never been invited," said Drew. "Hayley probably thinks I'm too much of an old hunk to accept."

Ranson laughed. "You're neither old nor miserly, but he plays it safe and only invites those men who indicate an interest."

"So the Home Office wants you to help put a stop to the Cyprian house parties? Doesn't sound important enough for their intervention."

"They wouldn't care a whit if it were merely a house party. It's what occurs during the event that makes it of interest to them," explained Ranson.

"More than just consorting with beautiful women, I suppose," said Drew.

"Some of the women have not returned from the house parties," Ranson revealed. "At first, it was assumed that they had decided to move on, perhaps to return home, or try their luck in Bath or Brighton. However, the disappearances have become too numerous to ignore.

"The men who leave the party without the women they have brought are closemouthed. Several theories are being bandied about to explain the men's silence concerning the missing women."

"Can't be good," Drew interjected.

Ranson nodded his head in agreement. "It isn't. Speculation is that Hayley has found a market for English women sold into slavery in the Far East, and that men who are short of funds or who are in debt to Hayley bring unsuspecting women to him to sell."

A sound of disgust emanated from Drew and he shifted on the plush squabs of the coach.

"That isn't all," warned Ranson. "The second theory is that men who have grown tired of their mistresses and are experiencing difficulty in ridding themselves of the women, turn them over to Hayley. They have found that it's the easiest and most inexpensive way to eliminate the problem of their unwanted fancy pieces."

The coach fell silent for several minutes when Ranson finished speaking.

"Don't like to think of a woman being kept as a slave," said Drew in a carefully restrained voice.

"Nor do I," acknowledged Ranson. "That is why I agreed to help. If men are foolish enough to fall into Hayley's trap and lose their money then that is their business; however, an unsuspecting woman who attends a party, ends up being sold and transported out of the country is something else altogether. The Home Office wants me to attend one of the parties to see whether I can find anything substantial in the rumors and, if so, to attempt to find concrete proof against Hayley."

"Anything I can do?" asked Drew.

Ranson looked out the window and realized they were already on Bow Street, fast approaching the theater. "Exactly what we are doing; help me find a mistress. Perhaps I need someone who is older and more experienced in the profession, who will be eager to accept my protection and less likely to leave it," he suggested. "Since the invitations to the house party will soon be issued, I have little time to spare."

"We'll find someone suitable," vowed Drew. "I have a few candidates in mind already."

"I didn't know you were such a fancy man," bantered Ranson.

"Not as much as you are, but I've been known to charm a lady or two."

Their mood was much lighter as they arrived at Covent Garden and entered through the Greek Doric portico. They made their way through the crush that filled the vestibule and ascended the staircase to their box.

The next afternoon Drew and Ranson were sitting in two comfortable chairs with a bottle and glasses on a small table between them at White's on St. James's Street. The gentleman's club was a perfect place to find both comfort and privacy while discussing the past evening.

"Meet anyone you think might do?" asked Drew.

"Perhaps, but I want someone who is perfect for the job."

"May be forced to settle for less," observed Drew, pouring each of them a drink.

"What do you think of Candice?" Ranson spoke of a woman both of them knew who had been a fixture of London's Cyprian society for several years.

"Lovely woman, to be sure, but she cannot keep her tongue between her teeth once she has a cup or two of Regent's punch."

Ranson stretched his legs out before him and slid down in his chair. His elbows rested on the chair arms, and his hands cradled his glass. "I will count her out then," he decided, "since I may need someone who can keep a secret. Do you have any suggestions?"

"Jeannette? She's younger than what you wanted, but she's awake on every suit and seemed to take a fancy to you."

"I'll keep her in mind," said Ranson, remembering the young woman he had met the evening before. "I still have a few days before I must choose and I want to visit a few other schools of Venus before I make a final decision."

"Where to this evening?" asked Drew.

"I must make an appearance at the Harringtons' ball before I renew my search."

"Suppose I should do my duty also," replied Drew.

"Good," said Ranson, straightening in his chair. "We'll go together, stay a few socially acceptable minutes, then continue looking for the perfect ladybird."

Lavinia's involvement in collecting Lord Weston's mistresses left her unaware of the stir she was causing among the single gentlemen of the *ton*. She was truly deserving of the title diamond-of-the-first-water. Slender and of medium height, she moved with an effortless grace that many women never achieved.

Her hair was black as a raven's wing and framed a face with delicate brows over blue-gray eyes. More than one poem had been written in praise of the delicious dimple near the right corner of her perfectly formed lips.

Her manner and reputation were unassailable and several men felt she would make their life complete if she would only agree to be their wife. Although Lavinia was unfailingly polite, she did not seriously consider any of them. They might have been surprised to learn that her plans did not include marrying until she had satisfactorily settled the matter of Lord Weston.

Lavinia and Jessica were at the Harringtons' ball, each holding a cup of punch while watching a quadrille take place on the dance floor.

"Did Thomas miss you yesterday?" asked Lavinia.

"I don't believe he even knew I was gone," replied Jessica, with a sad smile.

"Some women would call that a blessing."

Jessica sighed. "I know you are attempting to cheer me up, but if you had only seen Thomas when he was courting me. He sent flowers every day with lovely notes accompanying them. I vow, I don't believe there was an event held that Season that we didn't attend. It was such a happy swirl that my head was continually spinning with delight. He simply swept me away with his romantic nature and before I knew it he was offering for me and I was accepting."

"It sounds wonderful," said Lavinia.

"It was," Jessica agreed, "but as soon as we were wed Thomas began to change. He began going out alone more and more often. Soon, we seldom went anywhere together . . ."

"I believe I see Thomas coming our way," warned Lavinia, interrupting Jessica's account of her faltering marriage.

Jessica turned pale and lifted an unsteady cup of punch to her lips.

"Ladies," said Thomas Carter, coming to rest before them.

Lavinia studied him as she returned his smile. Carter was a striking man, tall and broad-shouldered, with unruly black hair and captivating eyes. A change of clothing and he would appear right at home on the deck of a pirate's ship. Lavinia could understand how Jessica had immediately fallen in love with him. It was unfortunate she could not have foreseen what marriage to him would be like.

"Mr. Carter," acknowledged Lavinia.

"Surely we are well enough acquainted for you to call me Thomas," he insisted, bowing over her hand.

"I will do my best," she replied, reclaiming her hand.

"Jessica," he said, turning to his wife. "I find this event deadly dull and am going elsewhere to find more satisfactory entertainment."

Jessica's face fell with disappointment. "Oh, Thomas, couldn't you stay just this once?" she pleaded.

"You will not even miss me," he replied, taking her hand and patting it. "Lavinia, will you keep my wife from running off with another man and see her safely home?"

"I'll be pleased to do so," acquiesced Lavinia.

"Then I'll bid you both good night," he said, bowing briefly before turning and striding quickly from the ballroom.

"It is like this nearly every evening," complained Jessica, watching her husband disappear into the crowd. "It is as if he cannot bear to be with me any longer."

"You know that isn't true," said Lavinia, attempting to comfort her. "There are not many men who like crowded ballrooms and punch."

"If it were only just that," replied Jessica.

"You will be better off not to dwell on it," advised Lavinia. "You are not going to sit out every dance this evening. We will each accept the next gentleman who asks us to dance."

"I couldn't," demurred Jessica. "I'm a married woman."

"Being married does not mean you are dead. Now, put a smile on your face or no one will approach us this evening."

"Have spoken to the Harringtons. Ready to take our leave?" asked Drew.

The two men stood inside the doorway of the ballroom, observing the assembly of the *ton*'s elite. A rainbow would be put to shame by the varying hues of the ladies' gowns, which stood out in stark contrast to the gentlemen's black evening dress.

"I was until I saw that Incomparable across the room. Do you know who she is?"

"Which one?" asked Drew, unable to distinguish which lady Ranson was admiring.

"The one with the shimmery dress and the black hair. I believe that's Lady Jessica Carter with her."

"Jessica's here?" said Drew, his usually calm façade sparking with interest.

"That's right. You were once taken with her, weren't you?"

"Nothing serious," commented Drew. "We went about together some, but she met Carter and was soon wed." Drew searched the room for Jessica. "Ah, I see her now."

"And the other woman?" insisted Ranson.

"Daughter of Pheneas Peyton, Lord Cranston," revealed Drew. "Heard he was in town for the Season. That would be Lavinia, who is the middle daughter. Has an older daughter, Barbara, who left England for the Continent several years ago. There's also a younger girl, I believe by the name of Abigail, who should be ready for her come-out soon."

Ranson paid little attention to the information concerning the older and younger daughters, for it was the middle daughter who commanded his full attention. In his eye, she stood out in the room like a candle in the dark. The luster of her silver silk gown gleamed beneath the crystal chandelier, as did her glossy black hair. He could not tell the color of her eyes from this distance, but he was certain they would be uncommon.

He suddenly grew impatient. He wanted to be near her—to speak words that would cause a flush to rise to her cheeks, to inhale the delicate perfume, which he was confident she wore, to look deep into her eyes and see himself reflected there.

"Introduce me," he demanded.

Drew glanced sharply at Ranson. He had never before known him to react so strongly to the mere sight of a lady.

"Good heavens! No!" exclaimed Lavinia, staring across the room.

"What is it?" asked Jessica, alarmed at her friend's outburst.

"It is Lord Weston; he's here."

"Where?" asked Jessica, peering about, searching for the figure of Lord Weston in the crowded room.

"There, by the door," whispered Lavinia, "and I believe he is looking at us."

"Don't be absurd," remarked Jessica. "Why should he show any interest in either of us?" Her eyes widened in dismay as a thought struck her. "Unless Felicity changed her mind and returned to his protection. If so, she would have confessed who lured her away, and he could be seeking you out to ring a peal over your head."

"I cannot believe Lord Weston would cause a scandal in the middle of the Harringtons' ball," replied Lavinia, not at all certain of her conclusion.

"Why, he is with Drew," said Jessica, a pleased smile on her face.

Lavinia forced her attention to the man who stood by Lord Weston's side. He was of medium height and build, with light hair verging on red. There would most probably be freckles scattered across a nose that appeared to have been broken at least once in his lifetime. His expression was pleasant and he looked as if anger would be completely out of place on his face.

"Who is Drew?" she asked, after she had completed her survey.

"Andrew, Lord Stanford," clarified Jessica. "We met at my come-out and for a while we . . . Well, until I met Thomas I thought something more serious might come of our acquaintance. He is a truly good man: intelligent, kind and gentle."

"But not dashing," Lavinia added.

"Back then I was unaware that dashing was not a good trait for a husband," Jessica confessed with a wry smile. "But, look, I believe you are right. They are coming toward us."

"Oh fie! What am I to do?" cried Lavinia in a hushed voice.

Jessica took her elbow tightly in her hand and squeezed until she had Lavinia's attention. "You will do exactly as you always do. You will smile and be a polite to a peer of the realm. If he knows you have been stealing his mistresses, it is too late to do anything. If he is unaware of your deeds then you need only endure a few minutes of his company before he will be gone."

"At all events, I have precious little choice," replied Lavinia, "for they are nearly upon us."

TWO

As he drew closer, Ranson found that his first opinion of Lady Lavinia's looks was accurate. She was, by far, the loveliest woman he had met all Season, and he wondered whether he would still be captivated when she spoke or whether she would be only another simpering miss.

"Lady Jessica, wonderful to see you again," said Drew, as the two men paused in front of the women.

Jessica extended her hand to Drew as color surged into her cheeks. "I am happy to see you also," she replied, holding his gaze until Ranson cleared his throat.

"May I introduce Lord Weston?" said Drew. "Lady Jessica Carter."

"Ma'am," replied Ranson, bowing over her hand.

"And this is Lady Lavinia," said Jessica. "Her father is Lord Cranston."

"Lady Lavinia," acknowledged Drew with another bow.

Ranson claimed her hand and raised it to his lips. It was no courtesy air kiss that he offered, but he pressed his lips against the softness of her skin for just a moment too long in society's eyes.

"Lady Lavinia, it is an honor," he said, as she pulled her hand from his grasp.

"My lord," she replied curtly.

"I do not believe I have seen you in London before."

Lavinia, grateful that he did not immediately charge her with removing his mistresses, breathed a sigh of relief. Evidently he had no idea that she had played such a large part in keeping his love nest empty.

Ranson heard her sigh and thought perhaps he had made a greater impression than he had first presumed. He was encouraged; since his involvement with the Home Office and their case against Hayley, he had little time to spend dangling after a lady.

Lavinia had no desire at all to speak to Lord Weston, but if she did not it might cause speculation as to why she was being rude without reason for it. As Jessica pointed out, Lord Weston was much sought after by the ladies of polite society.

"I was here when my sister came out," she revealed, "however, that was sometime ago. Since then my father has suffered ill health and has not been able to make the trip."

"I hope he is doing better now."

"He is in Town for my sake, but he is not fully recovered," said Lavinia. Weston's gaze was still fixed on her and it made her vaguely uncomfortable.

"I must call upon him and extend my best wishes," he said.

"Are you acquainted with my father?" inquired Lavinia.

"Not yet, but I fully intend for us to be quite close before the Season is over." Lord Weston's confident smile filled Lavinia with trepidation. She had absolutely no desire for him to work his way into the good graces of her father while she went about luring away each mistress he acquired.

He had been mistaken, thought Ranson. The sigh must have been for someone else, for the encounter was not going as he had planned. While Lady Lavinia was not the mindless green girl he prayed she would not be, she also did not indicate she wished to carry their acquaintance beyond an introduction. He could not allow her to slip away before he learned more about her.

"Would you care to dance, my lady?"

"I could not desert Jessica," she objected quickly.

Ranson glanced at Jessica and Drew. The two had moved a few steps away and were deeply involved in conversation. "It does not look as if she needs your company for the moment."

Lavinia saw that he spoke the truth and made a note to speak to Jessica about leaving her alone with Lord Weston if they should meet again. "The floor is quite crowded," she pointed out.

"I believe I can find a place for us," he replied, holding out his hand toward her.

Lavinia was certain that the smile he gave her would have sent most women into silent awe. All it did for Lavinia was remind her how helpless her sister had been against Lord Weston's renowned charm. However, there was nothing left to do but place her hand in his and walk with him onto the dance floor, or she would draw unwanted attention to herself.

The warmth of Lord Weston's hand engulfed hers as she accompanied him onto the floor. As he said, space miraculously appeared, and he guided her into a waltz. His touch burned through the thin fabric at her waist and she felt certain that the gown would require repairs once the dance was over. She did not dare meet his eyes, but kept her gaze purposely directed into the crowd eddying around them.

"Are you always so silent?" Ranson asked.

"I have nothing of note to say," answered Lavinia, allowing her irritation to slip beneath her guard.

"I cannot believe that," responded Ranson.

"We could speak of the weather, which has been uncommonly good," said Lavinia. "Or perhaps you would like to tell me about the latest bit of blood you have acquired at Tattersall's."

Ranson laughed, then leaned closer to her. A light scent of roses wafted up to him and he drew her nearer. "While I take great pride in my prime cattle, I would not think to waste time talking about them to such a lovely lady."

His voice was soft and his breath brushed the tendrils of hair that had been left in gentle curls around her face. Lavinia thought her heart would cease beating altogether when his lips brushed against her ear. She did not understand her reaction to Lord Weston, but decided to abandon her fruitless thoughts and gather her wits.

"You would not bore me, my lord, for I have ridden all my life and my father takes great pride in his stables."

"Ah. Something else we have in common," he remarked, looking down at her while keeping their bodies a little closer than what was thought acceptable in polite society. "I believe your father and I will get along very well indeed."

"I do not see that it signifies," grumbled Lavinia, wishing to discourage him from seeking an introduction to her father. Her revenge would be far more difficult if he became friends with her father. She wondered how he could contemplate such a friendship after what he had done to her sister.

"Nothing that you need to worry about," he replied, just as the music ended. Ranson did not want to allow her to leave his arms, but the dancers were dispersing, leaving the two of them standing alone. He could not ruin her reputation no matter how much he yearned to place his lips against the dimple in her cheek. Releasing her, he tucked her arm in the crook of his elbow and they began to stroll slowly off the floor.

"Since we are discussing animals, perhaps you would

care to ride in Hyde Park? I have a mare that would suit you very well."

Lavinia was alarmed at her continued response to his closeness. He was her enemy after all, and she should be pulling away from him instead of enjoying the texture of his coat beneath her fingers. "I have a horse," replied Lavinia shortly, in a vain attempt to discourage any further discussion.

"But not one such as this, I'll wager. She is black in color and has good bottom. Yet, she is gentle enough for a lady."

"I do not require a gentle animal," responded Lavinia.

Ranson smiled. "Then you need only ask and she will respond to any situation." They were nearing Jessica and Drew, who were still involved in conversation. "Will you ride with me tomorrow?" he asked, placing his hand over hers.

She almost yielded, almost agreed to ride with the man who had hurt her sister; then good sense reasserted itself. "I'm sorry, my lord, but I'm promised to another event tomorrow. Lady Clifton is holding a water party on the Serpentine in St. James's Park. I am told it will be quite a grand affair, with carpeted boats and supper from Gunter's. I'm certain you understand."

Ranson didn't understand anything that kept her from him, but they had reached Jessica and Drew and he had no further opportunity to convince her to see him again.

Drew and Jessica turned to them as they approached. "Don't see how you managed to squeeze onto the floor," remarked Drew.

"That is part of the enjoyment," said Ranson, looking at Lavinia. "Thank you for the dance."

"You are welcome, my lord," replied Lavinia, removing her hand from his arm.

"Would like to take you in to dinner," said Drew to Jessica, "but we are promised elsewhere."

"I understand," she replied. "It was delightful to see you again."

As the gentlemen bid the ladies good-bye, Ranson took time to address Lavinia in an aside. "If you should change your mind about riding . . ."

"I won't," she replied, quickly cutting him off.

He nodded, turned, and followed Drew from the room.

"You look pleased with yourself," said Lavinia to Jessica.

Jessica unfurled her fan and waved it before her flushed face. "He was as amiable as I remembered," she replied.

"You still retain a soft spot for him, don't you?"

Jessica hesitated for a moment. "More than I realized," she admitted. "And how did you get along with Lord Weston?" she asked once she had regained her composure.

"We shared a quite brief and common conversation," said Lavinia.

"But you danced; surely that was uncommon."

"Not as much as you would think from a man with such a reputation for charming ladies," prevaricated Lavinia. "I was more than happy when it was over."

"I wish I could have danced with Drew; however, Thomas would have heard about it and been angry. He knew Drew and I were going about together when he began courting me, and he has never gotten over his jealousy."

"It sounds as if you are sorry you didn't wait for Drew to offer."

"Perhaps, I am," confessed Jessica. "I admit I fell head over heels for Thomas when we first met, but my eyes were opened shortly after the marriage. If he hadn't rushed me into being wed I would have probably seen his true character and refused him."

"He was well aware of what he was doing," judged Lavinia.

"Of course," Jessica agreed. "Now I can see that he had it planned out like a military campaign, but then I only saw the roses and moonlight." She sighed, leading the way to a row of gilt chairs placed along the wall of the room, and taking a seat.

Lavinia sat down beside her, thankful to be off her feet for a while. "He must have loved you to have pursued you so relentlessly."

"I have come to the belief that he married me only for my money." Jessica bowed her head, staring at her hands clasped in the lap of her pink satinet gown.

Lavinia felt a stab of pity for her friend. "Surely you are mistaken," she objected.

"I had hoped so, but every day it grows clearer. I am telling you nothing new when I say Thomas had not even a modest amount of money before we wed. Father was against my accepting his offer—said I should marry someone with a title and at least some money—until I threatened to elope to Gretna Green. At that point, he agreed, but he made it impossible for Thomas to get his hands on any large amount of money. Father agreed to pay for our household expenses and my expenses; however he left little in Thomas's control."

"I suppose he gambles for his money as most men do," said Lavinia.

"I imagine," agreed Jessica, "but he does not do it well enough to earn a great amount. I suspect he's involved in something shady, but I am in no position to prove it."

"Ignore him and go your own way," advised Lavinia. "That is what many ladies do when their husband is less than perfect."

"It is demeaning to think that I cannot hold the interest of my own husband," said Jessica. "But, I suppose, no more than realizing he only married me for money."

"Do not allow this to destroy your spirits," advised Lavinia. "None of it is your fault, and it does not reflect on you, but on Thomas, who is totally unworthy of you."

A thin smile appeared on Jessica's face. "I don't know what I would do without you boosting my morale now and again."

"Come along," ordered Lavinia. "We are going to stop hiding in the corner and enjoy ourselves this evening." Linking her arm with Jessica's, she led her out into the crush of the ballroom.

"Was the lovely Lady Lavinia as enchanting up close as she was from across the room?" asked Drew, as he followed Ranson into the coach.

"A little cool, but I can deal with that," said Ranson confidently. "It is only a matter of finding the time."

"Don't let the lady hear you say that or it will be over before it's begun."

"I would never be that crack-brained," Ranson replied with a smile. "I'm only sorry I could not stay longer, but it's critical that I find a woman who is willing to attend Hayley's house party."

"We'll find someone soon," promised Drew. "Still have a few fancy pieces in mind that we haven't met."

"I will be happy to have this over and done with," grumbled Ranson. "I am anxious to begin my pursuit of Lady Lavinia in earnest to determine whether she is able to hold my interest for more than a fortnight."

"Could be she'll be taken by the time you get back from Hayley's," remarked Drew.

"Impossible," said Ranson, but a frown creased his forehead nevertheless.

* * *

Lord Cranston, Lavinia's father, was still awake when she returned home that evening.

"Are you feeling worse, Father?" she asked anxiously, crossing the room to lay her hand against his forehead.

"Not at all," he said, taking her hand and holding it in his. "I am feeling better and did not want to go to bed so early."

Relief flooded through Lavinia. She had attempted to put off her come-out until the next Season so that her father could completely recover, but he had insisted that he felt well enough to come to Town.

"Did you have a good time?" he asked.

"It was the same as usual," she replied, still thinking of Lord Weston and how his arms felt about her.

"Not tiring of London so soon, are you?"

"I have had too many late nights, so I came home early to get a few hours of extra sleep."

"I had hoped attending the Season would raise your spirits," he remarked.

"I may have a fit of the dismals now and then, but overall my spirits are fine," she objected. "You must attend to your health and not worry about me."

"You have been out of sorts since Barbara left and you cannot convince me otherwise," argued her father.

"I have missed her," admitted Lavinia. "But it is nothing for you to fret over."

"I hope not, for I'm certain she would have never left if she had known you would become down-pinned."

"I am nothing of the sort!" Lavinia protested again. "We are going to Richmond on a picnic tomorrow if the weather is fair. Does that sound like something I would do if I were on my last legs?"

Lord Cranston smiled up at her, having gotten the response he sought. "You have too much energy for me," he said, getting to his feet. "Come, we will walk upstairs together. It's time I retired, also."

"You will tell me if you begin to feel worse, won't you?" she asked as they strolled out of the room arm in arm.

"You shall be the very first," he assured her.

Thomas Carter's nose wrinkled as he climbed into the hackney he had hired. It was offensive both in appearance and odor. He was happy he did not have far to go in it.

"Is this the best you could do?" asked the woman who was already gingerly seated on the worn squabs.

Before Thomas was seated, the coach started moving over the cobblestones in a bone-jarring pace which proved without a doubt that there was nothing at all left in the vehicle to cushion the passengers from the jolts of the ride.

"I could find nothing else available on such short notice," he snapped. "I'm certain you've ridden in much worse."

"But I do not need to do so now," she replied in a miffed voice.

Thomas did not mean to lose her even if it meant putting on a pleasant front when his temper was so near the surface. "Now, Jeannette, bear with me." He took her hand and lifted it to his lips, holding her gaze with dark eyes he knew she could not resist.

"I am just as upset as you are that we must ride in such a ragged coach, but I promise this is the last time it will happen."

"Well . . ." she said, her anger beginning to melt before the heat in his voice, which promised a repeat of the night before.

"Stay with me and you will experience things you've never envisioned," he pledged, leaning over to brush his lips across hers tantalizingly.

"All right," said Jeanette, aware that she should not agree so quickly, but unable to deny his plea. She had been disappointed that Lord Weston had not paid more attention to her when she met him, but her vanity was appeased when Thomas Carter had seemed immediately taken with her.

"We have arrived," he said, looking out the window of the coach. "See, I promised it would be a short trip."

They had stopped in front of a brick town house which, while not in the best part of Town, was still far more respectable than any other Jeanette had entered. He was the first gentleman who had taken her to call on a friend. She allowed herself to dream that she was more than just another light-skirt to him.

Thomas handed her out of the coach and turned to follow her up the three shallow steps to the door. His booted foot came down on the hem of her skirt, but he quickly removed it as he heard the delicate fabric rip.

Jeannette gave a small cry of distress as she lifted her skirt and appraised the damage.

"I'm so sorry, my dear," said Thomas, looking abashed. "It was all my fault. I'm afraid I was paying more attention to you than to where I was stepping. I'm certain Lord Hayley will have a maid who can put it right in a few minutes."

Jeannette could not be angry with a man who couched his apology in such terms of flattery. "Do not give it another thought," she replied, lifting her skirt and stepping up the remaining two steps. "It is nothing that cannot be repaired."

The door was opened by a butler and they were ushered into a marble-floored foyer with oak-paneled walls. At nearly the same moment, George Melford, Lord Hayley, stepped into the hall from an adjoining room.

He was barely taller than Jeannette and of slight build; however, his dress was impeccable, which drew attention away from his small stature. His hair had been dark in his salad days, but silver was gradually encroaching into the thinning strands. Overall, his appearance did not live up to his reputation. He looked much more the gentleman than Jeannette thought he would.

"Carter, I see you have brought a lovely lady to visit," said Hayley, by way of greeting.

"I have," agreed Thomas. "This is Jeanette Norville."

Hayley moved closer and took her hand. "A pleasure, Miss Norville."

"Please, call me Jeanette," she said, meeting his gaze and at once realizing she had misjudged the man. His eyes were small and dark—bestial some might say—and she would not have been at all surprised if he had licked his lips in anticipation as he examined her from head to toe. It was all she could do not to jerk her hand from his.

She again recalled meeting Lord Weston only a few nights before, thinking she certainly had not wanted to pull away from him. He was ever so handsome and made her feel as important as any lady of the *ton*. She had heard he was looking for a mistress, and hoped more would come of their introduction; however, he had left without indicating she would see him again.

"We had a slight accident at your door," said Thomas, drawing her attention. "I stepped on Jeanette's skirt and caused a tear. I told her you would have someone who could help her repair it."

"How distressful," remarked Hayley. He turned toward the butler. "Jarvis, call Lizzie and have her accompany Miss Norville upstairs to mend her gown." He turned his attention back to Jeanette. "Lizzie is a wonder with a needle, I'm told, and I'm certain she will have you put to right in no time at all."

Jeanette was relieved to follow the small maid up the stairs and out of Hayley's sight. She did not like the man and would be happy when Thomas finished his business and they could leave.

The two men watched the maid and Jeanette until they disappeared from view. "She will do nicely," said Hayley. "Much the best of the others you've brought me."

"It isn't easy to find women who fill your specifications," complained Thomas.

"Don't tell me I've decimated London's prostitutes so quickly," replied Hayley, leading the way into the library.

"There have been too many disappearing lately and the others are becoming more selective. You would think they were all dukes' daughters choosing a husband, rather than the doxies they are," Thomas replied, his lips curling in a disdainful snarl.

"I'm confident you'll manage," said Hayley, reaching into his desk and pulling out a bag of money. He counted out a sum and handed it to Thomas. "After all, you have an incentive."

Thomas smiled thinly and tucked the money away. "For the time being," he agreed. "But as soon as I get my hands on Jessica's money, I won't need to be sweet-talking strumpets to turn over to you."

"I'll be sorry to lose your talent," replied Hayley. "You've been my most productive source."

"I'm certain my mother would have expected more from me than being a pimp," remarked Thomas, a sour expression on his face.

Hayley laughed out loud. "More of us than you would think are pimps in one way or another."

"Then I'll leave them to you," said Thomas. "And Jeanette, too. I'm glad to have her and her constant complaining out of my hands and into yours."

"She won't be complaining long," promised Hayley, an anticipatory gleam filling his eyes as he thought of the woman upstairs. If she was as unruly as Carter indicated, he would need to spend more time than usual with her. The men to whom he sold his wares liked their women docile.

Thomas nodded and stepped through the door to the outside. He stood for a moment and drew in a deep breath, feeling the need to cleanse his body of the air in Hayley's house. He descended the shallow steps and walked across the cobblestones, looking up at the upper stories of the house before he entered the coach. Jeanette's face appeared briefly at a window, hair disheveled and mouth opened in a silent scream, until she was jerked back into the dimness of the room.

Thomas patted the pocket where he had stored Hayley's money and climbed into the distasteful hackney, hoping no one would observe him in such an unseemly vehicle.

"Thomas had not returned home when I left to meet you," confided Jessica, as she and Lavinia strolled along a path in Hyde Park.

The two women had decided to forego a carriage ride in order to admire the beauty of the park from a closer vantage point. Flowers were in bloom and the grass was nearly too green to appear genuine. The sky was clear, with only a few wispy, white clouds scattered in the perfect blue expanse. Altogether, nature could not have cooperated more to enhance their walk.

Lavinia felt a twinge of regret that such a pleasant afternoon was going to be overshadowed by Thomas's wrongdoings. However, Jessica was her friend and at the moment an unhappy one. If talking about Thomas helped, then she would listen.

"Perhaps he was caught up in gambling and forgot the time," Lavinia suggested. "You know how gentlemen are when they gather around the green baize table."

"Do you think so?" asked Jessica, a hopeful note in her voice.

"I think it's highly likely," replied Lavinia, with more assurance than she felt. "You should be relieved that he does not subject you to such scenes as that."

Jessica followed Lavinia's gaze to see Lord Weston standing with a woman not far away. "She is . . ."

"A candidate for his next mistress, I'll wager."

"She is pretty," ventured Jessica.

"I wouldn't expect anything less of him," Lavinia commented.

"Look. She's leaving him standing there," remarked Jessica in disbelief.

Lavinia glanced again in Lord Weston's direction, and as Jessica had said, the woman was walking quickly toward the entrance of the park, leaving the earl staring after her in what appeared to be puzzlement.

A satisfied smile curved Lavinia's lips. "It looks as if that is one woman who is not impressed by his lordship."

"And one that you won't need to rescue from his clutches," added Jessica.

"I find that I'm enjoying our walk far more than I expected," said Lavinia, linking her arm with Jessica's and continuing down the path.

"What was that all about?" asked Drew, appearing at Ranson's side.

"I haven't the slightest idea. We met not two nights ago and I could not get her off my arm. But today you would have thought I was going to attack her at any moment," complained Ranson. "I supposed I can strike her off my list of possibilities."

"Don't let her put a damper on your search. Probably

wouldn't have suited anyway," remarked Drew by way of appeasement.

Ranson's face settled into a gloomy expression. "That's all well and good, but I'm beginning to think I won't find anyone to suit," he muttered.

"Takes time."

"And that is one thing I have little of," said Ranson.

"Might as well continue," suggested Drew. "Perhaps we'll find the perfect woman for your needs before we leave the park."

"There's always tonight," answered Ranson, rallying quickly. "I'm encouraged that we're going to visit Madam Vivian's establishment this evening. There's usually a multitude of lovely fancy articles there."

"Don't know how she does it, but she attracts the best," agreed Drew, matching his step to Ranson's as they proceeded along the path toward Rotten Row.

"Let's hope she doesn't disappoint me this time for I must make a decision quickly." Ranson had the urge to resort to the childish act of crossing his fingers for luck, but did not. Surely things could not get worse than they were.

"Is there something wrong with me?" he asked Drew that evening as they stood in Madam Vivian's drawing room.

Drew surveyed Ranson from top to bottom. "Nothing amiss I can see," he replied.

"Have I grown fangs? Hair on my face? Perhaps two heads?"

Drew leaned forward and peered at him closely. "Seem normal to me, but then, some might question my taste," he answered, laughing at his own jest.

Ranson scowled. "Look around us," he ordered. "Whom do you see nearby?"

"No one."

"That's just it! Here we stand in a room full of lovely women, and we are being ignored like the plague. Not one woman has approached us, and when I attempt to speak to someone, she turns and practically runs away."

"Does seem unusual," acknowledged Drew. "Ah, there's Madam Vivian. She'll know what's put everything at sixes and sevens tonight."

Madam Vivian had spent her younger days as one of the most popular courtesans in London. As the years passed, she had done what many Fashionable Impures could not. She had accepted her age and had opened a nunnery of her own. She was wildly successful and could match a gentleman with a woman of their qualifications for an evening's dalliance or for an extended period of time. Some called her the Cyprian Broker and she more than lived up to her name.

Madam Vivian gave Ranson a welcome smile as he and Drew approached. Both were favorites who treated her girls with more respect than other gentlemen.

"My lord, I'm happy to see you again. The evenings are always more lively when you are here."

"I doubt whether you will feel that way this evening," Ranson replied. "It seems I'm casting a pall over the festivities."

"What do you mean?" asked Madam Vivian.

"Whenever I approach any of the women, they scamper away like frightened mice."

After a sympathetic pause Madam Vivian spoke. "Oh, no, I was afraid of something like this. I apologize, my lord, I will speak with them immediately. I warned them not to listen to rumors, but once they get something in their heads they tend to act like silly children."

"Rumors?" questioned Ranson. "What are you talking about?"

"I see you are unaware," she murmured. "I don't like to be the one to pass on gossip."

"Since it is evidently gossip about me, I believe I have a right to know. Trust that I will hold nothing against you, madam. You know me better than that."

"I do," she agreed, "but it isn't pleasant."

"Then get on with it," he commanded.

"There is a rumor going about that three women who have been your mistresses have gone missing. That they accepted your offer of protection and then mysteriously disappeared."

"Is that all? It's true that they left suddenly," Ranson admitted, "but it was of their own accord. I had nothing to do with it."

"I told them as much and had quieted the gossip," she said. "Then came the news about Jeannette."

"Jeanette?"

"Jeanette Norville, I assume," interjected Drew.

"That's right," said Madam Vivian.

"She's the young woman you met several nights ago. One we discussed as a possibility," explained Drew.

"Of course, I remember her," responded Ranson. "A lovely young woman who might fit my needs."

"Then I'm afraid you must look elsewhere, for she has disappeared as quickly and as mysteriously as your mistresses did," revealed Vivian.

"And she is not the only one," the madam continued. "Women have been dropping out of sight since the last Little Season and there are no explanations for their disappearances. They do not say good-bye to anyone, or mention that they are leaving, or even leave a message. In many cases, their belongings are left behind, which is unusual for these women. They have little enough as it is and cling to what they have acquired.

"Earlier today they were discussing the missing women and that is when they discovered that three of them had been your mistresses. I'm afraid they decided that was more than a coincidence and determined that you were behind all the disappearances."

Ranson stifled a curse. "Why, that is ridiculous," he sputtered, his face going red.

"That is what I told them," replied Vivian in a soothing tone. "I had them convinced it was a farrago of nonsense until this afternoon when we received news that Jeanette Norville had joined the list of the missing. One of the women remembered she had been with you several evenings ago."

"But I scarcely know her," Ranson protested. "We met and spoke of things in general. She was a pleasant young woman and I admit I thought she might do if I did not find someone in the next sennight, but that is all I had to do with her."

"You need not convince me, my lord. I have no doubt of your innocence in the disappearances; however, it is difficult to convince a flock of flighty women once they have an idea firmly embedded in their minds."

"You must," demanded Ranson. " 'Else it will be all over Town that I am kidnapping the demireps of London."

"I will do my best, my lord, but I cannot promise that they will listen."

"They are probably whispering it into every ear right now," he said, looking around the crowded room.

Drew began to protest, but as he glanced at the others in the drawing room, he noticed that nearly every eye was fixed on Ranson. The women were clinging fearfully to the men's arms, while murmuring what was surely their horrible suspicions of Lord Weston behind their unfurled fans.

"Damnation!" growled Ranson. "This is insufferable."

"I'm sorry, my lord, I did my best," said Vivian apologetically.

"It is not your fault that I have mistresses who are so ill-mannered that they depart without the slightest hint of where they are going or why. In the normal course of events, I would ignore it completely. Unfortunately, I need a mistress."

"I wish I could help, but I doubt if you will find anyone here willing to accept your offer," observed Vivian.

"I only hope this rumor doesn't reach every courtesan in London before I find someone suitable," he grumbled. "Come along, Drew, we're doing no good here."

"If only I were younger," murmured Madam Vivian, as the two men left the room.

THREE

"I promised to pay my respects to my godmother," explained Ranson, as the coach traveled toward the West End of London.

"Might get your mind off Madam Vivian's."

"I will not forget what happened this evening," replied Ranson, swearing under his breath. "How I can lay the rumors to rest and acquire an adequate mistress before Hayley's house party, I don't know."

"Will find someone. As for the rumors, they only make you more desirable in Hayley's eyes if what you suspect is true."

Ranson was silent for a moment, mulling over what his friend had said. "Drew, I believe you're right. This is one time that a shady reputation might serve me well." He was in a much better state of mind as the coach stopped in front of the posh house on Park Lane.

"Quite a crush," observed Drew, as they stood just inside the door of the ballroom at Lord and Lady Brownley's home.

"I expected nothing less; however, I believe Lady Brownley has outdone herself this time," Ranson replied, surveying the masses of flowers decorating the room.

"Enough to get your mind off disappearing women?" queried Drew.

Ranson shook his head. "I'm still loath to acknowledge that anyone would believe I would do away with any woman, let alone my own mistresses."

"Mistress would be the easiest," said Drew. "Lives in your house and is at your beck and call."

"And it would be nothing unusual to go for a long drive or a trip to the coast," added Ranson.

"Heard of men who take great delight in torturing women," Drew said.

"Not men—monsters," replied Ranson, contradicting his friend.

"Agreed."

"You are looking very solemn this evening, my lords," said Jessica, as she peered around a huge vase of flowers at the two men.

"And you are looking lovely as usual," remarked Drew, his face lighting up at her appearance.

"More so, if that is possible," added Ranson.

"Fustian!" replied Jessica, laughing up at him. She stepped out from behind the flowers with Lady Lavinia following.

Ranson bowed over her hand. "Lady Lavinia, how pleasant to see you again." He thought her lovelier than ever, dressed in a gown which had a slip of peach satin with an overskirt of net. Small peach-colored blossoms were tucked in the ebony curls clustered at the back of her head.

"Thank you, my lord," she replied briefly, before pulling her hand from his grasp as if his touch burned.

Ranson wondered whether she had already heard the *on-dit* about him and studied her face closely as she greeted Drew. However, she did not look at him as the women had at Madam Vivian's, so he assumed his secret was safe for the moment.

"Would you care to dance?" he asked, hoping to have the opportunity to hold her in his arms again.

"I am sitting this one out," she replied stiffly.

"Nonsense. You are entirely too young and lovely to miss even one dance," he insisted. Taking her hand, he placed it on his arm and led her toward the dance floor before she could object further.

Lavinia did not like to be maneuvered and especially by such a man as Lord Weston. She would give him something to think about.

"I noticed you in the park this morning."

"You should have made yourself known," he said. "We could have walked together."

"Oh, you appeared far too busy to bother. You were speaking to a very attractive young lady."

"Er. A slight acquaintance," he explained.

"Although I suppose I could have called to you," Lavinia continued. "For not long after I spied you, she turned and walked—no nearly ran—away." Lavinia opened her eyes in wonder. "Now why would she do such a thing?"

"Ah. I believe she was late for an engagement," he muttered.

Oh, he was quick on his feet, Lavinia had to admit. However, he did seem a bit disconcerted, which left her feeling quite revived.

"I thought as much," replied Lavinia, "for I have not seen any lady ignore you."

"If that is so, how can you refuse to stand up with me?"

"I didn't know you had left me a choice," said Lavinia, as they stepped onto the floor and began moving to the music.

"I have been meaning to call on your father and make myself known to him, but circumstances have kept me away," remarked Ranson, changing the subject.

Lavinia did not want her father to come to know Lord Weston for he would most likely judge him a perfect match for his daughter. "Do not worry, my lord. My father is still weak from his illness and keeps to his rooms much of the time."

"Then I will wait until his health is better," he said, before changing the subject. "Have you ridden in Hyde Park yet?"

"I haven't had the time."

"You should do so," he urged. "It is at its loveliest, nearly untouched by the crowd that will soon fill it so that even the flowers will go unseen."

"I will make a point to go soon," she replied.

"Then come ride with me," he cajoled. "Let me bring the mare I mentioned, for she is exactly suited for you."

"Do you always know what is best for a person?" asked Lavinia, irked at his self-confidence.

Ranson tightened his grip on her hand just enough that she looked up at him. "For you I do," he said, with a meaning she could not ignore. Lavinia's desire was to push him away and walk off the floor; however, if she wished to avenge her sister she needed to put aside her personal desire and begin to allow him to think he was winning her over.

"My lord," she murmured, lowering her lashes and feigning confusion, "you put me to the blush."

Sensing capitulation, Ranson leaned closer, whispering in her ear, "Tomorrow?" he coaxed.

Closing her eyes and taking a deep breath, Lavinia nodded in agreement.

Ranson smiled triumphantly. The music ended and he escorted her back to Jessica and Drew, who were still engaged in conversation.

"Tomorrow at four?" he queried.

"I shall be ready, my lord," Lavinia agreed, removing her hand from his arm. Although loath to admit it, his charm was strong even with her. She found it difficult to keep revenge in mind when she was so close to him, and was grateful to be able to take a step away.

"You are back already," remarked Jessica, a trace of disappointment in her voice.

"The dance is over," replied Lavinia, amused at the blush that rose in Jessica's face. Perhaps she should not be glad that her friend found Drew attractive, but with the state of Jessica's marriage, Lavinia was happy her friend could find some enjoyment in the viscount's company.

"Unfortunately, we cannot linger in your delightful presence any longer," said Ranson. "We have some unfinished business we must attend to this evening."

"How regrettable it is that you must miss an evening of entertainment for something as bland as business," replied Lavinia, pouting a bit for his benefit.

"Regrettable, but necessary," said Ranson, bending over her hand. "Nothing else could take me from your side," he vowed, pressing his lips to her soft skin.

"Lord Weston seems greatly taken with you," said Jessica, as they watched the men's departure from the room.

"He is greatly experienced and can convince almost anyone to believe whatever it is he so desires. Anyone but me, that is," she clarified dispassionately.

"Perhaps you have misjudged him."

"Do not waste your sympathy on Lord Weston," Lavinia advised. "Remember, I have firsthand knowledge that he is not at all what he seems, and I intend to be the one to put a spoke in his wheel."

"Such a pity," Jessica said with a sigh.

"Seemed you were making progress with Lady Lavinia," commented Drew, as the men settled into the town coach once again.

"She is riding with me tomorrow," announced Ranson smugly.

"Not surprised. Haven't seen a woman turn you down once you set your mind."

A frown appeared on Ranson's face. "You may well see it before my search for a mistress is over. Where are we off to now?"

"Know several other places where the fancy pieces gather," said Drew. "We'll visit as many as we can tonight."

"I hope none of them have heard they will disappear completely if they're seen with me or the room will empty quickly."

Drew chuckled. "Doubt that will happen. There will be women who will not shy away no matter how undesirable the rumors."

"Should that make me feel better?" grumbled Ranson.

"Enough for some men," replied Drew, "but I know it does not suit you."

Ranson heaved a sigh and sank back against the soft squabs of the seat. "I must go on with my search no matter how my sensibilities suffer," he complained, "but I need not enjoy the process."

"You are doing this for your country," Drew reminded him with a chuckle.

"That is the only reason that motivates me and I am already beginning to regret it. I have just met a woman who holds my interest for more than a moment and I am forced to chase after light-skirts."

Drew grinned. Ranson had never mentioned more than a passing interest in any woman. Perhaps he could be caught in the parson's mousetrap after all. "Fate is cruel," he replied wryly.

* * *

The next afternoon Ranson rode slowly toward Lavinia's home. A groom leading the black mare he had recommended followed behind.

The night before had not been an unmitigated disaster, but had embarrassed him nonetheless. There had been stares and whispers when he and Drew entered the establishments that housed London's finest examples of fallen women. While no one ran from the room screaming, some women avoided him completely whereas others sought him out to demonstrate just how daring they were. He suffered through it all, dispensing smiles and compliments and appearing that everything was as it should be.

The men were more accepting, greeting him with smiles and mild quips about his luck with women.

Beneath the surface, Ranson simmered with anger at the three women who had left him so precipitously. As far as he knew, he had treated them well during the short time that they had been with him, and had not insulted them in any manner. For them to disappear without a word of explanation or farewell was inexcusable. If they had found someone who could offer them more, Ranson would have sent them on their way with his blessing. However, none of them had shown up on any man's arm since they had left his protection.

He shifted in his saddle. Was it possible the women had met with an unsavory end? Had they fallen into the hands of someone like Hayley? If so, they had gone willingly, for there were no signs of a struggle in any of their cases. Perhaps he should have been more concerned about their disappearance and investigated, but if he had come upon them with another man they would not have welcomed him at all. Once this business was over, he decided, he would see whether he could find the women to ensure that they were safe.

At the moment, however, he was forced to concentrate

on finding a suitable woman and then receiving an invitation to Hayley's house party. As Drew had pointed out, his current reputation should recommend him to Hayley.

Then there was Lavinia. Lovely, cool Lavinia. He was hoping to warm her up today. The short time he had spent with her had only increased his desire to know her better; however, she seemed reluctant to grant him that wish. He didn't consider himself vain, but he wondered why he did not seem to appeal to her, a problem he had never encountered before. Perhaps he could change her outlook about him today.

Ranson stopped in front of Pheneas Peyton, Lord Cranston's home. It was a large brick house, windows sparkling, steps swept clean, and brass knocker polished until it gleamed in the sunlight. The house bespoke wealth and pride of ownership.

Ranson tossed his reins to the groom and crossed the cobblestones to the front door. He had given only a brief knock before the door opened to him. Evidently alerted to his arrival, a black-clad butler stepped back and invited him in with a bow.

"I am here to call on Lady Lavinia," he said.

"And you are right on time," came the reply from the head of the stairs.

He looked upward and was rewarded with the vision of Lavinia descending. She was wearing a blue riding habit and a small hat with a feather which curled down from the side, touching her cheek. She was altogether charming and for a moment Ranson forgot to answer.

"As are you," he finally said. "And looking quite fetching."

"Thank you, my lord. I'm looking forward to riding the mare you mentioned."

"She's outside waiting for you." He smiled, offering her his arm.

Lavinia stood for a moment at the top of the shallow steps and studied the mare. "She's a fine-looking animal."

"You will not find fault with her," judged Ranson. "If you do, I'll sell her tomorrow."

"There's no need to promise that for I'm certain she'll not disappoint me," said Lavinia. "Besides I would not like to cost her what is evidently a good home."

After tossing her into the saddle, Ranson mounted his own bay stallion and they turned the animals toward Hyde Park.

"Did you enjoy the ball last night?" he asked.

"I did, but it was a smashing crush."

"That is the way of all of Lady Brownley's entertainments. Not only is she one of the most popular hostesses, she is my godmother."

"You are lucky," Lavinia replied. "I immediately admired her when we met."

Ranson was pleased that they agreed on at least one thing. "She entertains quite often, so I'm certain the two of you will become well acquainted before the Season is over."

Lavinia patted the mare's neck, then glanced at Lord Weston. "I heard—perhaps I should say—overheard the strangest thing during the ball."

"And what was that?" he asked, guiding his stallion closer.

"As you may remember, there were masses of flowers around the room," she began.

"Lady Brownley is prone to overdoing when it comes to decorating."

"Oh, no. I didn't mean to criticize," she remarked quickly. "It is only that I was standing beside a particularly large arrangement when I heard a conversation between two men who were on the opposite side of the flowers. Not that I was trying to listen, it is just that I could not avoid hearing what they said."

"I hope it was not something in poor taste," he commented.

"No. Nothing like that, but I have been puzzling over it since then. They spoke of women disappearing here in London. Do you know anything about it?"

Ranson silently cursed. He would like to get his hands on the two men who had spoken of missing ladybirds in the middle of a ball, but it was unlikely that he would ever know who they were.

"Were any names mentioned?" he asked.

"No. The music was playing and I couldn't hear every word that was spoken. One of them might have said something about Felicity, but I don't know of anyone by that name in the *ton*. I thought to ask Jessica, but we were parted and I didn't see her the rest of the evening."

Ranson breathed a sigh of relief. At least she did not know he was the man blamed for the women's disappearances. He was determined to put the matter to rest before it could spread any further.

"I would pay no heed to it," he advised. "It's probably just an *on-dit* begun by someone attempting to liven up the evening."

"What an odd way of doing it," she said. "I don't find a tale of missing women amusing at all."

"Nor do I," he answered grimly. Ranson needed to change the subject. He did not feel comfortable being less than truthful with Lavinia. "We are nearly at the park and it looks as if everyone is out to enjoy the afternoon."

Ranson's observation was correct. Carriages and riders crowded the paths, slowing the progression through the park. Both Ranson and Lavinia were greeted as they made their way through the crush. A lively group of young dandies separated them briefly and before Ranson could work his way back to Lavinia, he heard his name being called. Turning, he saw Madam Vivian along with three of her most beautiful women in an open landau.

"Come and see me," she said. "I believe I can help you."

"Lord Weston?"

Ranson turned. Lavinia had caught up with him and was glancing from him to Madam Vivian, a puzzled expression on her face. There was no concealing Vivian's profession, for her appearance and that of the women accompanying her left no room for doubt. Their gowns were cut far too low for any woman of the *ton* to be wearing for an afternoon in the park, and rouge had been applied with a heavy hand.

Without acknowledging Vivian, Ranson smiled at Lavinia. "I believe it is less crowded this way," he said, turning his horse out of the heavy flow of traffic.

"But what of your friends?" asked Lavinia, looking over her shoulder at the landau.

"She mistook me for someone else," he said, flushing slightly.

Ranson sent the groom home with the mare once he had returned Lady Lavinia to her home. He rode aimlessly through the streets, cursing the coincidence that had brought him to Vivian's notice at such an inopportune time. Lady Lavinia had not mentioned the encounter again, but she was inordinately silent for the remainder of their ride. Her farewell and thanks had been perfunctory and she had hurried inside before he had a chance to speak of seeing her again. All in all, the afternoon had not been the success he had wished it to be.

Straightening in the saddle, he attempted to shrug off the gloom that had overcome him. He could not allow himself to become downcast. He must put his mind to the task ahead of him and complete it quickly so he could return to pursuing Lavinia in earnest. The more time he spent around her, the more convinced he was that she was well suited to him.

He was nearing Madam Vivian's street and decided there was no need to waste more time. He would call on her and find out her reason for wanting to see him. He hoped it was worth the damage it had done to Lady Lavinia's opinion of him.

"How could he?" cried Lavinia, pacing swiftly back and forth across the drawing room floor in front of Jessica. "To acknowledge those . . . those women while he was with me."

As soon as Ranson had ridden away, Lavinia had called for the carriage and was driven straight to Jessica's house. She was too furious to sit at home alone and she could not express her anger to her father, for he had no idea what she was up to.

"Those women are the same as the ones you work so hard to save," Jessica reminded her.

Lavinia paused, looking a bit chagrined. "I'm sorry. I had forgotten for a moment. It isn't that I feel any different about helping the women. It's just that in that particular situation, it was an insult to me. At least, that is how it will appear to everyone who observed it."

"If the park was as crowded as you say, I doubt many noticed. You seem overly upset about a man you have sworn to destroy. Are you certain you don't feel something other than contempt for him?"

"What? Are you truly suggesting that I . . . that I . . ." Lavinia could not complete the thought. She forced herself to regain control of her emotions, then spoke in a much calmer voice. "I saw him only because it is important that I keep track of what he is doing. However, he did not reveal one thing, so I may need some help in that respect."

"I have some information in which you may be interested."

"What is it?" Lavinia asked eagerly, taking a seat across from Jessica.

"I heard it from Thomas last night. He returned home earlier than usual, but he was still in his cups. He had more to say about the missing women."

Lavinia clasped her hands in her lap, praying for patience. "What did he tell you?"

"It seems the rumors are increasing that Lord Weston's last three mistresses have disappeared."

Lavinia's hands rose to cover her lips and the smile that spread over them. "Go on," she encouraged.

"How do you know there is more," teased Jessica.

"You have that look. Now tell me before I fly into pieces," demanded Lavinia.

"I wouldn't want you to do that," replied Jessica, smiling at her friend's ebullient behavior. "Thomas said that discovery was enough to send every Cyprian within earshot up into the boughs. And as if that wasn't bad enough, it seems that a young woman—I believe her name was Jeanette—was last seen with Lord Weston just a few days ago and has also vanished."

"I don't understand," said Lavinia, a puzzled look on her face. "I haven't taken anyone to Hope House since Felicity."

"Then I suppose the last could be a legitimate disappearance."

"That doesn't mean Lord Weston had anything to do with it," replied Lavinia.

"Are you taking up for him now?" asked Jessica.

Only a few days before, Lavinia had explained the reason behind her aversion toward Lord Weston and Jessica wondered whether the story of his deception toward her sister had reached Lavinia without the truth of the matter being twisted.

Bright splashes of pink spread high on Lavinia's cheekbones. "Of course not," she objected. "You know how I feel about the man."

"Do I?" said Jessica, a sly smile on her face. "It looks as if he is being particular in his attentions to you."

"He is an odious creature who ruined my sister's life. Even so, I do not like to see anyone accused if they are innocent."

"Are you certain your feelings have not changed since you have come to know him?" inquired Jessica.

"I am acquainted with him," corrected Lavinia. "I do not know him well at all and do not mean to. My involvement with Lord Weston is only to allow me to avenge Barbara, nothing more."

Jessica was not at all certain that her friend realized her true opinion of Lord Weston, but decided not to pursue the matter at present. "Thomas said that the rumors were running wild last night and that Lord Weston was met with whispers and fear from the women. A few approached him merely to gain attention; however, most kept their distance."

"No wonder he was subdued today," murmured Lavinia.

"Well, it seems you are getting your revenge."

"It isn't the same," grumbled Lavinia. "How can I find satisfaction if I cannot see the results with my own eyes?"

"I have no idea," said Jessica impatiently.

Lavinia felt shame at her pettiness. "I sound like a child, don't I?" she asked. "I apologize. It's only that I have thought of nothing else but making Lord Weston pay for driving my sister from England for so long that it has become my sole objective. It is probably unhealthy for me to do so, but I cannot—no, do not, want to help myself. If I cannot make him suffer as Barbara did, I will not be able to live with myself."

"You are too hard on yourself," said Jessica. "If Barbara feels she was wrongly used by Lord Weston, she should go to your father and let him handle the matter."

"She cannot; she would be too ashamed."

"Then let it go, Lavinia. You should be enjoying the Season instead of plotting against Lord Weston."

"I wish him to perdition and I will enjoy it after I see him pay," repeated Lavinia stubbornly.

"He is paying," argued Jessica.

"But not due completely to me," countered Lavinia. "Because of this Jeanette person who probably decided to take a trip with her latest protector, or perhaps who moved to Bath on a whim."

"It's being said that all her belongings were left behind. That is one reason speculation is that she was taken away rather than leaving voluntarily."

"It is disheartening to think she was taken by force. I would not wish that for any person," said Lavinia with a shudder. "I must contact Hope House. Perhaps someone took her there and we are not aware of it."

"I pray that's the case," replied Jessica. "In the meantime, I shall ring for tea. It will fortify us for the evening ahead."

"I must apologize," said Madame Vivian, immediately upon Ranson's entering her private drawing room. "I would never have spoken had I known you were with a young lady."

Ranson waved his hand dismissively. "We had become separated in the crush, so you could not have known."

"You are kind to let me off so easily," she replied. "But perhaps I can make up for it. I believe I have found someone to suit your purpose."

"And she is willing to take a chance with a man who has done away with four women?" he asked, flashing a wry smile.

"She is new to London, but I explained what has taken place over the past few days. I also told her about you without revealing your name. She is willing to meet you and see if the two of you suit."

A sudden desire to explain himself to this woman who accepted him without question compelled Ranson to speak. "Perhaps you find it odd that I am anxious to acquire a mistress, but I have a very good reason—beyond the usual—for it."

"I have no doubt, my lord, and I will do what I can to help."

"This woman . . . what is her name?"

"Stephanie. Stephanie Morris."

"Is it possible to meet Miss Morris this evening?" he asked.

"You may meet her now, my lord. She is staying here for the time being and is upstairs in her room."

"Good. I would like that very much."

Madam Vivian sent for Stephanie and while they waited she fortified Ranson with a drink and spoke of inconsequential things. Ranson found it amusing that the most peace he had found in the past few days was in the drawing room of one of the most famous madams in London.

Ranson was pleasantly surprised when Stephanie Morris entered the drawing room. She was an extremely attractive woman of average height, who moved gracefully. Her hair was brownish-red and pulled back into a riot of curls, while green eyes sparkled from a delicately oval face. Her light green gown was more modest than most in her profession, but still allowed a man to admire the curvaceous figure it covered.

"Miss Morris, I'm delighted to meet you," said Ranson when Madam Vivian introduced him to the woman, then slipped from the room.

"And I you, my lord," replied Stephanie.

"Shall we make ourselves comfortable?" he suggested, indicating the settee with a wave of his hand.

Nodding in acquiescence, Stephanie seated herself and arranged her skirt around her.

Ranson claimed a chair across from her and leaned back, studying the woman. If he were seriously searching for a mistress, he could not have chosen better when it came to looks. She had the appearance of intelligence instead of the emptyheadedness often found in the Birds of Paradise frequenting London. He hoped he would not be proven wrong before their meeting was over.

"I suppose Madam Vivian explained I am in need of a mistress," he said.

"She did, my lord, but after meeting you, I am convinced you could not have a problem getting any woman you set your sights on."

"There are complications," he replied.

"I am aware of them," she revealed. "But Madam Vivian assured me that you are innocent of the accusations leveled against you."

"Then you would be willing to come under my protection?"

Stephanie fidgeted with her handkerchief a moment before answering. "There is something you should know before I answer," she said.

Ranson should have known she was too good to be true when she first walked into the room. He wondered what her secret was and whether it would be something

which would make her unacceptable for the position of
his mistress under the circumstances. Fatigue washed
over him; he was weary of the chase and had thought
it was at an end.

"You may as well tell me what it is, Miss Morris,"
he said dispiritedly.

"This is embarrassing," she declared, staring at the
floral design in the carpet spread beneath their feet.

"I doubt there is anything you can tell me that I haven't heard before," encouraged Ranson.

"Well, this is my first time . . . I mean I've
never . . ." said Stephanie, stumbling to a halt.

"You are not going to tell me you've never been with
a man before, are you?" he asked, eyes narrowed.

"Oh no," she replied, looking up at him. "But I have
never been a mistress before," she confessed quickly.

"What the devil made you start now?"

"My husband died after a long illness," she explained.
"I was left with just a few shillings in my purse and no
family to turn to. I do not have the education to be a
governess. I applied for several housekeeping positions,
but was told I would be a distraction to the young men
of the household." A slight flush rose to her face as she
repeated the comment. "At that time, I was just a few
days away from being on the street, so I was forced to
turn to the only profession left open to me. When I arrived in Town, I asked around and was directed to
Madam Vivian.

"It has not been easy for me, my lord. Even though
I have been poor all my life, I have retained my pride;
however, pride cannot put food on the table, nor a roof
over my head. I am willing to become your mistress,
but felt you should know of my inexperience in the matter."

Ranson was unable to believe his run of luck. While
Stephanie certainly had the looks to be a mistress, her

very inexperience could jeopardize his undertaking. If he chose her, he must wager that her intelligence would carry her through. He rose from the chair and walked to the window, looking out into the street. If he meant to be successful in procuring an invitation to Hayley's house party, he could not put off his decision any longer. He returned to his seat and looked across the short distance to meet Stephanie's gaze.

"You have been candid with me," he began. "Since you are new to London and all its intrigues, I should explain my situation before we agree to strike a bargain."

"You make it sound daunting."

"Before I am finished, you might think it so and change your mind," responded Ranson. "I am not merely looking for a mistress for my own enjoyment. I need someone to attend a Cyprian's house party which will take place in approximately a fortnight."

Ranson felt he should apologize for speaking to her so bluntly, but she had made the decision to enter the profession and he elected to forego the niceties.

"My attendance at the house party is not pleasure, but business. I am not at liberty to explain specifics of what I must accomplish for it is of a highly sensitive nature. I need a woman to accompany me to the party and act as my mistress."

"Act?"

"Yes. It will not be necessary for you to . . . er, fulfill any of the duties, but we must put forth the effort to look like a happy couple. No one must suspect that we are anything more than two people enjoying one another's company. It's of the utmost importance that you be able to carry this off. If you cannot, let me know now. There will be no hard feelings, I assure you."

"You mean all I need do is to enjoy myself?"

"I don't know whether you will consider it pleasant.

You will be consorting with a house full of Cyprians and their protectors."

"You forget, it is now my chosen profession."

"You may change your mind after this foray into the life of a demirep."

"You also forget I have no choice," said Stephanie, dropping her gaze.

At that moment, Ranson decided to help out the woman once the house party and all that it entailed was behind them. But first, he must see that Hayley's activities were curtailed.

"Then you are still of a mind to become my mistress?" he asked, smiling for the first time in their interview.

Stephanie returned his smile. "I believe I am, my lord."

"Remember, what I have revealed to you today must remain in absolute secrecy."

"I will not repeat anything you have confided, my lord."

"Good. Then we will consider it settled. We must begin our charade immediately. We shall attend the theater this evening. Have Vivian help you select new gowns and everything that goes with them. She will know what you need. The bills should be sent directly to me. I will also see you receive a sum of money so your pockets will not be empty."

"My lord," Stephanie began, plainly embarrassed.

"You have reminded me you chose this life and this is part of it," he said. "Tomorrow I will take you to a house I have here in Town. It will be your new home for as long as our association lasts. If there is anything you need, you must ask either me or the servants who will be there."

"Servants?" she asked, bewildered.

"I could not ask you to cook and clean for yourself,"

he teased. "I know things are happening quickly, but I have no choice. I'll be back this evening to go to the theater, then we'll make the rounds of some of the finer gentlemen's establishments. We must be seen in order to begin my plan."

"I shall be ready, my lord." She rose when he did and walked with him to the door.

"Until this evening," he said, taking her hand and brushing it with his lips.

FOUR

"Thomas, please hurry," Jessica pleaded. "We are already late."

"Should never have agreed to escort you," grumbled Thomas. "You know I can't abide these silly plays."

"Some of them are quite good," said Lavinia, hoping the couple was not heading for another argument.

"We'll see," he replied, offering each lady an arm and beginning to climb the staircase at Covent Garden.

The play had already begun when the three arrived at the box, however, they were able to slip in and take their seats quickly. It wasn't until the actors had left the stage at the end of the first act that Lavinia took the opportunity to look around the theater. Her breath caught in her throat as she stared into a box across from them.

"What is it?" asked Jessica.

"Over there," Lavinia choked out, nodding in the direction of the box.

"Why it's Lord Weston," said Jessica.

"And it looks as if he has chosen a new mistress," observed Lavinia.

"She's quite pretty," commented Jessica.

"I can see that," snapped Lavinia. "I'm wondering how I missed her."

"How could you possibly know every Cyprian in town?" asked Jessica. "Now that I think of it how did you meet Lord Weston's previous mistresses?"

"You will keep it to yourself?"

"Of course."

"We—that is the women who run Hope House—have a contact who was a Cyprian until age caught up with her; then she became a madam."

"You have actually spoken with her?" asked Jessica breathlessly.

"I haven't met her," admitted Lavinia, "but she does not seem to be the ordinary madam. There are times when she sees women who have had no choice but to become some gentleman's mistress. I understand there are some women who enjoy their profession, but there are also many who do not. When this particular madam sees a woman who is only becoming a mistress out of need she passes the name along and arranges a meeting with a representative from Hope House.

"I let it be known early on that I was especially interested in Lord Weston's mistresses. However, I was not advised of this woman," she said, once again indicating Weston's box.

"Perhaps the woman is happy where she is," suggested Jessica.

"It is more likely that Lord Weston's influence is stronger than what is best for the woman," judged Lavinia.

"You're upset," said Jessica, voicing the obvious.

"It disturbs me anytime a woman is exploited."

"Are you certain it isn't because you're beginning to feel something for Lord Weston?"

"Of course not! Lord Weston's bid for my attention does not concern me in the least," declared Lavinia vehemently, rousing Thomas from the light doze he had fallen into.

"What? Is it over?" he asked, blinking his eyes and straightening in his seat.

"No, but I am ready to go," announced Lavinia, rising from her chair and gathering up her shawl.

"But there is more to come," objected Jessica.

"Should bow to our guest's wishes," said Thomas, delighted to have an excuse to leave. The evening was still young and he would have time to visit some of his favorite haunts tonight.

The ride home was uneventful, with only sporadic conversation to break the silence. Lavinia was grateful to reach the solitude of her room, where she did not need to pretend to be calm. She had been upset when she had first observed Lord Weston with the woman and she now paced the width of her room, still unable to put the sight behind her.

Seeing him with his first three mistresses had not affected her in the least and she wondered what the difference was this time. Could it be that this woman was more attractive than the others? Or that Lord Weston had seemed to be more attentive to her? She had watched him lean close and whisper in the woman's ear; she had seen him raise her hand to his lips. Lavinia's face had grown hot and she had been glad of the dimness in the theater.

Perhaps it was because she had met him, had been in his arms on the dance floor, and had also felt the touch of his lips on her own hand. Her pacing increased and she hoped the sound of her rapid footsteps was muffled by the thick carpet beneath her feet. She would not allow herself to feel anything for a man who used women as did Lord Weston, the very man who had ruined her sister's life.

She would continue her campaign tomorrow. First she would find out about the woman, then devise a plan to steal her from Weston's protection, if indeed, they had progressed to that point.

Ranson had been so totally involved in making it appear he was completely besotted by Stephanie that he had not taken the opportunity to discover who occupied the other seats in the theater. Therefore, he missed Lavinia's late arrival and subsequent hasty departure from the box across from his.

After the play, he escorted Stephanie backstage so that she could meet the actors. He also hoped that Hayley would be present, but he was to be disappointed for the man was nowhere in sight.

They soon took their leave and began visiting establishments where Ranson thought he might find Hayley. As they were leaving the first one, they met Drew, who was just alighting from his coach.

"Been looking for you," said Drew after being introduced to Stephanie. "Have some news."

"And what is that?"

"Hayley has a new place open."

"I'm very happy to know about it. I've been attempting to run him to ground, but have so far been unsuccessful."

"Had a notion that might be your aim. Just learned about it this afternoon. Too late to catch you at home. Hasn't been open but a sennight, so Hayley should be there overseeing the operation," said Drew, then gave him the directions to the establishment.

"Thank you, my friend," replied Ranson, as he handed Stephanie into his coach. "Will I see you there?"

"Most likely," said Drew, closing the coach door and stepping back.

The house was brick with no embellishments of any kind. It was, of course, not in the best of neighborhoods, but it was neatly kept and the area in front was swept free of debris and appeared as if it had been recently washed. The burly man who stood guard outside to en-

sure the patrons' safety moved quickly to open the door
for them.

It was apparent as soon as they entered the foyer that
Hayley had spent a great deal on refurbishing the house.
The decor was garish, but was exactly what was expected in such an establishment: all red and gold, with
an abundance of gold-framed mirrors to reflect the men
and women filling the rooms.

The air was heavy with the mingling scents of the
women's perfume and the men's pomades. Ranson
wanted nothing more than to get away from the cloying
surroundings, but he reminded himself he had a mission
to accomplish and the sooner it was over with, the
sooner he could begin to court Lavinia in earnest.

"Lord Weston, what a pleasant surprise."

Ranson turned to find Hayley at his side. "I heard
you had a new establishment and decided to visit."

"Glad you did," said Hayley. "And you brought a
lovely lady with you."

"This is Miss Stephanie Morris. Our acquaintance is
short, but I hope to convince her to make it a more
permanent one."

"You have excellent taste, Weston," commented
Hayley, as if Stephanie were a painting Ranson had purchased. "Now, have you looked around yet? I think
you'll find most anything you desire for entertainment.
This is the social room. There are games of chance in
a room just down the hall on your left, and if you like
something relaxing to smoke, you can find it in the
small room at the back of the house. There's food and
drink across the hall and if you should need privacy,
there are rooms upstairs."

"You have everything well thought out," observed
Ranson.

"It's the key to my success," replied Hayley proudly.

"Well, I won't keep you. Look around, enjoy yourself. If you need anything special, let me know."

"What do you think of your chosen life?" Ranson asked Stephanie after Hayley had left.

"It is too soon to tell."

Ranson chuckled. "By that, I will assume you aren't impressed."

"Oh, I did not mean to be judgmental at all," she replied swiftly. "It is only that I am unaccustomed to everything that I've experienced since arriving in London. And it has happened so quickly."

"You need not apologize. Anyone with half an eye can see beyond this tawdry display to what it is hiding. However, we must pretend great interest and enjoyment in what is going on. We need not stay long since this is our first time here, but we will be meeting Hayley more often in the next few days. I must convince him we're worthy of an invitation to his house party."

While Ranson and Stephanie were winding their way through Hayley's rooms of pleasure, Lavinia was pursuing Lady Danforth at the Sanderfords' soiree. Gripping the woman by the arm, she gently but firmly steered her toward an unoccupied corner of the room.

"Edith, you must help me," she entreated.

Lady Edith Danforth was one of the earliest supporters of Hope House and would go to great lengths in order to aid any woman who needed it. She had been married to a much older man when she was barely out of the schoolroom and rumor had it after a few years of ill use at his hands she had helped him find his early departure from the earth.

Her husband's treatment of her had been well known to her friends, for he had made no effort to hide that he considered himself her master, so no one stepped forward to accuse her of any wrongdoing. Since then, she had used her husband's wealth to help other women begin new lives.

"What is it I must do?" Lady Danforth asked, smiling at the younger woman's earnest expression.

"I have heard Lord Weston has another mistress. I have even seen them together at the theater and if she is not his mistress yet, I feel she soon will be."

"And you want me to arrange a meeting with her?" guessed Edith.

"Do you think you could?" pleaded Lavinia.

Edith studied Lavinia for a moment. She had not questioned Lavinia's need to break up Lord Weston's love nest. At first, she had assumed the women had appealed to Lavinia's compassion enough that she wanted to help them out of their subservient roles. However, by the time Lavinia had snatched Felicity from under Lord Weston's nose, Edith was convinced that Lavinia had a personal vendetta against the earl.

"Why have you taken such an interest in Lord Weston's mistresses, Lavinia? This is the fourth woman of his that you have pursued. While they may be in need of our assistance, there are other women in London just as worthy of your attention."

Lavinia's face flushed under Edith's close scrutiny. "I have it on good authority that he is a scoundrel when it comes to women," she answered.

"He is no worse than most, and much better than many," replied Edith. "I have never heard that any woman has complained of his treatment. In fact, I understand that he is quite generous with his mistresses."

"That does not redeem him," shot back Lavinia.

"No, it does not," agreed Edith. "But I don't believe it's fair to single out one particular gentleman to hound unless he is proven himself worthy of our dedication. I don't want to draw attention to what we are doing. If word reached the wrong ears, all that we have achieved could be put in jeopardy."

"I don't want to harm our cause," murmured Lavinia, her eyes downcast. "But I would like to interview this woman. I promise, I will turn my efforts elsewhere if you will assist me this one last time."

Edith considered Lavinia's request. The young woman was one of the group's most dedicated converts since she had arrived in Town and she did not want to dampen her enthusiasm. Perhaps her concentration on Lord Weston had just been a coincidence. She would need to point out men who were more worthy of her attention in the future. For the time being, she would investigate the earl's current bark of frailty to see whether she appeared to be in distress.

"I will do what I am able, but I cannot promise success. This will be the fourth time within such a narrow span of time and Lord Weston may be more alert," she warned.

Lavinia smiled warmly. "Your best is all that I ask," she responded. "This is . . ."

"I know . . . it is urgent," said Edith, before Lavinia could get the words out of her mouth. "I will contact you as soon as I have anything to pass along."

"Thank you so much."

"Don't thank me yet for I've done nothing and may not be able to do anything. Now go along and enjoy the evening," she urged.

Lavinia spied Jessica across the room and made her way through the crush to her side. "I had given up seeing you here this evening."

"I was delayed," she answered shortly. Then, "I'm sorry. I shouldn't take out my temper on you."

"Think nothing of it," replied Lavinia. "Is it anything with which I can help?"

"If only it were that simple. As usual, it is Thomas.

He is becoming more impossible every day. I cannot say a word to him unless he jumps down my throat. And that isn't often, for I seldom see him anymore," Jessica complained. "He has used up all the funds available to him and is angry that my father will not advance any more. He blames me for not being able to persuade him. I don't know what to do," she exclaimed, blinking back tears.

"Perhaps it's best that you don't see him often if he is that embittered. Try to ignore him and enjoy the evening," Lavinia advised, repeating the advice Lady Danforth had just voiced to her.

"I believe that is impossible." Jessica sniffed.

"Perhaps not; I see Viscount Stanford just arriving."

"Where?" asked Jessica, quickly dabbing at her eyes with her handkerchief.

"I believe he's already making his way toward us," said Lavinia, pleased that the viscount had arrived in time to keep Jessica from sinking into a self-pitying morass.

Pleasantries were exchanged and Lavinia was encouraged to see a smile on Jessica's face once again.

"Is Lord Weston not with you?" asked Jessica, much to Lavinia's chagrin.

"Would have been here if he could, but had other obligations this evening and could not break free," explained Drew.

Lavinia could well imagine what *other obligations* claimed his attention and with Edith's help she meant to remove his obligation right from beneath his very finely formed nose.

Hayley poured himself a glass of brandy from the decanter on the table, but did not offer one to Thomas Carter, who had been shown into the library a few minutes prior. He had also not invited the man to sit, and he stood across the room, shifting from one foot to another like a recalcitrant schoolboy.

"You are failing me, Thomas," said Hayley, pausing to take an appreciative sip of the liquor.

"It is not my fault," replied Thomas in a belligerent tone. "Since the rumors have been going around about the disappearances, the women are far more wary than before."

"But you are not a stranger to them," Hayley pointed out. "They should trust you."

"It is such a poor state of affairs that many are trusting no one," Thomas grumbled, wondering whether to take a chance and sit down without an invitation. Perhaps not, with Hayley in his present humor.

"Come, come, Thomas. Surely you can convince one or two of them to visit your old friend. That is an innocent enough invitation. I have requests that must be filled or else I will lose many of my most important buyers."

"Your house party is coming up," Thomas pointed out.

"I doubt that will give me as many women as I need. I will pay you a premium on any you bring to me before the house party," he offered, hoping to entice Thomas to increase his efforts.

"I could use the money," Thomas admitted, scowling at the scuffed toe of his Hessians and wondering whether he would ever be able to afford a competent valet.

"Then go out tonight and use your charm. Bring me a woman worthy of my customer and I will make it worth your while."

"I'll do what I can," Thomas agreed grudgingly.

"See that you do," replied Hayley. There was a warning note in his voice that had not been there before. "It would be tragic if a rumor started that it was you and not Weston who was responsible for the missing women. Your father-in-law might cut you off completely." He smiled at Thomas, then turned his attention back to the paper on his desk.

Thomas quickly left the room, never doubting Hayley's threat. He was beginning to be sorry he had ever met the man.

Lavinia had spent a restless night, not falling asleep until dawn was beginning to lighten the sky. She nonetheless arose early and picked listlessly at breakfast. When she had drawn that out as long as possible, she chose her favorite chair in the drawing room and took up her embroidery, determined to fasten her attention on something else other than Lord Weston. As she worked, she decided she must make time to see Miss Linwood's needlework pictures, which were on display in Leicester Square. They were said to be as lovely as an oil painting.

As usual, her sewing brought her a measure of calm. She enjoyed working with the rich color of the threads and watching the design of flowers take place in her hands. However, peace seemed destined not to prevail long, for Lady Danforth was announced.

"Edith, I didn't expect to see you so soon," said Lavinia, rising to greet her.

"I happened to have the opportunity to make inquires sooner than I expected," explained Edith, seating herself across from Lavinia.

"And did you discover anything about Lord Weston's new companion?"

"I did," Edith stated. "The woman is new to London and the first gentleman she met was Lord Weston. It seems he wasted no time in establishing her as his current paramour. I don't know whether you have heard the *on-dit* yet, for it is only whispered about, but his name is being linked with women who have gone missing. We know what happened to three of them, and I find myself feeling guilty about not being able to come to his defense and explain the disappearances. However, I know nothing about the fourth woman, and I have it on good authority that Lord Weston was seen with the woman a short time before she vanished."

"I have heard about it," admitted Lavinia. "But I did not know whether to give it any credence."

"I cannot credit that he would harm any woman," confessed Edith, "yet public opinion is beginning to turn against him."

"And what of his current mistress?" asked Lavinia, bringing Edith back to the subject at hand.

"Her name is Stephanie Morris and there is no use in attempting to lure her away from Lord Weston," replied Edith. "My source tells me she has vowed to remain with him for at least the remainder of the Season and that she is a woman who keeps her word. There is also no indication that she is unhappy or that she desires to leave his protection."

"But . . ."

"Lavinia, you know I am the first to help a woman who wants it; however, I will not force our efforts on anyone. That would be the quickest way to draw attention to ourselves and that, in turn, could lead to the end of Hope House."

"I understand," said Lavinia.

"And I hope you won't go off on your own," warned Edith.

"You may depend upon it that I will keep my counsel," promised Lavinia. "As much as I would like to convince Miss Morris to leave Lord Weston, I do not want to put Hope House at risk."

Edith breathed a sigh of relief. She had been afraid that she could not quell Lavinia's enthusiasm for stealing away Lord Weston's mistresses. "I hope one day you will be able to tell me what's behind your obsession with him," she said.

"I am not . . ."

Edith held up her hand. "I know, it is nothing personal. You are merely intent upon helping save women who all just happen to be connected to Lord Weston."

Lavinia could not contain her embarrassment. "I hope it will help to assure you that I have good reason for what I do."

"I'm certain you believe so," Edith agreed. "However, I wonder whether it would appear that way to an uninvolved person?" She waited a moment, hoping that Lavinia would confide in her, but that was not to be. "Well, I must be going. I have an appointment with my modiste and I cannot keep her waiting if I want my new gown in time for the Bramtons' ball."

Lavinia walked with her to the foyer, thanking her for her effort in finding out about Miss Morris. After the door closed behind Edith, Lavinia wandered back into the drawing room and absentmindedly picked up her discarded embroidery. It seemed she would be unable to part Miss Morris from Lord Weston. Even if she had wanted to attempt it on her own, Edith had made it clear that her effort could irreparably harm Hope House, and that she did not want to do. She was serious in her desire to help women move up in life and as soon as she was finished with Lord Weston, she meant to increase her endeavors to do just that.

Lavinia jabbed her needle into the fabric, releasing her irritation at being powerless to continue her vendetta against Lord Weston. Surely, there was something more she could do to reveal him for the blackguard that he was. Her conscience would not allow her to perpetuate the lie that he had done away with three of his mistresses; however, she had not been involved with the fourth woman. Was Weston responsible for her disappearance? It was difficult to believe that he was guilty of the very rumor her actions had begun; however, stranger things had happened and she was not disinclined to dismiss it out of hand.

Perhaps she could find out more about this Jeanette and her connection to Weston. If he had caused any harm to come to the woman, that alone could ruin him with the *ton*. Society lived for scandal and would accept any easily believed gossip that slandered one of their own.

Lavinia applied her needle more gently now that she had decided upon a course of action. Perhaps Jessica could learn more from Thomas about the woman. She could even hire a Bow Street Runner to help her as long as she concealed it from her father. Not only would he disapprove of her plan to ruin a peer, but he would force her to disclose the reason behind her animosity toward Lord Weston. Barbara had never divulged to their father her reason for leaving England. Lavinia did not want him to discover it now when he was still weak from his illness.

The knocker on the front door sounded and Lavinia smiled broadly when she heard Jessica's familiar voice. *Just in time to help me with my new inquiry,* thought Lavinia. Perhaps she could salvage her plan despite the setback.

When Jessica arrived at the Peytons' household, Lavinia was too involved with her own plans to notice that she was unusually quiet. Lavinia explained the circumstances surrounding Stephanie Morris and her inability to steal her away from Lord Weston. She then revealed her idea to investigate Jeanette's disappearance to see whether she could find a connection to the earl.

"What do you think?" she asked Jessica when she had finished.

A silence ensued and Lavinia saw that Jessica was staring into the distance. "Jessica?" she said, but there was still no response. "Jessica?" She spoke louder and finally gained her friend's attention.

"Lavinia, I'm sorry. My mind was wandering, I'm afraid." Jessica looked down and toyed with the lace at the end of her sleeve, which fell partly over her hand.

"What is it? You are never this distracted. Tell me what is bothering you."

"I don't like to bore you with my problems. It seems that is all I can talk about lately."

"We are friends," Lavinia reminded her. "We should be able to tell one another everything."

"Are you certain . . . ?"

Lavinia interrupted her before she could finish. "I am absolutely certain," she said reassuringly. "Now tell me what is wrong."

"I'm afraid it's Thomas again. He is nearly beyond bearing and I don't know what to do."

"What has he done now?" asked Lavinia.

Jessica pushed up the sleeve of her gown and folded back the lace. A dark, ugly bruise encircled her wrist. There is a matching one here," she said, raising her other hand.

Lavinia's mouth opened, but she was too shocked to even gasp or cry out. She had seen some of the new arrivals at Hope House bearing bruises from the men who bought their favors, but she had never encountered a lady of the *ton* whose husband had misused her.

"You must leave him," she said, once she had regained her speech.

Jessica's laugh was shrill. "And go where? If I leave Thomas, my father would insist upon knowing the reason and once he did, he would no doubt call him out. My father is no longer young and he would probably lose. I cannot risk it." She pulled down her sleeve and adjusted the lace so that it covered every sign of her mistreatment.

Lavinia rose and closed the doors leading into the hall. "Why did he do this?" she asked, when she had returned to her chair.

"It was the usual argument over money. I assume that Thomas must be gambling and losing quite heavily for he never seems to have a shilling to his name. He demanded I give him whatever money I had and when I refused he grabbed me by the wrists and jerked me to my feet. He would not let me go, but pulled me from room to room attempting to force me to show him where it was. I was afraid," Jessica confessed, tears beginning to course their way down her cheeks. "I had never seen him so enraged, so I finally gave in and told him where he could find it. I am so ashamed."

Lavinia moved to the settee next to Jessica. She wiped the tears from her face with her lace-edged handkerchief, then took her hands gently in her own.

"You should not be ashamed. It is not your fault," Lavinia assured her. "Thomas is certainly no gentleman, nor a man of any kind, or he would not treat you so."

"I believe he is so desperate that he is not himself."

"Or perhaps his true colors are showing," Lavinia suggested.

"I fear to think what he may do next. I did not have enough money to last him one evening if he is gambling and what will he do then?"

"Well, he will not ill-use you any longer, that I will assure you," Lavinia said belligerently. "I will not allow it!"

"What can you do? I cannot permit my father to know about this," she repeated.

"He will not know," Lavinia promised. "If Thomas continues on this course I will let him know he will answer to someone else if you suffer any more of his attacks. My father can deal with Thomas without even leaving the house. He knows everyone who is worth knowing and Thomas will find himself on a ship heading toward a land where he will have ample reason to use his fists on someone more worthy than a woman."

"You couldn't."

"I can and I will," said Lavinia stubbornly. "That is, unless you cannot live without him."

"If I never see him again it will be too soon," vowed Jessica. "But I cannot let you put yourself at risk for me."

"I risk nothing. Once I explain the circumstances to my father, Thomas will not have time to retaliate; he will be too busy surviving."

"If he goes into a rage as he did today, I will not have time to call for help."

Lavinia gave the matter some thought. "Is there any way you can stay here?"

"I don't know what excuse I could give," said Jessica.

"Tell him my father is returning to the country for a short time and that you are going to stay to keep me company. The aftereffects of his illness keep him in the house and Thomas will never know whether or not he is at home."

"Do you think it will work?"

"Of course it will," said Lavinia. "He will decide that earning favor with my father might benefit him in the future, so I do not believe he will raise any obstacle to your visit."

"I wish I had your self-confidence, but Thomas has made me such a wretched, foolish thing."

"You are not at all foolish. You are wise to be wary of a man who is as unstable as Thomas. We will work this out so that you will escape his grasp."

"But I cannot stay with you forever," said Jessica. "I

must return to our house someday and then he could be far worse."

"At this moment, I don't have a solution," confessed Lavinia. "But your visit will allow us time to plan further. We can discuss it with my father with the assurance that he will keep it confidential. He can surely come up with an answer."

"All right," said Jessica. "When should I tell Thomas about our plan?"

"Perhaps you should wait a few days so it will not appear that you are reacting to your argument. Of course, if you believe he is going to hurt you again, you must come immediately."

An expression of distaste spread across Jessica's face. "I probably will not see him for days. He will gamble and drink and womanize, then come crawling home."

"That might be the perfect time to approach him with the news. If you can arrange to inform him in public he will not be able to go into a rage and, with luck, you will be packed and gone before he returns home."

A tiny giggle escaped from Jessica's lips. "You sound like Wellington planning a campaign."

Lavinia was encouraged that Jessica could find some humor, however slight, in the situation. "And Thomas is my Napoleon," quipped Lavinia, "and I know exactly how to spike his guns."

FIVE

"Have you abandoned Miss Morris this evening?" Drew asked Ranson. It was early evening and the two men sat side by side at White's.

"No. We are beginning later than usual. Stephanie needed the extra rest since she is unused to such hours, and I was not adverse to having a little time on my own."

"Finding the life of a rake not to your liking?"

Ranson chuckled and rested his head against the back of his chair. "I'm getting too old for all this," he complained. "Remember when we were nothing but young cubs, how we welcomed each sunrise before we fell into bed to rest up for the next night's revelry."

Drew nodded. "Enjoyable at the time, but couldn't do it now," he admitted.

"Nor can I," concurred Ranson. "The only joy I get out of these endless rounds is watching Stephanie's reaction to what is going on around us." He was silent for a moment before continuing. "I must be getting old, for I continually struggle against feeling guilt at introducing her to such a life."

Drew gave him a sharp glance.

Ranson shook his head at his friend. "Do not think it. I assure you I feel nothing more than friendship for Stephanie. It is only that she was a contented wife until her husband died and she had nowhere else to turn ex-

cept to the life of a demirep. Since I am her first protector, I suppose I feel a certain responsibility toward
her."

"There will be others," Drew predicted.

"Perhaps not," replied Ranson pensively. His elbows
rested on the chair arms, with his fingers steepled before
him, and he appeared deep in thought.

"You aren't considering anything rash, are you?"
asked Drew.

Ranson laughed, lowering his hands and meeting
Drew's gaze. "No. I'm aware that society will not accept
Stephanie as any more than she is now. Regardless, I
have been considering how I can help her once this business with Hayley is finished."

"Have heard of a group that helps women who want
to escape the demirep life. Said to be quite successful."

"I'm amazed at the things you know," said Ranson.

"Just keep my ears open," responded Drew, pouring
them each a drink of the fine brandy that White's
stocked.

"Then see if you can locate a contact with whom we
can speak. I'm assuming this is done discreetly since
I've never heard a word about it."

"Secrecy is the reason for their success," said Drew.
"Although, I believe I can uncover the information
you'll need."

"No doubt," replied Ranson wryly.

Now that his conscience had been eased concerning
Stephanie's plight, Ranson found his thoughts drifting
to Lavinia. He wondered with whom she had been
spending her time the last few days. Which men had
held her in their arms while guiding her around the
dance floor? Who had sent her flowers, penned a poem
to her, or kissed her hand? Had anyone dared to lead
her onto a darkened terrace to taste the sweetness of her
lips? Anger rushed through Ranson and he sat upright

in his chair, spilling some of the liquor from the glass he held tightly in his hand.

"What now?" asked Drew, startled by Ranson's abrupt movement.

"Nothing. Just some unpleasant thoughts." He tossed down the remaining contents of the glass as if it were Blue Ruin instead of aged brandy, and rose to his feet. "Shall we see what the members of the *ton* are doing this evening?"

"What of Stephanie?"

"She is not expecting me until later."

"Suppose you will want to hunt down Lady Lavinia," said Drew, finishing his own drink.

"No more than you will Lady Jessica," Ranson replied, a devilish glint in his eyes.

"She is a married lady and I've learned to avoid any involvement when a husband is present."

"I wonder whether their marriage is all it should be for I seldom see Carter with her. Perhaps he would not mind if she acquired an admirer of her own."

"Already admire her," confessed Drew. "If Carter had not appeared and swept her off her feet we might have been married by now and setting up our nursery. But I cannot fault her for marrying for love."

"It wasn't love I saw in her face the last evening when I observed the two of them together. Carter seemed vastly annoyed with her and left her standing looking after him as he stomped out the door."

"Noticed her discontent as well," revealed Drew. "Unfortunate that divorce carries such a stigma or we might still be together yet."

"You care for her that much, do you?"

"Wouldn't admit it to anyone else but you," said Drew.

"Your secret is safe with me," vowed Ranson. "I hope something will work out between the two of you. In the meantime, there is nothing wrong with enjoying her company."

"Take the opportunity every time I have a chance. Now that you're pursuing Lady Lavinia, it makes it much easier for me."

"I don't think you can say I'm pursuing the lady," protested Ranson.

"Looks like it to me," insisted Drew.

Ranson laughed. "I suppose you're right. I think I'm reluctant to admit that I might be ready to be caught in the parson's mousetrap. Once this business with Hayley is over with I may be asking you to stand up with me, that is, if the lady is willing."

Still bantering, the two men left White's and directed their driver to the first of the entertainments they planned to attend before duty called Ranson away.

Lavinia and Jessica arrived later than usual at Lady Swearington's soiree. Lavinia had insisted upon dressing for the evening and accompanying Jessica to her home in case Thomas had returned.

However, the house was quiet when the two women arrived and Jessica's maid reported that Mr. Carter had not been seen since that morning. Jessica quickly changed into an evening gown and the two women departed a short time later.

"You are being quite brave about this," said Lavinia as they made their way up the stairs at the Swearington house.

"I have no choice but to see it through," Jessica remarked shortly.

Lavinia laid a hand on her friend's arm. "Remember, you are not alone."

Jessica smiled, but had no opportunity to respond since they suddenly stepped into a crush of people.

"Lady Swearington's soiree appears to be exceptionally successful," judged Lavinia.

"I have never known her entertainments to be anything less," replied Jessica.

The two women entered the large drawing room. Additional chairs had been positioned around the room and a great many animated conversations filled the air with an indecipherable buzz.

Lavinia noticed Jessica peering about the room. "You must be looking for Viscount Stanford."

"Not at all. I'm merely interested in who is here."

"You cannot fool me," replied Lavinia. "It is Drew who holds your interest."

Jessica appeared to be discomfited. "Am I absolutely dreadful to be thinking about another man while I am planning to leave my husband?" she asked in an undertone.

"One has nothing to do with the other," said Lavinia. "You are leaving Thomas because he has harmed you and will, no doubt, do it again. Perhaps the next time will be far worse. Drew, on the other hand, is an example of the perfect gentleman. I don't believe he would treat a woman any differently in private than he does while in the company of others. Your interest in Drew is not a sudden occurrence. You have known him for some time and the two of you were attracted to one another before you met Thomas."

"You put up a good argument," said Jessica.

"It is only the truth, and you should remember it whenever a doubt crosses your mind. And smile," she ordered, "for I see Drew just across the room."

"There are the ladies," said Drew to Ranson. They had searched the other rooms and this was the last before

Ranson would be forced to give up the pursuit in order to reach Stephanie at the appointed time.

"Nearly too late," grumbled Ranson.

Drew pulled out his pocket watch. "Still time to spare. At all events, should at least pay our respects," he said, beginning to make his way across the room.

Ranson followed, still believing there was too little time to undo the damage Madam Vivian's notice had caused. If only the Prince Regent had not chosen him to work his way into Hayley's inner circle, he was certain he would have been on close terms with Lady Lavinia by now.

The two parties met and pleasantries were exchanged. Drew noticed that Jessica appeared wan and wondered whether all was well with her.

At the first blush, Ranson thought that Lavinia's smile appeared forced and he speculated whether she had heard any rumors about him.

"Lady Lavinia, allow me to show you Lady Swearington's collection of art." Ranson offered his arm and although Lavinia's hesitation was slight, he noticed it.

"You seem conversant with the house," said Lavinia as he led her into the hall and up the stairs.

"I have practically run tame in this house since I was in leading strings. Lady Swearington's son is a good friend of mine."

A frown crossed Lavinia's face. "I don't believe I've met her son."

"He's been serving with Wellington for the past four years. Nearly broke his mother's heart when he left, but he considered it his duty. I've received several letters from him, but none recently."

"I hope he's well," said Lavinia.

"I'm convinced we would have heard if he wasn't. In the meantime, I call as often as possible in an attempt to keep Lady Swearington's spirits up."

"That's extremely commendable, my lord."

Lavinia wondered how a man who would visit his friend's mother could treat her sister as he had. Pushing aside the sympathy she had been feeling for him, she forced herself to concentrate on the reason behind her desire to ruin him.

"Ah. Here we are," he announced, stepping into a long chamber whose walls appeared to be covered with all manner of framed paintings.

"Lady Swearington appears to be a dedicated collector."

"This is only a small part of her paintings," divulged Ranson. "The remainder are at her country estate. She began collecting while on her honeymoon and hasn't stopped since."

"Perhaps someday I'll have the opportunity to see the rest," remarked Lavinia.

"Oh, I'm certain you shall," he replied, moving further into the room. "Let us begin here and stroll around the room."

They reached the far end of the chamber, where they stood admiring an early portrait of Lady Swearington.

"She was very lovely, wasn't she?" observed Lavinia.

Ranson spoke without thinking. "No more lovely than you."

Startled by his comment, Lavinia looked up, candlelight softly illuminating her face, leaving her eyes dark and mysterious.

He was tempted beyond belief and allowed himself to give in to his desires. He lowered his head, watching her face for any sign of distress.

Lavinia could do nothing but stand frozen in place and watch Lord Weston bend toward her. There was no doubt as to his intentions, but she was powerless to stop him. All thoughts of her sister and revenge, of his past three mistresses and his current one, were swept from her mind as his lips touched hers.

She had been kissed before, but nothing she had experienced compared with the feelings Lord Weston's kiss aroused in her. Her legs grew weak and she clung more tightly to his broad shoulders, depending upon his strength to support them.

Ranson's arms encircled her completely and he drew her closer. She could feel the warmth of his muscular body against hers through the thin material of her gown and she reveled in their closeness, thinking she never knew she could feel such pleasure in a man's arms.

Ranson raised his head, lifting his lips from hers. She complained with a small feminine whimper and pulled him back to her. They were lost in one another: hands were caressing soft curves and hard muscles, the kiss was becoming more intimate by the second and neither of them seemed to remember where they were until voices interrupted their private idyll.

Ranson was the first to realize they were not alone. He stepped away from Lavinia, slipping the sleeve of her gown up over her shoulder and straightening his coat. By the time the couple saw them, they were strolling down the opposite side of the room, giving their full attention to the paintings hanging there.

"What were you thinking?" hissed Lavinia, as soon as they were out of earshot. "My reputation would have been ruined if we had been seen."

"I was overcome by your beauty," said Ranson.

"Fustian! You have never been overcome once since we have met. What possessed you to lose your common sense at this particular time?" She stopped, hands on hips, awaiting his answer.

She was altogether lovely in her fury and Ranson could not help but smile.

"Don't you dare laugh at me," she snapped, stomping her foot against the highly polished floor.

At that, he burst out laughing. "I am sorry," he apologized once he had gotten himself under control. "I admit I shouldn't laugh, but you are absolutely adorable when you're angry, and your beauty makes me smile."

"I am not adorable," she protested. "Kittens are adorable; I am infuriated."

Ranson was wise enough to hold back his laughter. "There was no harm done," he pointed out.

"There very well could have been. You wouldn't be laughing if I had been compromised and you were pressured into a marriage you didn't want," she raged, still seething with anger.

Ranson stared down at her. Perhaps that was the answer, he thought. He could escape all the wasted time courting her with just one small public kiss. No, he was allowing her nearness to overcome his good sense. He did not want to begin their life with a forced marriage and a blot on her reputation. Good God! He had just admitted he wanted to marry her. Had he lost all sense after one kiss? He had only met her a handful of times and he was already thinking of setting up his nursery.

"You're right," he said, taking both her hands in his, noting that she did not pull away even though she remained angry. "I sincerely apologize for endangering your reputation and I will be careful not to do so in the future."

Amazed that she felt totally undone by his charm, she ungraciously mumbled, "I suppose there was no harm done."

"Shall we return to Drew and Jessica?" he asked, placing her hand on his arm and starting down the hall.

She could do nothing more than follow and allowed him to guide her back to the drawing room, where Drew and Jessica remained deep in conversation.

"Unfortunate we had to leave so soon. Seemed you were making progress with Lady Lavinia," said Drew, once the men had left Lady Swearington's and were traveling toward Madam Vivian's nunnery.

"I don't know whether to call it progress, but we certainly came to know one another better," remarked Ranson. "Now I must spend the rest of the evening visiting the underbelly of London."

"Will have Stephanie with you. Cannot be the worst position in which to find yourself."

"I suppose you're right. I could have ended up with an emptyheaded chit and that would have been intolerable. However, I am still anxious to have this over and done with. I am in hopes that Hayley will extend an invitation to me if I see him tonight. We have spoken quite often and at greater lengths each time we meet. Do you think it would raise suspicions if I brought up the subject of the house party?"

"Don't see why it should. It isn't a secret. Would seem natural since you have a new mistress and might want to spend more time in a pastoral setting such as Hayley's estate."

The coach came to a stop outside Madam Vivian's.

"Are you coming in?" asked Ranson.

"Don't think so," replied Drew. "You won't be there long and I don't feel the urge to visit with the ladybirds. Will probably go to White's."

"I wish I could join you," said Ranson, as he stepped out of the coach.

The men bade one another good-bye and went their separate ways

Lavinia was in her room, spending another sleepless night after returning from the Swearington soiree. Although she had not revealed what had happened between her and Lord Weston, Jessica had clearly seen that her attention was elsewhere. However, each time her friend asked if something was wrong, Lavinia insisted she was fine as five pence. But now that she had privacy, she did not need to conceal her agitation.

Lavinia had once again paced her room until fatigue finally forced her to take a chair before the cold fireplace, considering again what had occurred that evening.

When she began her crusade for revenge against Lord Weston, she never thought she would end up kissing him in the art gallery of one of London's prominent hostesses. That she would encourage his kiss was unthinkable, but she could not refute that that was exactly what she had done.

Her face burned and she shifted uneasily in her chair as she remembered how she had clung to him and pressed her body against his. Although she had railed at him immediately afterward, she had experienced a sense of loss when she watched him leave the soiree.

How could she feel any emotion toward a man who flaunted his courtesans in front of her? If he felt anything toward her, he would never allow her to see him with another woman, particularly a Cyprian.

But now that she thought of it, Lord Weston had never said he cared a whit for her. Perhaps she was merely another conquest about which he could brag. Lavinia rubbed a shaky hand across her forehead. She should not even be thinking such thoughts. It did not matter how Lord Weston felt about her, for she felt nothing for him except anger, wanted nothing from him but revenge.

She must put him out of her head and concentrate on finding out what happened to Jeanette. If the earl was the reason for her disappearance, perhaps she could use it against him. In the meantime, she would attempt to keep a close eye on Stephanie Morris, and at the first sign of discontent, she would contact the woman. The

Season was at its height and if Lord Weston lost a fourth mistress it would certainly not go unnoticed.

Lavinia climbed into bed and lay awake thinking how sweet revenge would be against the earl, then she dreamt of being in his arms again, his lips pressed gently to hers.

Thomas Carter stepped out of the gambling hell into the vile-smelling street; his pockets were empty and his head ached from the cheap Blue Ruin he had consumed. His good sense told him the games were crooked, but when he was flush with blunt, he felt he could beat all odds. However, that had not been the case tonight, and he was left with only Hayley's need for women to replenish his gambling funds. He would make the rounds of the usual establishments and see whether he could entice a woman to visit Hayley's new house with him.

Night was not quite over when Thomas, a woman on each arm, entered Hayley's door. Even at that hour there was a respectable number of people milling about. The gambling room was filled with smoke and the sound of slurred voices. Thomas watched as glasses were filled and cards were dealt. He could tell the losers by the desperation in their actions. They nervously rearranged their cards—as if looking for one they had missed—then drank deeply from the glass of liquor at their elbows, as if it would change their fortunes. But Thomas knew from experience that theirs was a lost cause. They would lose their current hand as surely as they had the others.

Leaving the women at the door, he strolled around the room, searching for Hayley. He found him seated in a shadowy corner, keeping an eye on the activity in the room.

"Busy night, I assume," he said, taking a seat at the table.

"Business has been better each evening since we opened," bragged Hayley. "The ladybirds encourage the men to come here. They like the idea of having a drawing room where they can relax while the men gamble. Then there is the dinner room and even music if they should want to dance. I could not have planned better for my new venture."

"Not to mention the rooms upstairs," added Thomas.

"That's been quite lucrative, also," agreed Hayley. "There's only one area where I'm lacking and that is women. Are you able to help me yet?"

"I've brought two women with me, but they are not the quality of the last one."

"That's too bad, she was perfect for my needs," replied Hayley, remembering the young woman's horror when she realized what was happening to her. "Where are the ones you brought?"

"Over there, by the door. I don't know whether you can see them clearly through the haze."

"Introduce me," ordered Hayley, rising and taking out a beautifully enameled snuffbox. Thomas had no doubt that the snuff it contained came from only the best: Fribourg and Treyer in the Haymarket. Hayley did not offer the box to Carter, but took two delicate sniffs before continuing. "If they will do, I have a special room upstairs where we will send them. They won't be aware of their fate until it's too late."

The two women were introduced to Hayley and after a few minutes of conversation he gave a surreptitious nod to Thomas.

"Ladies, why don't you go upstairs and wait for me?" said Thomas. "I have some business to complete with Lord Hayley, then I will join you. I promise I won't keep you waiting for long." He offered them his most flattering smile.

They simpered and agreed they could use a little time to freshen up.

"I'll have someone show you the way," said Hayley. He made his way to one of the black-clad men standing in the hall and held a short conversation before returning to Thomas and the two women.

"If you'll just follow Barkley," he said, indicating the man standing a few steps away, "he will show you the way."

Barkley bowed to the ladies and they followed him down the hall and up the stairs.

"What happens next?" asked Thomas.

"They'll be offered some wine, which will make them very sleepy indeed. When they awaken they will be on their way to my country estate to await a trip to Dover. You aren't feeling sorry for them, are you?"

"Not at all," replied Thomas. "Just curious."

"I suppose you want your money," said Hayley.

"I wouldn't be doing this if I didn't," responded Thomas. "By the way, I may be bringing you a prime article soon."

"How prime?"

"The best you can ask for: one with beauty, brains, and grace."

"Sounds too good to be true," said Hayley, "but I could certainly demand a high price for a woman like that. How do you know this fancy piece is so talented?"

"Because she is not a fancy piece—she's my wife."

SIX

"I have hired a Bow Street Runner to help locate Jeanette," Lavinia said to Jessica as she held two shades of ribbons up to the light.

The two women were in Bailey's linen draper's shop on Oxford Street searching for ribbon to match one of Lavinia's gowns and Jessica glanced around to see whether anyone had overheard her friend's announcement.

"How did you manage to do that without your father knowing?" she asked.

"I enlisted Lady Danforth's aid. She contacted the man and we met at her house yesterday afternoon. He is going to search for Jeanette and determine whether Lord Weston had anything to do with her disappearance."

"And what will you do if he did have a hand in it?" inquired Jessica.

Lavinia paused, still holding the ribbons in front of her. "Why, I haven't thought that far," she replied, surprised she had not considered it before. "I shall use the information against him in some manner, I suppose. Perhaps I shall ask Jeanette to give an account to the newspaper."

"But that will call attention to her, and you are working to help the women, not harm them."

"She could not reveal her name and leave town immediately," argued Lavinia. "She could go to Hope House and begin a new life."

"But will her story be accepted? Lord Weston's name is an honorable one."

Lavinia laughed. "You've seen how much good his honorable name has done since the disappearances have been laid at his doorstep."

"Not everyone has believed it."

"But many have and if it is proven he had a hand in Jeanette's disappearance, then the rest will be believed."

"It's difficult to credit you hold such animosity toward him. When you are around him you treat him no differently from anyone else. You have danced with him and even viewed Lady Swearington's pictures with him."

Jessica's remark reminded Lavinia of Lord Weston's kiss and the confusion she felt each time she had thought of him since then. Disconcerted, she selected one of the ribbons she was holding and handed it to a clerk to cut.

"I cannot allow him to discover my personal feelings. He would demand a reason and I am not yet ready to confront him. The time will come when I will reveal all to him, but not until I exact every drop of revenge that I can."

"Perhaps you're mistaken in Lord Weston," suggested Jessica.

"Trust me, I am not," said Lavinia.

The two women moved on to inspect a new shipment of lace. "I spoke to Thomas about staying with you," said Jessica, as she studied the fragile threads.

"You should have waited until we were together to have mentioned it to him."

"I didn't want to get you or your father involved unless it was absolutely necessary."

"What did you tell him?" Lavinia asked.

"Exactly what you suggested. That your father was

returning to the country for a time and you could not remain alone in the house."

"And what was his reaction?"

"I don't know whether he even listened to what I was saying. He merely grunted and continued reading the paper. I chose to accept that the plan had his acceptance and did not bother him further."

"You are learning," said Lavinia, smiling her approval. "When may I expect you?"

"I thought perhaps in a few days' time. There are instructions I need to leave with the staff and new window hangings should be delivered tomorrow. I want to make certain the color is right before they are hung. Then I will need to pack."

"I wish you could come sooner. I don't like to think of you near Thomas any longer."

"I've been issued a reprieve," said Jessica. "He is ignoring me again, which means he has been lucky at the tables and has won sufficient funds for his needs at present."

"Are you certain you are in no danger?"

"It's possible that I will not even see him from now until the time that I leave," said Jessica.

"Then I will not dwell on it any further. On the day you decide to leave, I will send my coach for you and your trunks."

"I cannot hide forever," said Jessica.

"You are not hiding. You are merely visiting until we can determine a solution as to how to solve your problem with Thomas."

They left the draper's shop and strolled down the street, Lavinia's abigail trailing behind.

"There is something I'd like to discuss with you," said Jessica.

"You sound mysterious," teased Lavinia.

"I think . . . I think my feelings for Drew have returned. We have been seeing one another more than you know. We have arranged to meet at various functions and have even walked in the park one day."

"How wonderful," exclaimed Lavinia.

"Do you think so?" asked Jessica, surprised at her friend's reaction.

"It is exactly what you need," she said. "Drew is a wonderful person. I believe he is still more than halfway in love with you."

"No," said Jessica.

"Yes," replied Lavinia. "Besides, he will keep your mind off Thomas and you will be able to rely upon him if need be."

"I could not . . ."

"You do still have feelings for him?" Lavinia asked.

"I believe . . . No, I am certain I do, but I don't think it's fair to encourage him since I am married."

"You are married, not dead," replied Lavinia. "You and Drew should enjoy whatever time you are able to spend together."

"You don't mean . . . I couldn't," protested Jessica.

"I'm not suggesting anything except to enjoy what you can when you can. You know that the *ton* will overlook a married lady's indiscretions—even applaud them in some cases."

"Lavinia," said Jessica, choking back something between a gasp and a giggle.

Lavinia stopped and turned to her friend. "Jessica, I don't want to hurt you, but do you believe that Thomas never looks at another woman?"

Jessica studied a display of gloves in a shop window nearby before meeting Lavinia's gaze. "I know that he does more than look. I have smelled their perfume on him when he returns after a night out."

"I'm truly sorry, Jessica."

"There's no need. Not long after our marriage, I was

forced to admit that Thomas was not faithful to me. I have attempted to accept it as a weakness shared by all men, and have been fairly successful. However, since Drew has reappeared in my life, I find I no longer care what Thomas does."

Lavinia stared at Jessica a moment then burst into laughter; a moment later Jessica joined her. Their laughter had died down to sporadic giggles by the time a voice interrupted them.

"It isn't at all ladylike to be found acting like school-girls in the middle of the street on a sunny afternoon," said a deep voice from behind Lavinia.

"Robert!" cried Jessica, turning to embrace a tall, brown-haired man. "When did you arrive?"

"This morning," he said.

"Lavinia," said Jessica turning to her, "this is my brother Robert. Robert, this is my very best friend, Lady Lavinia."

"I am happy to meet you, my lord. Jessica speaks of you often."

"Please, call me Robert. Since you are such a close friend of Jessica's, I'm certain we'll see one another quite often."

Lavinia was impressed with Jessica's brother. "And you must call me Lavinia."

"What took you so long?" demanded Jessica. "I expected you a fortnight ago."

"A few problems in the country kept me," said Robert. "But I won't bore you with plantings and ditches." He smiled, his teeth white against his sun-browned face. He was a man who was not ashamed to admit he enjoyed running his estate.

"Well, I hope you are here for the remainder of the Season. Lavinia and I are looking for a tall, handsome gentleman to escort us around Town."

"Tall and handsome? Ummh. It seems that I remember you once calling me odious."

"I was only eight then and as I recollect you had used your guillotine on my favorite doll. Her head never fit right after that, no matter how many times Nurse repaired it."

"A boy must learn somewhere," quipped Robert. "But I am glad you've forgiven me after all these years."

"Forgiven you? Never. I am merely waiting for the right opportunity to pay you back."

They grinned at one another, evidently having had this same discussion many times previously.

"Where are our manners?" asked Robert. "We are ignoring Lavinia."

"Pay me no heed," responded Lavinia. "I am enjoying it. It reminds me of my sisters, whom I sorely miss."

"They are not in Town for the Season?" asked Robert.

"I'm afraid my older sister has been out of the country for the past several years and my younger is still in the country."

"Then we shall attempt to keep you entertained with sibling rivalry," promised Robert. "Now where are you two ladies off to next?"

"We've completed our shopping," said Lavinia, "and had thought to stop at Gunter's."

"I see my sister still has a sweet tooth," teased Robert.

"She is not the only one. I have been known to sneak down to the kitchen at night for another piece of Cook's cake," admitted Lavinia.

"Then the two of you are well suited," said Robert. "And if you will allow me, I shall be happy to join you at Gunter's." He held out an arm for each lady.

Lavinia took a moment to send her abigail home and then the three continued down the street.

* * *

Ranson could not get the short time he had spent alone with Lavinia at Lady Swearington's out of his mind. He repeatedly recalled the softness of her lips beneath his, and the sweet curve of her waist as he held her. It was true she had been angry after they had nearly been caught, but at the time she had been as responsive as any lady he had known. No, he should not compare her to other women, for she was far above the others in looks and intellect. He smiled to himself at the thought. There was no doubt he was in love.

The problem was with this whole Hayley operation. Ranson rued the day he had agreed to help investigate Hayley. If he had not done so, he and Lavinia would most likely already be betrothed. Now she had seen him in the park with a light-skirt and had been riding with him when one of the most infamous madams in Town had hailed him from her carriage. It was no wonder she was furious when they were nearly discovered in one another's arms. She doubtless thought he consorted with fallen women every day. He shook his head in amusement. These days he would not be able to refute the charge, for most of his evenings were spent with Stephanie, pursuing the elusive invitation to Hayley's house party.

Hayley had been welcoming whenever Ranson visited his establishment, but he had not yet mentioned the Cyprians' house party which was fast approaching. Ranson wondered whether he should bring up the subject, but decided to give Hayley a few more days. He did not want to appear too anxious and arouse Hayley's suspicions.

Ranson was in one of the better jewelry shops in London, considering a selection of emerald necklaces. The previous evening, he had noticed that Stephanie was the only woman in Hayley's house who did not wear at least one piece of jewelry. He had not thought to buy her any because she was not occupying the same position that his previous mistresses had filled. However, if he hoped to convince Hayley that he was so smitten he wanted to spend time with Stephanie at the house party, he would need to be convincing. Jewelry would go a long way to proving his devotion, particularly the excellent quality of the emerald necklace and earrings he decided to purchase.

"Isn't that Weston?" asked Robert.

Jessica peered around. "Where?"

"In the jewelry shop. Although I can't be certain from here, I do recognize the family's crest on the coach outside."

Lavinia looked through the windows of the shop and had no doubt about whether it was Lord Weston standing in front of the displays.

"Let's say hello," Robert suggested. "I haven't seen him for some time."

"We shouldn't bother him," protested Lavinia. "He appears to be busy."

"Nonsense. He will not mind in the least," answered Robert, escorting them to the door.

Lavinia watched as Ranson nodded and picked up a necklace from the display. It consisted of emeralds and glittered in the afternoon light that made its way into the shop. Lavinia did not need to wonder who would receive the necklace and the thought caused her to feel ill remembering Ranson's kiss. How could she have allowed him to even touch her after all she knew about the man? It was true, she wanted to keep in contact with him to learn all she could, but it did not mean she need kiss him. She wanted to rub her hand across her lips, but it was not the place to do such a thing. Besides, she could not wipe away the memory of his kiss no matter how hard she tried. The contradictory feelings waged war inside her and she was decidedly uncomfortable with them.

"Come along," said Robert, urging them toward the shop door.

Lavinia could no longer protest or she would draw too much attention to herself. She followed Jessica into the shop and watched while Robert greeted his old friend. Then the two men turned toward the women.

"Ladies," said Ranson, once he stood in front of them. "My day is complete now that we have met."

"Gammon!" replied Jessica, laughing at him. "You cannot turn us up sweet with such blatant flattery."

"You wound me," replied Ranson, placing his hand over his heart. "It is only the truth."

"We are going to Gunter's," said Robert. "Would you like to join us?"

Ranson had immediately noticed Lavinia's lack of response to his nonsense. Her expression was impassive and she offered him no encouragement at all. He could not help but wonder why a kiss should put her on her high ropes if that indeed was the reason.

"I would enjoy it if the ladies do not mind my presence."

Jessica immediately hastened to add her entreaty to her brother's, which left Lavinia the only one remaining silent. Ranson's gaze rested on her and she realized she must say something.

"Please do, my lord," she said, her voice stilted, for she was not a good-enough actress yet to appear completely comfortable in his presence.

Ranson hesitated a moment longer, then said, "I will be delighted. We must take my coach; it is right outside."

Somehow Lavinia found herself seated next to Ranson in the luxuriously appointed town coach. The squabs were so soft Lavinia knew she would never become stiff from traveling in this coach. There was even a small vase attached to the wall of the coach with a few calla lilies which scented the small area with a sweet perfume.

Lavinia was relieved that the conversation was carried on mainly by Robert and Ranson. She did not know whether she would be able to reply in a reasonable fashion, sitting so closely beside a man who kept her emotions in such chaos.

The time they spent at Gunter's seemed endless to Lavinia, but she supposed she responded naturally since no one stared at her in a curious manner. There was no time for private conversation, for which she was thankful. However, when the carriage reached her home, Lord Weston handed her down the steps and walked with her over the cobblestones to her door. "You have been quiet this afternoon," he said. "I hope you are still not upset over the other evening."

How could he bring that up to embarrass her? wondered Lavinia. "I don't know what you mean," she replied, knowing exactly what he was talking about.

"Our, er, experience at Lady Swearington's."

"Oh, that," she replied, her answer sounding false even to her own ears. "I haven't given it another thought. It is only that I received a letter from my sister this morning and I suppose I am more subdued because I miss her so much."

"Do you expect her to return soon?" he asked.

"She did not say, but I don't know whether she will ever come home. She had such a painful experience that it drove her out of the country." Lavinia watched his expression closely.

"I'm sorry to hear it. I hope you'll be able to convince her to return."

Lavinia wanted to call him to book for his treatment of Barbara, but it was too soon. She was filled with disgust. She was certain now that Lord Weston did not even recall her sister, for no one could appear as guile-less as he did at the moment, and her outrage mounted because he did not deem Barbara important enough to remember.

"It is my fondest wish," Lavinia answered evenly, thinking she could match his calmness. She would divulge nothing until she was ready. "Will you be at Lady Danforth's ball this evening?"

"I wish that I could be," he said sincerely, taking her hand in his. "But I am promised elsewhere. Would you consider riding with me again? Perhaps the day after tomorrow?"

Lavinia wanted nothing more than to jerk her hand from his and tell him she never wanted to see him again. But that was not how the game was played. "Only if you allow me to ride that wonderful mare again," she said, looking up at him from beneath her lashes.

"I am honored you admire her. Shall we say at four again?"

"At four," she agreed.

"Why did you agree if you did not want to go?" asked Jessica later that evening at the Danforth ball.

"You know I need to keep in contact with him or else how will I know whether my plan is working. I'm also able to ask seemingly innocent questions which disconcert him. It just infuriates me that he does not even remember Barbara, or so it seems."

"Are you certain it was Lord Weston whom Barbara accused?"

"Absolutely. I am not mistaken in that."

"Lavinia, I wish you would let this urge for revenge against Lord Weston go. I have only known him to be kind. There isn't a mother in the *ton* who wouldn't give her last shilling to have him offer for her daughter. He

* * *

At the same time that Lavinia was discussing marriage with Jessica, Ranson and Stephanie were entering Hayley's again.

"I feel as if I live here," grumbled Ranson as he handed Stephanie out of the coach.

"It is rather stifling night after night," she agreed.

"You are very lovely tonight," said Ranson, looking her up and down. He had told her to wear green this evening and she had done so. The low-cut gown hung on her shoulders by the merest scrap of a sleeve, leaving an expanse of bare skin where the emerald necklace he had purchased that day was displayed. She had pulled her hair back so that the matching earrings could be seen. All in all, he thought she would be the most striking woman at Hayley's that evening. Perhaps it would be enough to cause Hayley to invite him to the house party. He had not meant to use Stephanie as a lure, but if the man was selling women, he could not find one more captivating. He might think if he got her to his country estate, he could persuade Ranson to part with her. Revulsion overwhelmed him at the thought and he decided again that he must help Stephanie stay out of prostitution when Hayley was finally out of business.

"Well, here we are again," he murmured, too low for the guard to hear. "Can you keep smiling tonight?"

Stephanie laughed as if he had whispered something witty in her ear. "Why, my lord, I believe that is a most improper question." She winked at the guard as he opened the door.

"You're certainly getting the knack for this," said Ranson.

"I've been keeping my eyes open, watching the other women. I think I will be able to put on a good front if need be."

is wealthy, titled, and handsome; no one could ask for more. It is difficult to believe that he would act in the manner your sister related."

"Are you saying you don't believe me?"

"No. I am merely suggesting that perhaps there was a misunderstanding between the two of them."

"I will not argue the facts," said Lavinia. "I only know what Barbara passed along to me and unless she tells me differently, I will continue to believe it."

Jessica could see that she was making no headway in changing Lavinia's mind. She admired her loyalty to her sister, but continued to wonder whether Lavinia had the complete truth of the matter. She had known Lord Weston for some time since he and Robert were friends and she had never known him to be cruel to a lady.

Lavinia did not want to argue with Jessica, so she changed the subject to something she knew would get her friend's full attention. "How has Thomas been behaving?"

"I haven't seen him much," replied Jessica. "He was out until early this morning and was still abed when I left. We met last evening at dinner and he was as polite as I could have expected. I believe he has gotten some money from somewhere because he didn't demand any more from me. But I know it will just be a matter of time before he is out of funds again. Even if he wins at gambling, he continues until he loses everything he has gained.

"I believe it is a sickness with him, one that many other gentlemen have. Did you hear that Lord Trent lost everything that wasn't entailed in a game at Lord Hayley's two nights ago?"

"No," said Lavinia, aghast. "What of his family?"

"I don't know what they will do. They can reside at the country estate, of course, but how they will survive is questionable. Their manner of living will certainly be reduced."

"I am so sorry for his family," said Lavinia.

"There's something more I should tell you," began Jessica. "I don't know whether you know about Lord Hayley. He has always been known to have gambling nights which have ruined many gentlemen such as Lord Trent. Thomas told me that he has opened a new establishment and that Lord Weston and his latest mistress have been at Hayley's house nearly every night since it opened."

"Is it Stephanie Morris?" asked Lavinia.

"He didn't mention her name, but says she has the greenest eyes he's ever seen."

"That's Stephanie," said Lavinia, thinking that the emeralds Weston was looking at in the shop would set off such green eyes.

"Of course, that means that Thomas has been at Hayley's, too," Lavinia pointed out.

"I've accepted what Thomas is and will make no further effort to change him. If I can somehow live separately from him, I will do so, but it will take some time to arrange. I don't want to bring my father in on it; however, I may be forced to do so. Staying with you will begin the break with him. Although he may not realize I'm gone for days since he is so seldom at home."

"I'm glad you haven't changed you mind about visiting with me. I'm looking forward to having someone else in the house. Father is always in his study and is little company. We shall even be able to stay in one night if we wish."

"Never say you are tired of this social round?" teased Jessica.

"Some of the parties do seem the same," admitted

Lavinia. "I will be at a ball when sudde[...] I've done this exact same thing the nigh[...]

"I know how you feel, but I do not wa[...] alone either. We can have a quiet evening[...] ever, we cannot allow it to be more or els[...] considered on the shelf."

"That would not be unwelcome, particul[...] think of the men who leave their wives a[...] spend the evenings with their mistresse[...] Lavinia.

"You must not let that—or my poor exa[...] you off marriage. There are many happy marr[...] many gentlemen who never take a mistress. M[...] slipped away when I chose Thomas over Drew[...] too late now. All I can do is enjoy Drew's [...] when I can."

"I am not completely put off marriage by what I've seen," Lavinia confessed. "I still hold out hope that I will find a man such as Drew to set up housekeepin[g] with. As for your marriage, there is precious little y[...] can do about it now except play least in sight for[...] long as possible. Thomas cannot harm you if you[...] not close at hand."

"Do you realize we have been here for at le[...] hour and neither of us has had one dance yet?"[...] Jessica.

"We have been huddled in this corner talkin[...] plied Lavinia. "Perhaps we should station o[...] where we are readily available if we expect to b[...] to dance."

"I hope Drew is here tonight," said Jessica,[...] glistening with excitement. "Dancing with hi[...] not draw gossip, should it?"

"I think not, or else nearly every woman[...] be the object of an *on-dit* tomorrow, for th[...] dance with everyone but their own husband[...]

"We'll see, for here's our host now."

Hayley stepped out of the drawing room and raised his quizzing glass to examine Stephanie. "You are looking quite lovely this evening, Miss Morris. And may I compliment you on your emeralds. I am an experienced judge and they are exquisite."

"Thank you, my lord," she responded with an arch glance. "Lord Weston just presented them to me this evening." She clutched Ranson's arm with one hand and ran her other hand down his forearm to his hand where her fingers intertwined with his.

"You see," Stephanie continued, "my lord has promised to take me on a trip as soon as he can get away from Town, but he has not been able to yet." Her lips formed a pout and she glanced up beneath darkened lashes.

"Perhaps you would be satisfied with a trip to my country estate, my dear. I am planning a house party within a fortnight and you and Lord Weston are certainly welcome to come if you choose to. I assure you there will be enough to keep you entertained."

"Oh, could we?" asked Stephanie, clutching Ranson's arm even tighter and looking as if she had just been invited to dinner with the Prince Regent.

Ranson could not believe his ears. With a flick of an eyelash Stephanie achieved what he had been attempting for weeks.

The next morning, Lavinia sat in the drawing room, awaiting Mr. Harry Black, the Bow Street Runner she had hired to find Jeanette Norville. Mr. Black had called the previous afternoon while she was out and left word that he would call the next morning. Lavinia hoped he had word of Miss Norville's whereabouts.

She did not have long to wait, for the butler showed Mr. Black into the drawing room a few minutes later.

"My lady, it is good to see you again."

"And you, Mr. Black. That is if you have news for me," replied Lavinia.

"I have *some* news for you; however, not all that you wished to know."

Lavinia was disappointed. She had hoped to be able to put the question of Jeanette's disappearance to rest today. She was the only person in Town who knew for certain that Lord Weston had not had a hand in the disappearance of his three mistresses. However, as far as she knew, no one was positive beyond all doubt that he was innocent of planning Jeanette's fate—whatever that was. If Jeanette's vanishing could be laid at Lord Weston's doorstep, then he could possibly be worse than she had anticipated.

"Any information would be more than I have now. So tell me what you have discovered," she demanded.

"Miss Norville is new to her profession," he began. "She arrived in Town at the beginning of the Season and has enjoyed success with the gentlemen since then. She is from a small village north of London, where she was one of a large family of tenant farmers on the estate of Lord Drysdale."

Lavinia searched her mind for anything she might know about Lord Drysdale, but could remember nothing. "I do not know him," she murmured.

"I'm not surprised that you do not," Harry Black responded. "Lord Drysdale has no family of his own. He is interested exclusively in his dogs and horses and comes to Town only when absolutely necessary. I hope my plain speaking will not distress you."

"No, no. My father did not raise a pea goose, so go ahead with whatever it is you have to say."

"Lord Drysdale made it a practice to dally with the local barmaid. That is, until a newly grown-up Jeanette caught his eye. He held the livelihood of her family in his hands and when he made advances toward her, it did not take Jeanette long to determine that she should cooperate if she wanted her family to prosper.

"To be fair to Lord Drysdale, Jeanette did well by the arrangement, but eventually she grew bored and decided to move to Town where she might find more excitement. She has been enjoying herself immensely if rumors are to be believed. She had several men vying for her permanent attention and was nearly ready to make a choice. Then she heard that Lord Weston was searching for a new mistress and decided to see whether they would suit. She arranged to meet Lord Weston and it appears he did spend a short time with her one evening before she disappeared, although I have learned that it was not the night she disappeared but the evening before.

"She let it be known to him and his friend, a Lord Stanford, that she was quite taken with the earl and would be agreeable to becoming his mistress. I understand he thought she was a lovely young woman, but was not ready to make a decision that evening."

"Was she seen after that?" Lavinia asked.

"She most certainly was," replied Mr. Black. "The next evening she was back at the house where she had met Lord Weston. I believe she felt he might return there, although he did not as far as I know. The last anyone saw of her was when she was hurrying out of the house. She told one of the other women that she was meeting one of the handsomest men in all London."

"And who would that be?"

"I don't know," he confessed. "The woman I talked to says that Miss Norville did not mention a name. She swears, however, that the man was not Lord Weston for Miss Norville had not been gone long before the earl and his friend arrived. She told him he had just missed

Jeanette for she thought he had expressed an interest in her the night before. He thanked her for the information and mentioned that he would, no doubt, see her the next evening."

Lavinia had suddenly become concerned for this young woman who had escaped life on the farm only to fall into trouble instead of living life as she dreamed it. Who was to say that she would not have been happy in the life, even though Lavinia found the thought appalling. She must find the girl and help her if she could, or at least see that she was safe wherever she was.

"You must find out whom she met that evening," directed Lavinia.

"I can try," he said, "but I cannot promise results. The women are very protective of their own and will keep their tongues between their teeth rather than talk to an outsider."

"I have complete confidence in you, Mr. Black. You have proven that you can glean information where others have failed. Talk to the women; convince them that you are attempting to find Miss Norville for her own good—that she will benefit greatly from it."

He raised his brows, but did not say a word.

"I am sincere, Mr. Black. I wish to help Miss Norville find a respectable life. She sounds as if she is an intelligent young woman and would listen to sound reasoning."

Mr. Black rose from his seat. "I will do my best, my lady." He executed a small bow and left the room.

Lavinia listened as the front door closed behind him. From what Harry Black had told her, she did not believe that Lord Weston was responsible for Jeanette's disappearance. Now she must find out whom the girl had met the last night she was seen. If she could accomplish that, perhaps she could save another woman from slipping into the life of a prostitute.

As for Lord Weston, Mr. Black had proven the rumors false. She was reluctant to tell Jessica, for she would again insist that Lavinia was entirely in error about the earl, and that she could not believe.

SEVEN

"I have never been to Vauxhall before," said Lavinia.

Robert reached out to help her from the boat. "So Jessica told me. I thought you might enjoy arriving by water since that was the only access when the gardens first opened. However, I've arranged for a coach to take us home since the boat will probably be too cool by the time we are ready to leave."

"It was a wonderful trip," replied Lavinia.

Robert turned and handed Jessica out onto solid ground. "I'm certain you will enjoy the evening," she said, coming to stand by Lavinia. "We will have a delicious dinner, then music and a grand demonstration of fireworks among other entertainments."

"Come along, ladies," said Robert, "I've reserved a supper box and we don't want to lose it."

Their box was one among a hundred or so and was located next to the Grove, where the concert was performed. They dined by music from Haydn and Handel, performed by Mr. James Hook, who was the organist.

Lavinia was delighted by the paintings which decorated the inside of the box. There were scenes from the maypole dance, colorfully and realistically reproduced.

Jessica's assessment of the food served at Vauxhall had been correct. There was the famous muslin-thin slices of ham, made famous long ago by a carver who bragged he could cover the entire surface of the Gardens with one lone ham. Though a person might be able to read *The Morning Post* through it, the flavor of the ham was the most savory Lavinia had ever tasted.

Next came perfectly prepared, minuscule chickens that seemed no larger than a robin. They were accompanied by an assortment of biscuits, cheesecakes, strawberries and ice cream, all washed down by a delicious punch.

"I shall never move again," groaned Lavinia, after taking a last bite of ice cream.

Robert chuckled. "I'll wager you'll be treading the Grand Walk within the hour," he predicted.

"And there is much more to see," added Jessica.

"Then it will need to wait," replied Lavinia, laying her serviette by her plate and leaning back in her chair.

"We must find a suitable place from which to view the fireworks," Jessica insisted.

"Can't we watch it from here?" begged Lavinia.

"We could, but there are much better vantage points," said Robert, confirming his sister's remark.

"I will accept your decision." Lavinia sighed, rising to her feet. "But the view had better be spectacular for me to abandon such a comfortable seat."

They left the box and started down the broad path, following the crowd to the best area from which to observe the fireworks display in all its fiery glory. The initial impact of the display caused Lavinia to grip Robert's arm. There were noisy wheels sparkling with varied hues, rockets that hissed and blazed as they shot off across the dark sky along with a multitude of other fireworks.

As Lavinia became accustomed to the noise, she looked around at the many faces turned upward. In a sudden burst of light, she thought she saw Lord Weston a short distance away. Moving slightly into a better line of vision, she waited for the next explosion. When it came it confirmed that what she thought she had seen was real. Lord Weston was there and at his side was Stephanie Morris. Another explosion, followed by an even brighter flash of light allowed her to note that a magnificent emerald necklace adorned Miss Morris's neck.

Lavinia regretted the dinner she had eaten for her stomach rebelled at the thought of being with Lord Weston as he was purchasing a gift for his mistress. She was not upset with the woman, for she hoped Miss Morris emptied the earl's pockets before her time with him was over. Her emotion arose from the fact that he could juggle both mistress and a lady with whom he had shared a passionate kiss without a crack in his genial expression.

"I think we could see better over this way," said Lavinia to Robert and Jessica as she led them farther away from Lord Weston. She did not want to run into him when the fireworks display was over.

When the last rocket had been fired, they returned to their box, where they met friends who had also elected to come to Vauxhall rather than attend any of the *ton*'s activities that evening. They danced to the orchestra, which was now playing, and Lavinia drank far more arrack than was good for her. She covertly studied the crowd, keeping an eye out for Lord Weston; however, she did not see him for the remainder of the evening.

Robert had left them alone for a moment to locate their carriage when Lavinia told Jessica about seeing Lord Weston.

"You should have said something at the time," admonished Jessica. "We could have left immediately."

"And what excuse would you have given Robert?"

"A megrim, perhaps. The fireworks were certainly loud enough to cause anyone's head to ache. In any event, you should have confided in me." Jessica appeared to be hurt because of Lavinia's oversight.

"I'm sorry," said Lavinia. "But I was so dismayed at the moment that my instinct was merely to escape his notice."

Jessica seemed appeased by her explanation. "Did you see them again?"

"No, and I am gratified that I didn't. Can you imagine if we had come face-to-face? What would we have done? While it is not proper to introduce a mistress to your friends, surely he could not have pretended she did not exist. The circumstance would have been too lowering by half."

"Well, it did not happen, so put the whole matter out of your mind," suggested Jessica.

"That is all well and good for you to say, but I am promised to ride with him tomorrow afternoon in Hyde Park."

"Oh, my," was the only response Jessica could make.

"So you saw Lady Lavinia at Vauxhall this evening," said Drew, repeating what Ranson had just told him.

As soon as he was able to get out of the Garden, Ranson had taken Stephanie home and had retired to White's to determine what he should do next. Drew was already there, seated in a comfortable chair with a bottle of brandy at his elbow.

"Just got here myself," said Drew when Ranson took a seat. "Have been looking for Jessica, but she wasn't at any of the entertainments I attended tonight."

"I know where she was," replied Ranson, and then proceeded to relate the events of the evening, which had led to Drew's remark.

"I certainly hope Lady Lavinia did not see me. We

moved back into the crowd as soon as possible and left immediately; however, it may have been too late."

"Did you see her looking at you?" asked Drew.

"No, but that does not mean she did not. I am to ride with her tomorrow afternoon and I am in a quandary as to what to do."

"Nothing for it but to act as if nothing is amiss. If there is, she will let you know, you may be sure of that."

"That is what I'm afraid of," said Ranson, in a worried tone. He poured a drink of brandy and quickly downed it. "I have never cared how a woman felt about me until now, and it's a devil of a time for it to happen. Here I am, involved in a task for the Home Office that does nothing more than put me in a bad light and I cannot refute anything without endangering the assignment."

"If Lady Lavinia cares for you she will forgive everything once this is all over," conjectured Drew.

"Ha! By then, she will never want to see my face or hear my voice again."

"Sound like a hysterical woman," joked Drew.

"It is fine for you to jest," said Ranson, "but you are not in my shoes."

"Nor would I want to be. Have another drink," Drew suggested. "Will not change anything that happened this evening, but will cause you to care less."

Drew was wrong, thought Ranson, the next morning. The brandy had not caused his anxiety to lessen, it had merely given him a headache to go with it.

The hours passed too swiftly the next day for Lavinia's peace of mind and before she was prepared, Lord Weston was at her door. He was impeccably dressed as usual; from his expertly tailored jacket to the highly pol-

ished and tasseled Hessians, he was a gentleman few
could rival.

As for Lavinia, she was wearing a dark green riding
habit which she had admired until she donned it and
was reminded of emeralds. However, she had torn the
hem of her blue habit and it had not yet been repaired,
so she had no choice but to wear the green. Cursing her
luck, she lifted the skirt and descended the stairs to meet
Lord Weston.

"I am hoping the sun will come out," said Ranson,
as they stepped out into the cloudy day.

"It will not make a whit of difference," remarked
Lavinia, without thinking.

Ranson looked at her strangely. "I'm sorry," she said,
"I was thinking of something else."

Soon they were on their way toward the park. The
day seemed to be getting darker and Ranson wondered
whether they should have put off their ride until the next
day.

"Have you heard anything more about the missing
women?" asked Lavinia suddenly.

"Er, no, but then I haven't pursued the matter."

"Neither have I, but I cannot avoid the *on-dits* nevertheless. I have heard that the last one to go missing
said she was going to meet one of the most handsome
men in London."

"Where does all the gossip come from? I believe
there are people in the back rooms of the newspapers,
dreaming up stories to keep the public buying their pa-
pers."

"I heard this on good authority," insisted Lavinia,
"and have no reason to doubt it."

"Then if it is true, it could be one of many men. It
would be difficult to narrow down the gentleman with
no additional information."

"I understand there is a private inquiry going on,"

continued Lavinia, longing to crack his calm façade and scramble his logical explanations. She was gratified to see his hands jerk on his reins, causing his stallion to impatiently throw his head up and down in protest.

Ranson patted his mount's neck and prayed that whoever was looking into Jeanette's disappearance didn't decide to delve into his own activities over the past week. If they did, they might well discover his unusual conduct and wonder what was happening. Which, in turn, could lead to more suspicion and ultimate ruin of all he had done.

"Who is doing such a thing?" he asked, in what he hoped was a disinterested tone.

"That is being kept private, I believe," she replied. "However, some of the results have become known."

"It sounds like merely more of the *ton's* gossip. I believe many thrive on being the bearer of the most preposterous rumors their minds can conceive."

Lavinia's anger grew as Ranson shrugged off her information about Jeanette in a bored voice. "Even though you may not know the woman, my lord, it would seem that you could spare a modicum of sympathy in case some harm has befallen her."

Ranson turned away so that Lavinia could not see the grimace that crossed his face. There was a fine line he must tread between caring too much and too little and it seemed he could not judge properly in her estimation.

"I do not mean that I am indifferent to her fate. I only question whether she is in danger or whether she has merely gone off on her own."

From what Lavinia had learned thus far, it could be very likely that Jeannette had gone on a trip with the man she was meeting. Perhaps he had told her to leave everything behind and he would buy her something better. She could be living a comfortable life at this very moment: wearing the best of clothes, eating the most delicious foods, and traveling in style.

However, the reverse could also be true. She might be locked away somewhere, suffering from hunger and much worse. Until she was certain, Lavinia could push the subject no further. She hoped Mr. Black would bring her news soon.

They reached the entrance to the park and joined the parade of carriages and riders. It was not as crowded as usual, probably because the day was becoming darker as time passed. Many were being cautious and returning home before the storm broke and gave them a drenching.

"As much as I dislike suggesting it, perhaps we should shorten our ride and return on another afternoon when the weather is less threatening," said Ranson, eyeing the clouds that rolled menacingly overhead.

"Are you afraid of a little rain, my lord?"

"Not at all, but your habit is too attractive to be ruined in the rain."

"Do you like it, my lord? I was unsure about the color."

"You could not have chosen better. I am fond of green."

"I am certain you are. Does it remind you of emeralds?" she asked innocently.

Puzzled, he repeated, "Emeralds?"

"I noticed the other day when we met at the jewelry store you were choosing an emerald necklace. Of course, I cannot compare my riding habit to an emerald necklace except it is green and, as you say, you are fond of green."

Ranson did not speak; he could recognize anger when it simmered beneath the surface just waiting to erupt, and Lavinia was a prime example. He decided that the best course was to keep silent.

"Eyes," she said suddenly. "Are you also fond of green eyes, my lord?"

The light finally broke over Ranson and it wasn't sunlight. Stephanie! Dammit, she knew about Stephanie! If this had happened with anyone else, he would have given her a set-down she would never forget. But this was the woman with whom he wanted to spend his life. Was there any explanation he could give that would pacify her?

"Lady Lavinia . . ."

But she continued as if he had never spoken. "Emeralds would go very well with green eyes. I hope the necklace is for someone with green eyes, but then it is none of my concern, is it?"

"Lavinia . . ." He spoke firmly, determined to gain her attention and cut off the nonsense she was spouting. "There are things you do not understand . . ."

"There are many things I don't understand," she corrected him. "Then there are things that need no explanation at all. You might be interested to know that I was at Vauxhall Gardens last night. I had never been there before and was absolutely spellbound by the fantastic display of fireworks. But I need not tell you for you saw it yourself. You were not far away, standing with a woman who wore an emerald necklace and possibly a dress this same shade." She motioned disdainfully at her riding habit. "And I would wager that her eyes were green also."

"Lavinia . . ."

"It is no business of mine whether you have a mistress," she remarked, speaking far too bluntly for a lady. "I understand it is common practice for many men; however, I do resent your attention to me while you have another woman in your keeping. You have attempted to make me think you were interested in me. You have pursued me at various functions, you insisted we ride together, you practically forced me to dance with you and you kissed me. All the while, you were deciding what jewels to buy for your mistress. Should I be flattered? I think not.

"Now I am going home and I am going by myself. I will allow your groom to escort me so that he can return the mare. You can stay here in the park and admire all the shades of green around you. Perhaps you will find another pair of green eyes. But for your pocket's sake, I hope not, for you could bankrupt yourself buying emerald necklaces."

She turned the mare toward the park exit, then paused, twisting in the saddle so that she could see him. "And I gave you no leave to call me by my first name. If you ever do address me again, it will be Lady Lavinia." She tapped the mare with her riding crop and rode away, not looking back.

Ranson motioned for his groom to follow, then sat his horse, watching until the two disappeared around a curve in the path.

The rain began before Lavinia reached home. It did not commence with a gentle splatter of raindrops which warned of more yet to come and allowed a person to reach shelter. Instead, it seemed as if a huge hand poured a bucket of water directly on top of Lavinia's head. She was soaked to the skin in mere moments and was forced to wipe the water from her eyes in order to peer through the gray curtain of rain so as to determine how close she was to her home.

She was vastly relieved when the groom clipped a lead onto her mare's bridle and guided her the remainder of the way. She had only to cling tightly to the saddle in order not to be washed away.

When she reached home, she slipped from the saddle

without waiting for his help, threw the heavy rain-soaked skirt of her infamous green riding habit over her arm, and plodded up the steps, her boots squishing water with every stride.

Ignoring the butler's astonished stare, she stormed up the stairs, threw her riding crop to the floor, and jerked her hat from her head, sending it flying after the crop.

"Maria," she yelled, standing in a gathering puddle just inside the door.

"Oh, my lady," said Maria with a gasp, when she came running into the room and first spied Lavinia. "What has happened to you? You must get out of that right away or you'll catch your death of a cold."

"I'm certain there is at least one gentleman who would not be sorry to learn the news," replied Lavinia, through gritted teeth.

"You cannot mean it, my lady," protested Maria, attempting to undo the drenched fabric-covered buttons.

"No, I don't suppose I do," agreed Lavinia.

"These buttons will not give way," muttered Maria, as she continued to struggle with the small, slippery buttons.

"Cut them off," snapped Lavinia, her patience wearing thin

"But, my lady . . ."

"You heard me; cut them off. Then throw the dratted habit in the dustbin, or give it away, or make dusting rags of it. Do what you will with it as long as I never see it again."

"Yes, my lady," replied Maria, as she ran to get the scissors. She quickly returned and began snipping off the buttons, sending them flying about the room.

"And, Maria, the first thing in the morning do away with every green gown that I own."

"My lady . . ." protested Maria.

"I do not want one speck of any green hue to remain

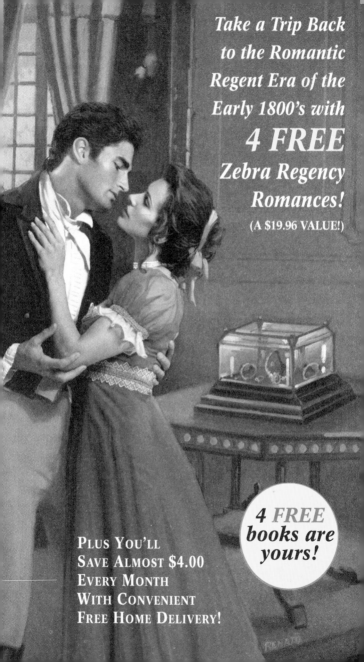

We'd Like to Invite You to Subscribe to Zebra's Regency Romance Book Club and Give You a Gift of 4 Free Books as Your Introduction! (Worth $19.96!)

If you're a Regency lover, imagine the joy of getting 4 FREE Zebra Regency Romances and then the chance to have thes lovely stories delivered to your home each month at the lowest price available! Well, that's our offer to you and here how you benefit by becoming a Regency Romance subscriber:

- 4 FREE Introductory Regency Romances are delivered to your doorste
- 4 BRAND NEW Regencies are then delivered each month (usually before they're available in bookstores)
- Subscribers save almost $4.00 every month
- You also receive a FREE monthly newsletter, which features author profiles, discounts, subscriber benefits, book previews and more
- No risks or obligations...in other words, you can cancel whenever you wish with no questions asked

Join the thousands of readers who enjoy the savings and convenience offered to Regency Romance subscribers. After your initial introductory shipment, you receive 4 brand-new Zebra Regency Romances each month to examine for 10 days. Then, if you decide to keep the books, you'll pay the preferred subscriber's price.

It's a no-lose proposition, so return the FREE BOOK CERTIFICATE today!

Say Yes to 4 Free Books!

Complete and return the order card to receive this
$19.96 value, ABSOLUTELY FREE!

If the certificate is missing below, write to:
Regency Romance Book Club
P.O. Box 5214, Clifton, New Jersey 07015-5214
or call TOLL-FREE 1-800-770-1963
Visit our website at www.kensingtonbooks.com.

FREE BOOK CERTIFICATE

YES! Please rush me 4 Zebra Regency Romances without cost or obligation. I understand that each month thereafter I will be able to preview 4 brand-new Regency Romances FREE for 10 days. Then, if I should decide to keep them, I will pay the money-saving preferred subscriber's price for all 4...that's a savings of 20% off the publisher's price. I may return any shipment within 10 days and owe nothing, and I may cancel this subscription at any time. My 4 FREE books will be mine to keep in any case.

Name _____

Address_____ Apt._____

City_____ State____ Zip_____

Telephone (   ) _____

Signature _____ RN032A
(If under 18, parent or guardian must sign.)

Terms and prices subject to change. Orders subject to acceptance by Regency Romance Book Club.
Offer valid in U.S. only.

lll..l..lll....llll.l.l.l.l..l.l.l.l..lll.l.l..l

REGENCY ROMANCE BOOK CLUB
Zebra Home Subscription Service, Inc.
P.O. Box 5214
Clifton NJ 07015-5214

PLACE
STAMP
HERE

in my wardrobe by noon tomorrow. If there is, you will be responsible for explaining to my father why I have run screaming into the street. Do you understand."

Maria's eyes were wide open as she stared at her usually mild-mannered mistress. "Yes, my lady. I'll do it first thing," she promised.

EIGHT

It was nearly eight in the evening and Drew had joined Ranson at his town house for dinner. They were in the small dining room at a round mahogany table laden with ham, beef, pheasant, chicken, fish, and at least twice as many vegetable dishes. Ranson had no doubts that the dessert selection would be just as varied.

"Envy you your cook," said Drew, as he sliced into a crisply baked Cornish hen.

"You've said that for years," bantered Ranson.

"Only because it's true. Someday I'll lure her away from you."

"Then expect me to be at your house for every meal," Ranson warned him.

"Perhaps I should reconsider," he joked. "Ready to tell me why it was so important I come to dinner at such short notice?"

"I need to discuss what happened on my ride with Lavinia . . . Lady Lavinia today. And you are the only person I can trust to keep silent on the subject."

Ranson repeated what had occurred that afternoon and waited for Drew's reaction.

"Why the big smile?" was his first question.

"Isn't it apparent? She is not indifferent to me," Ranson exclaimed, his smile growing wider. "If she didn't care, she would not be angry about the necklace or green eyes or anything else."

"Could be she felt played for a fool."

"That could be," said Ranson, frowning, "but even so, if she were not interested she would never have come riding with me. She would have had the butler convey her regrets and cut me dead the next time our paths crossed. Instead she warned me to address her as Lady Lavinia the next time we spoke."

"That can hardly be considered encouraging," objected Drew.

"Near enough," shot back Ranson. "I'm convinced I can win her over."

"Not while you are out every evening with Stephanie."

"That will end soon, and then I will tell Lavinia everything," said Ranson.

"Lady Lavinia," corrected Drew.

"No matter," said Ranson absently. "Tell me what you think about this search for Jeanette."

"Don't know enough to draw a conclusion. If we can believe the gossip to have any truth to it, someone is evidently concerned enough to attempt to track her down. Nothing to do but wait unless you want to mount your own search."

"I have three missing mistresses already, why should I take on one who isn't even mine?"

"To prove to Lady Lavinia you didn't kidnap her. If she's heard all the *on-dits,* then she knows your name has been linked with at least three other missing women. You are also rumored to have been seen with Jeanette shortly before she disappeared, and the ladies certainly consider you one of the most handsome gentlemen in Town."

"Surely she cannot seriously consider that I did away with four women," said Ranson, in disbelief. "She is too levelheaded for that."

"Never underestimate what people who are head over heels will believe," warned Drew.

"Do you think she is? Head over heels, I mean," Ranson clarified.

"Don't know. Suppose whether she is or not will hang on how soon you can be through with Hayley and get back to normal. Any woman would suspect a man who has been acting as you have been since the two of you met."

"I know," agreed Ranson, "but there is nothing I can do. Do you think apologizing would help?"

"What? Squeeze her in between trips to visit your mistress?" asked Drew. "That is exactly how she will view it until you make it obvious that Stephanie is no longer in the picture."

"You know I can't do that until after the Cyprians' house party," complained Ranson. "By the way, Hayley issued an invitation last night."

"Congratulations," said Drew.

"It wasn't due to my efforts," Ranson admitted ruefully. "Stephanie turned him up sweet and had him practically begging us to attend with two blinks of those green eyes that Lavinia dislikes so much."

"Don't think Lady Lavinia said she didn't like them, just that you liked them too much," quipped Drew.

"As soon as this is over and I can concentrate on Lavinia instead of Hayley, she will forgive me," boasted Ranson confidently.

"Lady Lavinia," said Drew, reminding him again. "Hope you're right. Would be a shame to lose the only woman in whom you've ever been interested."

Ranson considered Drew's words and the smile faded from his face.

Jessica had joined Lavinia in her sitting room, where the two women sat embroidering in front of the fireplace. The rain continued that morning, making the warmth of a small fire a welcome addition to take the chill from the room.

Lavinia glanced out the window at the gray day. "I'm surprised you braved this horrible weather to visit," she said.

"I couldn't bear to remain in the house. I have finished all the decisions on the new window hangings and have given instructions to the housekeeper. There was nothing left to do but sit and feel sorry for myself and I decided to do that no longer."

Lavinia's sewing rested unnoticed in her lap as she gave her attention to her friend. "Are you ready to leave Thomas then?"

"I believe that I am," replied Jessica. "I have given orders to Betsy on what to pack and we should be ready tomorrow. I hope it will not inconvenience your household if I bring her along."

"Of course not. We have plenty of room for her here and Maria will welcome her company."

"I suppose the plans remain the same and you will send your coach for my trunks in early afternoon," said Jessica.

"If you will come along at the same time, we'll have dinner here before we go out for the evening."

Jessica smiled for the first time that day. "That is an excellent plan," she said. "You make it sound as if I am doing you a favor when it is you who are helping to save me."

"I'm pleased that you will be keeping me company. Now, how do you plan on informing Thomas of your departure?" asked Lavinia, once again picking up her embroidery and beginning to ply her needle.

"I have no doubt he will be gone tomorrow when I am ready to leave, so I will leave him a letter. I will tell him your father has been called back to the country sooner than he thought and that you cannot stay in the house alone. I don't believe he will question it since he is familiar with the quirks of the *ton*. Once I am gone, it will be difficult for him to drag me from your house; however, I do not believe he cares enough to expend the energy."

"You should be grateful if he does not, for it will make it far easier for you."

"I don't know what he will do when he realizes I am not returning to him," said Jessica.

"Perhaps it would be best to confide in your father. You know that he will help you once he deals with Thomas and will continue to support your household if that is what you choose."

"I believe Thomas is capable of anything when he is in a rage and I fear he might harm my father or worse," she confessed.

"He would not dare," said Lavinia firmly. "And you are not to worry about that. We should be able to put that decision off for at least a fortnight at the earliest."

"All this depresses me," said Jessica. "Tell me about your ride with Lord Weston."

"You do not want to know," Lavinia warned her.

Jessica looked up in surprise. "Of course, I do. I believe he is seriously interested in you, Lavinia, and this is the first time in my memory that he has paid such particular attention to a lady."

"Let me tell you the story, then you might want to reconsider Lord Weston's interest in me."

It took some time for Lavinia to relate what had occurred, for she revealed everything she had previously held back, including the kiss. When she finished repeating her orders to Maria to burn every green gown and article in her wardrobe, Jessica could no longer contain her laughter. After a moment, Lavinia joined her and neither could stop until their sides were aching and tears ran down their cheeks.

At one point, the butler opened the door and solemnly intoned, "Is anything wrong, my lady?" which only set them off again. He quickly closed the door and they did not see him again until Lavinia rang for tea.

"Oh, my," Jessica gasped, still patting at her eyes with a fine linen handkerchief, "I have not enjoyed such a laugh for ever so long."

"Nor have I," agreed Lavinia. "Even though it was at my own expense."

"Do not feel I was laughing at you," said Jessica, concerned for her friend's feelings. "It was the situation and how Lord Weston thought you would never know a thing about his activities. Perhaps he is merely blind in this one area, for he surely knows the ways of society and that he could not avoid being seen with his mistress, nor could he hide the necklace."

"He has made no move to conceal his current flame," replied Lavinia. "On the contrary, he seems to be flaunting her instead."

Jessica frowned and when she spoke the laughter disappeared from her voice. "That is not like Lord Weston. I cannot believe that he would seriously pursue you and at the same time so blatantly carry on with another woman."

"Perhaps he is not pursuing me," suggested Lavinia. "He could be merely amusing himself at my expense."

"Definitely not," Jessica quickly replied. "That I know he would never do. Drew would not claim friendship with such a man and they have been friends since they were in leading strings."

Lavinia selected the brightest yellow thread she could find and began embroidering a pansy. "In any event, it does not matter," she remarked. "For I am not at all interested in Lord Weston. Have you forgotten that his actions drove my sister from her home?"

"Have you?" asked Jessica, turning the question around.

"No, I have not and I never will. The only reason that I've tolerated his presence has been to watch him as he loses his mistresses and to see his reaction as he is blamed for their disappearance. Before this is over he may be forced to leave England just as Barbara did. It will be interesting to see how casually he accepts that."

"There has been no hint that action will be taken against him for the disappearances. Most people are convinced that the women left of their own free will and the rumors are dying for lack of interest."

"Surely my work will not go to waste," moaned Lavinia.

"If you are depending upon a public outcry then I believe you'll be frightfully disappointed. However, if you mean to disconcert Lord Weston, then you have attained your goal. I understand from Drew that he is determined to locate his previous mistresses in order to ascertain their safety. As for the last girl, Jeanette, Drew says that Ranson only spoke a few words to her on one occasion, and he doesn't expect anything to come of it except for some bantering from the gentlemen."

"Bantering! About the disappearance of a woman? Does that tell you how much value men put on the women who serve them? Once I am finished with Lord Weston, I intend to devote myself to liberating every demirep in London," she proclaimed.

"I am of the opinion that many of them are happy with their way of life and would not change were the chance given to them."

Lavinia recalled the women at the theater who were dressed to the nines and surrounded by men. "I suppose you are right, but a few might accept my offer. I will concentrate on those, hoping to free them from that particular slavery."

"I should be getting home to check on Betsy's progress," said Jessica without much enthusiasm.

"It is still raining," observed Lavinia. "At least stay for luncheon. Perhaps the sun will be out by the time we are finished."

"I should be embarrassed to give over so easily, but I must admit I do not look forward to returning home and possibly meeting Thomas when I am so close to getting away from him."

"Forget him for the moment. I have a new book which I will read from while you sew. Then Cook will serve us a delicious luncheon before you go out into the damp again. And keep in mind that soon you will no longer share the same roof with Thomas."

"That is uplifting," responded Jessica.

"I shall begin," said Lavinia, picking up *Emma,* a new novel by Jane Austen.

"I enjoy her books immensely," said Jessica.

"As do I," agreed Lavinia. "This one is dedicated to the Prince Regent. I understand Miss Austen turned down the suggestion that she write a history of the Prince's family. I believe her excuse was that her meager talents could not do him justice."

"She has a wonderful way with words, doesn't she?" asked Jessica.

"Surpassed only by my tirade to Maria on the color green in my wardrobe," joked Lavinia, which set both women laughing again.

The night stayed wet and miserable and Lavinia thought of the many hostesses whose events would be lightly attended because of the inclement weather. Both she and Jessica had decided to stay at home that night, meeting again the next evening when Jessica would arrive with her trunks for an indefinite visit.

Lavinia had alerted the staff that a guest would be staying with her and warned the footmen about allowing Thomas Carter free access to the house. He was not to be invited in without the express permission of either her or Lady Jessica.

She spent the evening reading, and thoroughly enjoying *Emma*. Then she snuggled down in the softness of her bed and fell asleep to the sound of the continuing rain.

The next morning was bright with sunlight glinting on the damp cobblestones in front of Lavinia's home on Berkeley Square in Mayfair. She was glad to be out and stepped lightly around the lingering puddles without complaint and into the coach. She meant to visit Hatchard's for new books, then stop by the Carter household to visit with Jessica. They had not settled on a definite time for her to arrive today, and Lavinia did not want her waiting for the coach.

It was nearly one o'clock in the afternoon before Lavinia was admitted to Jessica's home.

"I hope I'm not interrupting," she said as Jessica descended the stairs to join her.

"Of course not. Come into the drawing room," she said.

"I'm afraid I don't have the time," said Lavinia. "I have a myriad of things to do before we depart this evening. I stopped by to settle on a time for my coach to arrive."

"The sooner the better."

"Good. Then I will send the coach at five. That should give us ample time to relax and enjoy our meal before we leave."

"I am so looking forward to this," said Jessica, her eyes sparkling with excitement.

"We are going to vastly enjoy ourselves," predicted Lavinia, as she turned to leave.

Lavinia's prediction would prove to be false, for her coach returned from Jessica's that evening empty.

"But where is she?" asked Lavinia, when the butler passed on the information.

"She left no message for you, my lady. However, her husband sent word that she had decided to visit friends in York."

Lavinia was completely bewildered. "York?" she said, echoing the man's words.

"That is what he said," affirmed the butler.

"Call a footman," she ordered. "I wish a note delivered to Lord Bates with all due haste."

As the butler left, Lavinia moved to the small writing desk in the corner of the room. She swiftly penned a note to Robert, explaining the circumstances surrounding Jessica's unusual decision to visit someone in York and begged him to call at his sister's home to see what he could discover.

After dispatching the footman, she paced the drawing room, wondering whether Jessica's fear of Thomas had proven true. She was not forced to wait long before Robert was striding into the room.

"She is not at home," he began without preamble. "Thomas is not there either. I was told that Jessica's trunks were in the hall ready to be loaded as soon as your coach arrived. Evidently Thomas appeared without warning, saw the trunks, and went upstairs to Jessica's rooms. He ordered Betsy out and closed the door behind him."

"Oh, no," exclaimed Lavinia, afraid of what she would hear next.

"When they next appeared, Thomas had Jessica by

the arm. The coach was waiting out front, so he had her trunks loaded and they drove off. Betsy attempted to speak with Jessica, but Thomas would not allow it. She said that Jessica was exceedingly pale and did not say a word to anyone."

"But what of Thomas? He was there when my driver arrived to bring Jessica here."

"About an hour after Thomas left with Jessica, he returned alone. He told the staff the same thing he had told your man, that his wife had decided to visit friends in York."

"I cannot believe it, can you?" asked Lavinia.

"I do not know any friends of Jessica's who live in York and I believe that I know all of her acquaintances. I intend to hunt Thomas down and demand he tell me where Jessica has gone."

"Robert, I am sorely afraid for Jessica's safety. I don't know whether she has told you everything." Lavinia went on to explain all that had happened between Jessica and Thomas of which she was aware. "Jessica was apprehensive that he might refuse to allow her to leave when the time came."

Robert's face was dark with anger and he stifled a curse. "She should have confided in me."

"She did not want to involve either you or your father for she feared blood would be shed," answered Lavinia.

"And she would have been right," Robert confirmed. "Once I find that coward, he will get what he rightly deserves." He made an effort to control himself before he spoke again. "Try not to worry. I will let you know as soon as I find out anything. You should go ahead as you had planned. Perhaps you'll learn something this evening that will help."

"I will do my best, but promise you will come here first thing in the morning so that we may exchange information."

"I will come immediately after breakfast if that is not too early."

"Why not join me for breakfast?" suggested Lavinia.

"I will see you then unless our paths cross this evening," he affirmed

After Robert departed, Lavinia could not sit still. She jumped up every few minutes, pacing to the window, then returning and dropping into the chair again. When tea arrived, she did not touch any of the saffron cake, which was her favorite.

The staff whispered and the rumors circulated as to why their mistress was behaving so strangely. But Lavinia noticed none of it, for she was far too worried about her friend.

Although his heart was not in it, Ranson had no choice but to continue with his investigation of Hayley. He and Stephanie were again at Hayley's establishment, although they had arrived later than usual because Ranson did not want to stay any longer than necessary.

He was nearly ready to leave when he noticed Drew enter the room. Ranson raised his hand and caught his friend's attention, then watched while he threaded his way through the crowd. Drew's usually genial expression had been replaced with a grimness Ranson had seldom seen.

"I'm surprised to see you here this evening," said Ranson, as Drew arrived at his side.

"Was looking for you. Have some news."

"Nothing's happened to Lavinia, has it?" he asked, even though Stephanie stood close enough to hear every word.

"No, not Lavinia, but perhaps to Jessica."

"What! Tell me what has happened," he demanded.

"Met Robert tonight at White's. He was searching for

Thomas. Said he had taken Jessica from the house, all white and scared-looking. Had returned a short time later saying she had gone to visit friends in York."

"And Robert believes he's lying?"

"As far as he knows, Jessica isn't acquainted with anyone in York. Her trunks were packed and waiting to be taken to Lady Lavinia's. She was going to spend a fortnight or so with her. Instead Thomas came home, found the trunks, spent some time locked in Jessica's rooms with her, then led her down the stairs and into the carriage."

"Can't the coachman tell you where he took her?"

"Don't know. Thomas has the coach and driver with him wherever he is. That's why Robert is searching."

"Can we help him?" asked Ranson.

"That's why I'm here. Told Robert we would also search. We're to meet back at White's later in the evening."

Ranson turned to Stephanie. "I'm afraid we must cut our evening short."

"Do not apologize, my lord. I will welcome a good night's rest. I hope you can help your friend," she said, placing her hand on his arm and looking up at him.

"I'll send you home in my coach," he said to her, then glanced at Drew. "We'll use yours to search."

Drew nodded and the three left the gambling room, walking down the hall to the front entrance to the house.

"You're leaving so soon?" asked Hayley, stepping through the drawing room door into the hall.

"I'm afraid we must," replied Ranson.

"Not getting bored with the entertainment, are you?"

"Not at all, but something's come up that needs our attention. You'll see us again soon."

"We're so looking forward to the house party," added Stephanie, with a coquettish glance.

"And I look forward to having you as a guest in my home," replied Hayley with a small bow. He opened the door for them himself and watched as Ranson handed Stephanie into his coach, then joined Drew in the other. "I wonder what that is all about," he murmured to himself, rubbing his chin with two fingers.

A little after two that morning, Hayley spied Thomas entering the gambling room. "I didn't expect to see you again so soon," he said, once Thomas had approached.

"I'm a little nervous about our deal. I wanted to see whether all was going well."

"You know better than to doubt me," chided Hayley.

"I do, but if I could only see indisputable proof with my own eyes I would rest much easier."

Hayley detested men who whined; however, Carter did bring him many of the prime articles that made his business successful. It wouldn't hurt to humor him this once, particularly since the baggage was so special.

"Come along then, but there is not much to see," he warned.

Hayley led the way up the staircase and down the hall to the last room on the right, where a man stood guard outside. "Anything?" he asked.

"Not a peep," confirmed the guard.

Hayley selected a key and inserted it in the lock. It turned easily and he pushed the door open and stepped inside. Thomas followed close behind.

At first, Hayley blocked his way and Thomas could not see anything. Then Hayley stepped aside, and in the dim light of a single candle, Thomas saw Jessica lying on a bed. He moved closer until he was standing directly over her. She was so white and still that he thought she might be dead.

"Is she . . . ?"

"I assure you that she is perfectly all right. I merely had to administer a heavy dose of laudanum since she was in such a state when you brought her here. She will sleep quite peacefully until the morning. Perhaps by then, she will realize she has no option but to cooperate or conditions will become much worse very quickly."

"If her father or brother finds out, I'm a dead man."

"They will not find out," replied Hayley, forcefully. "But you must not lose your nerve and allow anything to slip. You are doing nothing more than what you have done before."

"But none of the others was my wife," Thomas pointed out.

"She is a woman just like the rest. I'll move her to my country estate until the remainder of the women join her, then we'll remove them all after the house party is over. Once I get her to the coast she will never be seen again. Then you can go about collecting all that money she has at her disposal."

"If her father does not interfere," grumbled Thomas.

"You had her write a will indicating you should inherit everything, didn't you?"

"Of course I did," snapped Thomas. "But that doesn't mean the old man will give up without a fight. He disliked me at first sight."

"And with good reason it seems," broke in Hayley.

"Clutch-fisted old fool arranged Jessica's money so that I could not touch it, and I have had to go about purse-pinched since we walked down the aisle."

Hayley gestured toward the bed. "You can see you need not worry. Soon you will be able to afford whatever you want."

"And my fee for her?" he asked, nodding toward Jessica.

Hayley looked incredulous. "You mean you want to be paid for your wife?"

"Why not? She has caused me a great deal of difficulty and her disappearance will surely bring all manner of questions. I should receive something for my troubles."

"I suppose she means no more than the others you have brought."

"And not as much as some," replied Thomas, dealing the ultimate insult to his unconscious wife.

NINE

Lavinia was already at the breakfast table when Robert entered the next morning. "Did you find her?" she asked anxiously.

"Not a sign of her," he responded, dropping into a chair across from her and rubbing his face with both hands.

"And Thomas?"

"Nor him either. It's as if they both dropped off the face of the earth or at least from this part of it. Did you learn anything?" he asked, his weary eyes meeting hers.

"Nothing. And I made a point of attending as many functions as I could. There were no rumors about Thomas, although many people asked about Jessica. Of course, Thomas seldom attends any of the *ton* events unless it's a card party."

"I hope you don't mind that I asked . . ."

He was interrupted by noise from the hall.

"That must be them now," he said, rising to meet Ranson and Drew as they entered the room. "I was going to say I hope you don't mind that I left word for these two to join us, but I spoke too slowly. They helped me search last night and I thought we could compare notes."

"Of course, I don't mind," replied Lavinia. Although she had not seen Lord Weston since their argument in the park, she would accept any help if it meant finding

Jessica. "Please fill your plates from the sideboard and take a seat."

Although she appeared tired, Ranson thought Lavinia brightened the room in her yellow gown. She made no sign that she was still angry and he harbored a small hope that she had put it behind her. He ladled buttered eggs and a large slice of ham on his plate, selected a biscuit and bravely took a seat next to Lavinia.

"We were just beginning to discuss what we discovered last night," she said.

"And that was?" asked Drew, reaching for the red currant jelly.

"Nothing," replied Robert succinctly. "Did you have any luck?"

"We found several places Carter had visited earlier in the evening," answered Ranson.

Even though Lord Weston sat near Lavinia, she found her fear for Jessica had overcome her disgust for the earl. If he could find her friend, she would never utter an unkind word about him again.

"Did not mention where he was going next," Drew explained.

"I stopped by his house early this morning, but he had not returned," added Robert. "I waited until dawn but he still did not show up."

"Holed up somewhere, no doubt," concluded Drew.

"But where?" pressed Robert. "He has no real friends, only gambling acquaintances who would not put themselves out for him."

"Perhaps a woman," suggested Lavinia. "He seems to be able to charm them very easily."

"You may be right," agreed Ranson, "but there's no way to find him until he comes out of hiding."

"We cannot just sit and wait; she could be harmed." Lavinia's voice shook and she gripped her serviette tightly in her hand.

"I intend to keep searching," said Robert. "No matter what her age, she is still my little sister and I will have no harm done to her."

"We will help, of course," offered Ranson, and Drew nodded his agreement.

"Do not leave me out. I can't just sit here all day," protested Lavinia.

"Make the rounds of the at-homes today," suggested Ranson. "See whether anyone knows anything about Carter. Someone might have seen him last night. The best known hostesses seem to get all the gossip before it makes the rounds, so call on them first."

They continued discussing the problem and what each of them could do to help discover where Thomas had taken Jessica. When the men rose to leave, Ranson lingered behind, detaining Lavinia in the dining room while Robert and Drew continued into the hall.

"Lady Lavinia, you were angry the last time we met and I want to apologize for offending you in any way."

In the confusion of Jessica's disappearance, Lavinia had forgotten they had been at daggers drawn in the park. "There is no need," she answered.

"But there is," he insisted. "Lady Jessica's well-being is more important than our dustup. We must combine our efforts in finding her and bringing her home. I suggest we put aside any differences we might have, at least until she is safe."

"I agree," replied Lavinia. "I cannot think of anything else but Jessica. If only I had sent the coach a little earlier, she might have been here now."

"Don't blame yourself; you were doing all you could to protect her. You couldn't know that Carter was going to take her away so quickly."

Lavinia buried her face in her hands. "I cannot believe she is gone."

Ranson took hold of her wrists and pulled at them

gently until her face was visible. "We will get her back," he murmured, gathering her hands in his.

Lavinia looked up at him, the pain of Jessica's predicament apparent in her bearing. "Do you truly believe that?" she asked, begging for reassurance.

"I truly do," he confirmed with a gentle smile. "Try not to worry too much. We'll see you here again this evening, or earlier if we have news."

She nodded, unable to speak around the lump in her throat.

He raised both her hands to his lips and placed a warming kiss on them before he turned and joined the two other men in the hall.

Lavinia stood as he had left her until she heard the door close behind them. Then she returned to her rooms to dress for her morning calls.

Ranson, Drew, and Robert had spent the morning searching for Thomas Carter. They had visited every gambling hell that was open, thinking he might still be at the tables. Robert mentioned that Carter had interests in boxing and horses, so the three men stopped at Gentleman Jackson's Rooms, then continued on to Tattersall's, where they saw prime horseflesh being auctioned off at enormous prices, but no sign of the man they sought. Although Carter was not known for swordplay, they also called in at Angelo's Haymarket Room to no avail.

They were now at White's. Having just consumed a cold luncheon, they were considering what to do next.

"Must visit Madam Vivian's and all the rest this evening," said Drew. "Carter's a favorite with the women, though don't know why."

"It's his looks and the charm that he turns on and off

at a whim," said Robert. "He snared Jessica before she knew she was being used."

"Damn shame," remarked Drew.

"I believe she has regretted it since the first month," said Robert.

Drew looked at him sharply. "Didn't think she appeared happy," he commented.

"She isn't. I believe she meant this visit with Lavinia to be a permanent separation."

"Once we find her, she should have no problem ridding herself of Carter," said Ranson.

"He will be gone forever if he values his life," Robert growled, his hands curling into fists.

"Will be glad to help," said Drew.

"But first we must find her," remarked Ranson. "Drew's right. We'll need to visit all the houses again this evening. I will stop by the Wilson house even though I don't expect to find him there. Then there are the theaters and the gardens."

"Leave the theaters till last," suggested Drew. "According to Jessica, Carter did not care for them at all."

"First, we should call on Lavinia. It's possible she might have heard something on her rounds today. Then we will go by Jessica's home. I left a man watching to see whether Carter returned today. If so, he was to follow him and then report to me immediately."

"Let's be on our way," said Drew, rising to his feet and straightening his jacket. "No time to lose."

Robert and Ranson followed him out the door and into the waiting coach.

Lavinia arrived at her door at the same time as the men. She ordered refreshments and invited them to make themselves comfortable while she disposed of her hat, gloves, and pelisse.

"There is something I have not told you," Ranson

said to Robert, as the men settled into chairs in the drawing room.

"And that is . . . ?" asked Robert.

"I am leaving Town tomorrow," Ranson replied. "It's a trip that I can't put off or I would stay and continue the search for Jessica."

Robert did not voice his apparent disappointment. "Drew and I will finish what is left to do. I am convinced that Jessica is no longer in London and I will hire men to search for her if I cannot persuade Carter to tell me of her whereabouts once I find him."

"There is more you should know and I must ask you to keep this absolutely secret," said Ranson.

"Of course," replied Robert, a puzzled look on his face.

"I am attending Hayley's Cyprians' house party."

"What!" exclaimed Robert, unable to conceal his surprise and disgust.

"I am not going for pleasure," explained Ranson. "I've been asked by the Home Office to help investigate Hayley. They believe him guilty of many things and one of them is the increasing disappearance of women from the London demireps.

"It is thought he has a market for them on the Continent and that certain men assist him in procuring women to sell there."

Robert's mouth opened, but he did not utter a word.

Ranson held up a detaining hand to silence him. "I have lost three mistresses already this Season and have been marked as the last man to be seen with a woman by the name of Jeanette Norville. So you can see that I have a great interest in finding the truth of the matter and whether any of these women were taken by Hayley."

The implication suddenly dawned on Robert. "Jessica," he gasped. "I have seen Carter with Hayley numerous times. Do you think he . . . they . . . ?" He could not finish the question that filled him with horror.

Ranson would have liked to have given Robert more hope; however, it was necessary for him to be aware of the danger that might threaten his sister.

"It's possible Carter could have arranged for Hayley to take Jessica off his hands. He would have rid himself of a wife who had tired of his ways and could have gotten paid for it."

"Jessica's a lovely woman. Carter would have received a handsome sum for her," added Drew, seeming to choke on the words.

"Let's confront him now; search his house," said Robert, leaping to his feet.

"Just a moment," said Drew, following and taking hold of his arm to lead him back to his chair. "Would like nothing more than to call him out, but must think of other things."

"Drew's right," said Robert. "That is why I'm explaining this to you when I should keep my tongue between my teeth. We are not certain that Jessica is there and if we move now we could warn Hayley off and never be able to catch him and make him pay for his crimes. The Home Office has been watching him for months and it would be a disaster for their case against him if we made the wrong move now."

"The Home Office be damned! We are talking of my sister. I cannot sit still and do nothing," objected Robert.

"And you won't," said Ranson. "We will continue with our plans for tonight. I will do my best to search for Jessica when I reach Hayley's. I'll keep in touch while I am in the country and let you know what I've found out. But you must not tell anyone about what I'm doing or the whole thing could blow up in my face. It could endanger not only me, but the woman who has agreed to go on this trip with me."

"Does she know?" asked Robert.

"Part of it. I thought it only fair to tell her what she was getting into. She is a decent person and deserved to make a choice in the matter."

"And you will let us know the moment you find anything out about Jessica?"

"I swear on my honor," said Ranson.

"That is good enough for me," answered Robert. "I only hope you know what you're doing."

"So do I," agreed Ranson with a wry grin. "So the plan is to visit all the spots we mentioned earlier, then the two of you will continue tomorrow. As for me, Stephanie and I shall travel to Hayley's country estate in the morning where we shall attend his infamous Cyprians' house party."

After Lavinia had invited the gentlemen into the drawing room and ordered refreshments brought to them, she hurried upstairs to remove her outer garments. She smoothed her hair, then quickly descended the stairs, eager to hear whether the men had found out anything about Jessica. Just as she was ready to step through the door, she heard Ranson reveal that he would be attending Hayley's house party with Stephanie. Lavinia could not believe what she was hearing. How he could consider attending such an event at all was a mystery, but particularly when Jessica was missing. She took a few moments to compose herself and then entered the room when there was a pause in the men's conversation.

"I'm sorry to have taken so long," she apologized. "I hope you have some good news to impart."

"I'm afraid not," spoke up Robert. "We have been all over Town, but have little to report."

"Carter was seen around and about yesterday afternoon and early evening, hasn't been seen since," added Drew.

"We intend to search again this evening. Like many miscreants, he may come out of his hiding place, once darkness falls," said Ranson.

"When we find him, I have some hard questions for him to answer," said Robert, grimly.

"You heard nothing?" asked Drew.

Lavinia shook her head. "No. Many of the women asked me about Jessica. I told them she had suffered a slight summer chill and they seemed to accept it."

A silence fell over the group until Drew said, "Must go and change for the evening."

"Yes," agreed Robert. "We have places to search this evening."

Lavinia fretted because she was not able to go with them. "Is there anything I can do?" she asked.

"Continue keeping your ears open for any *on-dits,*" said Ranson, rising to join the two men who had made their farewells and were walking toward the door.

"Lord Weston, may I have a private word with you?"

Drew and Robert had paused, waiting for Ranson to join them. "Go ahead," he instructed, "I'll only be a moment."

"Will wait in the coach," replied Drew, as the two men left the room.

Lavinia did not move until she heard the outside door close, then she went to the drawing-room door and closed it.

Ranson wondered what she had to say that required such confidentiality. Perhaps she had fallen head over heels for him and meant to declare her intentions. Ranson smiled at his private joke, thinking that was the last thing she would say after the incident with the emeralds.

"I'm glad you can find something to smile about, my lord, for I see nothing amusing in this situation."

"Nor do I," replied Ranson, wiping away all semblance of a smile from his face. "But I was pleased to see you looking so well and could not help but smile."

"I am perfectly well," she confirmed. "Even though I should be the one with a chill after my last outing with you."

"Er, yes, the groom said you did get a drenching in the rain and I apologize for that. I should have canceled our ride once I saw the darkness of the day; however, my desire to see you overrode my common sense."

"It seems that happens often," replied Lavinia.

Ranson was stung by her remark. "How can you say that?"

"Simply by proof. When I came down the stairs earlier, I could not help but overhear your conversation."

Ranson winced. He should have been more careful of what he said, but he had been anxious to explain his absence to Robert. They had known one another for years and Ranson did not want Robert to think he was running out on him when he needed him most.

"What is it you heard?" he asked, already knowing the answer.

"That an extremely important engagement will not allow you to search any longer than this evening for Jessica. And that the event that takes you away is Lord Hayley's Cyprians' house party. Am I correct thus far?" she asked.

"Yes, but . . ."

Lavinia cut him off. "And that you are taking a woman by the name of Stephanie with you to keep you company. At least, that is one way to describe her duties."

"Lady Lavinia, you don't understand . . ."

"I understand only too well. I know that ladies are not to acknowledge they know anything about men and their mistresses, but that does not mean they are blind and deaf to what is going on about them.

"I spoke to you earlier about women missing in London and you seemed to know nothing about them," she charged. "I don't know how many women have disappeared, but I do know that three of them were your mistresses and that you have not done one thing to see whether they are safe."

Lavinia felt a small pang of guilt thinking that she had been the one to help the women vanish, but then she considered the others who had gone without anyone knowing or caring about them. She decided that men of Lord Weston's rank should bear some responsibility for them.

Ranson stood stiffly in front of her, attempting to contain his anger. If Lavinia had been a man, he would have planted her a facer. It was a moment before he could speak calmly. "I had nothing to do with the women disappearing. It's my intention to find them and make certain they are well as soon as I finish some urgent business."

"I suppose your urgent business is more important than the well-being of your friend's sister."

"No, it isn't," he denied.

"Then why, for God's sake, are you going off with your mistress while Jessica's very life could be at stake?" Lavinia clenched her fists, praying she would not completely lose her temper and strike out at him.

A slight crack appeared in Ranson's control. He stepped closer to Lavinia and took her upper arms in his hands. He did not shake her as he wished, but he pulled her nearer until the light scent of her perfume wafted up to him.

"It is something I cannot change," he said, from between clenched teeth.

"Cannot or will not," she mocked.

"Cannot," he insisted. "If I could explain it I would,

but it's impossible to do so at this time. You must trust me in this,"

"Ha! Trust? That is a peculiar word to mention in the same breath with your name since they are not at all compatible. Is that what you tell your women? Trust me," she said with a sneer.

A muscle pulsed in Ranson's cheek as he looked down into Lavinia's angry face. He drew a deep breath. "One day you will find that you are wrong about this," he predicted.

"You may be right, but it will be too late to save Jessica," she argued.

"I can see there is nothing I can say that will change your mind."

"There is not," she affirmed, attempting to pull away from him

"I hope you will not think less of Drew or Robert because of this."

"They are my friends," she said, "and they have not tried to hoodwink me."

"All for a good cause," he insisted.

"I do not believe it," she declared hotly. "You have had four mistresses this Season alone. You are well enough acquainted with Lord Hayley—a man with one of the worst reputations in London—to attend his house party. All this while both your friends are doing all they can to find Jessica. How can you be so callous. You could spend every night with your mistress here in Town. Isn't that enough for you?"

At that moment, with her color high and her eyes brilliant, she was the most beautiful woman in the world to him. He ached for what he was doing to her and would have done anything in his power to save her this pain. However, he could not reveal his secret to her.

Divulging it to Robert had been more than the Home

Office would allow if they had known, but he had been forced to explain it to him. The more who knew, the greater the chance it would find its way back to Hayley and ruin the entire plan. No, he could not tell Lavinia the truth and he was afraid it would ruin his chances with her forever.

The thoughts flashed through his mind, and when he realized she might never want to see him again, he could not resist. Pulling her closer, he leaned over her, pressing his lips to hers more in anger than in love. She struggled slightly at first, but her lips soon parted to accept his. He felt her weight rest against him and quickly put his arms around her to mold her body to his. Never was a kiss more sweet, never was a kiss more heartbreaking, for it could be their last.

He finally lifted his head and she rested her forehead against his chest for a moment before raising her gaze to his.

"This does not change anything," she whispered sadly.

"I know," he agreed just as softly.

They both straightened and he stepped away. "I will be gone for at least a sennight and perhaps longer, but I have arranged to keep in touch with Drew and Robert. I have not, as you think, completely lost interest in Jessica."

"Little good you will do in the country with a houseful of men and their demireps," spat out Lavinia, again forgetting for the moment that she was speaking of the very women she had sworn to save.

Ranson had no reply to her comment. "I mustn't keep the horses standing any longer. I will bid you good day."

Lavinia said nothing. She stood where she was as he opened the drawing room door and stepped into the hall. There was a muted murmur of voices and the front door opened and closed. A moment later, the butler appeared at the door.

"Is there anything you wish, my lady?"

"Yes, clear away all this," she said, pointing to the refreshments that had been brought for the gentlemen. "And bring me tea, as hot as cook can brew it."

As Ranson climbed into the carriage, Drew and Robert examined his solemn face.

"Trouble?" asked Drew.

Ranson leaned back into the squabs before he spoke. "She overheard what I said about the house party," he revealed.

"Lud!" said Robert.

"By George! What poor luck," exclaimed Drew. "Were you able to explain it?"

"She had heard enough," said Ranson. "There was nothing I could do. She has no hard feeling for the two of you, so keep in touch with her. I don't want her to become angry enough to tell anyone what she overheard."

"Will talk with her daily," promised Drew.

"As will I," Robert assured him.

"She still doesn't know that I'm working for the Home Office. She thinks this is all for my pleasure."

"Couldn't you have told her?" ask Robert.

"I wish that I could have," replied Ranson. "It might have saved me from her scorn. But I couldn't risk the chance that the news would get out before I got to the house party. The only way is to keep that information among the three of us. No, I must accept that Lavinia is going to think the worst of me, and hope that when all this is over I can explain it to her satisfaction."

"If anyone can do it, you can," said Robert.

"Won't be easy though," added Drew.

"Nothing worth having ever is," replied Ranson. "However, Hayley has made it nearly impossible and I look forward to settling the score. I hope tonight marks the beginning of the end for him."

TEN

Lavinia was fortunate to have an aunt such as Lady Fitzhugh. Aunt Hope had introduced her to the *ton* and had gone about with her until Lavinia met Jessica. Since Jessica was married, she had taken Lady Fitzhugh's place in lending propriety to Lavinia's ventures into London society.

Once Jessica disappeared, Lavinia had been forced to call on her aunt to once again attend events with her. Aunt Hope was a vivacious woman who had married young and lost her husband after only a few years of marriage. She had a substantial estate and was able to do as she pleased without any interference.

It was no coincidence that Hope House carried her name. The house itself had been the home of her late husband's mistress and she felt it only right that it be used to help women get out of the life.

Lady Fitzhugh had lost respect and love for her husband when she first realized she was not the only woman in his life. From that time until his death, she tolerated him. As soon as Lord Fitzhugh was laid to rest in the family tomb, she called upon the woman who was his mistress. She explained what she had planned for the house and told her she was welcome to be the first resident if she so desired. The woman agreed and was Hope House's first success, going on to marry and raise a fine family.

Lady Fitzhugh continued to be the driving force behind the project, slowly drawing other ladies to help the cause. The house had been instrumental in turning many women's lives around and always had a waiting list of women who wanted to become respectable people in society.

Lavinia had called on her aunt immediately upon Jessica's disappearance and told her what was going on.

"My dear, we must do whatever we can to help," her aunt had exclaimed.

"There is not much we can do except keep our ears open for any rumors of her whereabouts," Lavinia had responded.

"Then we shall begin right away," Aunt Hope had replied. "I will accompany you this evening and we will attend every event that is possible in one night. You will circulate among the younger people and dance with the men. I will sit with the dowagers and absorb whatever gossip is making the rounds. If anything is said about Jessica, we will surely hear of it."

"Thank you, Aunt Hope. I knew you would be willing to help," Lavinia had said. And they had done just that, but without any success.

Lady Fitzhugh had called on Lavinia to hear the latest on the search for Jessica.

"Robert and Drew are visiting wherever gentlemen gather in order to find Thomas," said Lavinia, "but he seems to have disappeared, too."

"More like hiding out," surmised Aunt Hope. "I attended the wedding; a hasty affair, I might add. I realized at first glance what kind of man Carter was, but knew that it would do no good to warn Jessica. She was completely taken with him and her eyes were blinded by his good looks and charm. I recognized it for the same thing that had happened to me years ago. The only good thing was that Fitzhugh died before wasting too many years of my life."

"Aunt Hope!"

"It's true, Lavinia. I would have still been sitting home waiting for him to put in an occasional appearance if it had not been for him trying to take a fence while he was foxed. Not that I wished for him to die, but it might have come to that before many more years had passed. In any event, I was left well off and have been able to indulge myself ever since."

"You have also done a great deal of good," said Lavinia.

"You mean Hope House? I suppose I have. It's ironic that Fitzhugh's mistress inspired such a project. If he knew, he would probably be furious that his money was being spent to transform the Fashionable Impures into ladies. But that is far behind me; we must now plan how to help Jessica."

The two women spent the next half hour deciding which entertainments being held that evening would most likely yield useful information. When she returned home, she sent a note to Robert, providing him with the list that she and her aunt had agreed upon so that he could get in touch with her if need be. Then she climbed the stairs to her room to rest before the long night began.

"I have heard nothing useful," complained Lavinia, as she and her aunt traveled from Lord and Lady Cochran's ball to the Hendersons' soiree.

"It is early yet," said Lady Fitzhugh, attempting to console her niece.

"Not for Jessica. She is probably counting every minute, wherever she is."

"Do not torture yourself, Lavinia. There is nothing more we can do until we hear from Robert or Drew."

"I hope I will see them soon and they will tell me they have found Carter and he has told them where she is."

"I'm certain they will let you know as soon as they have news," said Lady Fitzhugh. "Now here we are; put a smile on your face."

Lavinia and Lady Fitzhugh entered the Hendersons' home and were immediately swept up in the crush of people.

"I am going to sit over there," said Lady Fitzhugh, indicating a group of women who were occupying chairs set along one side of the room. "And you continue to circulate among the others."

Lavinia grimaced. "There are so many people here."

"The more the better," said her aunt. "You will be crowded so closely that you should be able to listen without anyone suspecting. When you have made the rounds, return to me and we will go on to the Lawtons' card party."

"All right." Lavinia sighed. "But I am already weary of this. A spy's life cannot be a pleasant one."

Lady Fitzhugh offered her niece an encouraging pat on the arm, and made her way toward the group of dowagers at the opposite side of the room.

Lavinia inched her way through the crush of people, speaking to those she knew, and attempting to listen to all the conversations going on around her. Her head was beginning to ache when she spied Robert and Drew enter the room and begin looking around.

They were searching for her, she knew. Praying they had good news to convey, she began making her way in their direction. However, when she reached the door they were nowhere around. She wondered whether they had gone into the supper room as she stepped through the door into the hall. The two men were huddled together, speaking in low tones. She opened her mouth to draw their attention when she heard the desperation in Robert's voice and paused.

"I am convinced she is already in Hayley's hands. Carter has grown close to him and the rumors we heard are near proof positive that he may well have turned Jessica over to him."

"He's a slippery fellow," replied Drew. "Don't know for certain."

"For God's sake, man! We may not have it in writing, but I'm as certain as I can be without hearing it from Hayley's mouth."

Robert rubbed his hands across his eyes and made an effort to control himself. "I believe we should concentrate on the house party. It's likely he has already taken her to his country estate. If so, he means to dispose of her with the rest of the women who will be left there. That gives us a few days to perhaps work our way into the party ourselves."

"Won't do," replied Drew. "Neither of us has a mistress and without one we could not get an invitation. Besides, the house party begins tomorrow and Hayley most likely has a full house by now."

"Then we'll hire a Bow Street Runner to find a position at the estate where he can tell us what is going on."

"Don't imagine Hayley hires strangers for this kind of thing," said Drew. "Suppose we'll need to rely upon . . ."

Drew heard a noise and turned to see Lavinia standing a short distance away. Her face was pale and her eyes wide. He moved quickly to her side and took her arm.

"Lady Lavinia, are you all right?"

"What . . . I overheard . . ." she stammered to a halt.

"Perhaps we should find a more suitable place to talk," suggested Robert, coming to stand by her side. "Let's see whether there's a room down the hall where we may be private." He led the way to a small parlor at the back of the house. The noise from the supper room was muffled to a soft hum.

"Lady Lavinia, what did you overhear?" Robert asked.

"That Lord Hayley has Jessica," she replied bluntly. "Is it true?" She looked from one man to the other for an answer.

"Don't know for certain," replied Drew.

"I must know everything," she insisted. "I want to know about Hayley and the other women and what the house party has to do with everything."

Robert and Drew exchanged glances. "She has heard too much; we must tell her all," said Robert. At Drew's nod, he turned back to Lavinia.

"Perhaps you had better sit down," he suggested, indicating a group of chairs at one end of the room. When they were all seated, he took a deep breath and began.

He explained the missing women and the reports of women not returning from Hayley's house party. He repeated what they had learned just that evening: that Carter had been seen with women who later had not returned to their rooms. He appeared to be close to Hayley, seeing him almost daily at one or another of his establishments.

Hesitantly, he recounted his fears that Carter had handed Jessica over to Hayley to get rid of her in an attempt to wring as much money as he could from her estate. They had not been able to track Carter down in any of his usual haunts, and assumed that he had already departed for Hayley's house party.

Lavinia had grown progressively paler as he recounted his story. One hand spread over her heart while the other clutched the skirt of her gown in an unsightly clump.

"What are we to do?" she gasped out, when Robert

finished his story. He had been careful not to mention Ranson.

"Must find out whether Hayley has Jessica," muttered Drew.

"Lord Weston is there," said Jessica, her face brightening. "All you need do is contact him. No matter what I think of him, surely he will not refuse to help Jessica."

Drew had to keep Ranson's secret that he was working for the Home Office. "Too obvious," he said. "There are too many people at the estate during the party. Couldn't get to Ranson without someone reporting to Hayley."

"I will think of something," she murmured, a thoughtful look on her face.

"Do not worry," said Robert. "Drew and I will handle this."

"But how?" she asked. "Neither of you can go alone, and even if you could obtain an invitation this late, you do not have a woman to go with you. I overheard that much."

"Will make do," said Drew. "Will not allow Hayley to put his dirty hands on Jessica."

Lavinia straightened in her chair. "Promise you will do nothing until you talk to me again tomorrow morning. Come to breakfast," she ordered. "I may have an idea by then."

"What?" asked Drew, a wary expression on his face.

"I do not have it completely worked out yet, but I will by dawn," she advised them. "Go home and get a good night's rest, for you will need it from now until Jessica is found."

Lavinia rose and leaving the two men seated in the small parlor, she made her way back to the ballroom. Greeting the women who were seated near her aunt, she then complained of a megrim and the two women took their departure.

In the coach, Lavinia related her conversation with Robert and Drew and her idea of how to save Jessica. Aunt Hope was not shocked by Hayley's actions, merely saddened. She had seen much inhumanity in the world and only hoped they would be able to help Jessica before she was lost to them. The two women retired to Lady Fitzhugh's house, where they sat up until the small hours of the morning, planning their attack. Lavinia finally took her leave to catch a few hours' sleep before confronting Drew and Robert.

Lavinia had ordered Cook to be certain that breakfast was varied and robust in nature since Robert and Drew would be joining her. She allowed them to fill their plates and take the edge off their hunger before she brought up her plan, for she knew their food would probably go untouched once she broached the subject.

"Cook is to be commended," said Drew, as he accepted a second cup of coffee.

"That she is," agreed Robert.

"I'll pass that along; she'll be pleased that two gentlemen appreciate her skill," said Lavinia.

"You mentioned a plan last night," said Drew.

"I admit we have thought of nothing that would work," confessed Robert.

"It is this," said Lavinia. "Drew and I are going to Hayley's house party."

Drew nearly choked on his coffee. "What!" he sputtered, dabbing at his mouth with his serviette.

"Do not be alarmed," exhorted Lavinia. "There will be no danger to anyone involved, including Jessica, if she is at his estate."

"Always danger in dealing with Hayley," replied Drew.

"Not if we pretend we are merely a couple who would like to enjoy the pleasures of his house party."

Both men stared at her as if she had grown two heads.

"Listen to me before you judge what I am suggesting," she pleaded. "There is a village near Hayley's estate which has a well-established inn. My aunt and I have stayed there several times when we have needed to break our travel. Aunt Hope and I shall take a room there, as will you, Drew.

"Then Drew and I will call on Hayley at his estate. I have never met the man so he will not recognize my true identity. I will dress in a manner that will cause him to believe I am your current ladybird. You will tell him that we were traveling through and that you remembered his house party was going on. That you had always wanted to attend since you had heard it was vastly entertaining. We know that his house is full and he will not be able to invite us to stay; however, we can suggest that we take rooms at the inn and join the activities of the party during the day and evening."

"Preposterous!" remarked Drew.

"I think not," said Lavinia. "Hayley is a nasty piece of work. He is a greedy man who will look at you as another gentleman to fleece by one means or another and will want to garner your goodwill. Since you have expressed an interest in the house party, he will already be adding your name to the next list of invitees and will be wondering how much he can win from you at the tables, both at the house party and once you return to London."

"It might work," said Robert thoughtfully.

"Your vision is clouded," said Drew. "I'm as anxious as you to rescue Jessica if she is there, but this plan will never work."

"Why not?" demanded Lavinia.

"Simply will not do," declared Drew stubbornly. Ranson would probably call him out if he turned up at Hayley's door with Lavinia in tow. Pistols for two, breakfast for one, he thought, without his usual amusement when he heard the remark.

"You are only saying that because I will be involved. I know what I am doing," she assured him, "and I will bring no harm to any of us. This is the only chance we have of proving whether Jessica is at the estate. As guests, we will be able to wander over the house and grounds without suspicion. We cannot do so in any other way."

"Perhaps we should seriously consider it," said Robert.

"Absolutely not," asserted Drew.

"Then I will go without you," announced Lavinia.

"You cannot," insisted Drew.

"I am free to travel wherever I desire," said Lavinia. "I will go to the inn, and if I must, I will present myself at Hayley's alone. From what I hear of him, he will not turn down a woman."

"That is insanity," argued Drew. "You could end up in the same position as the other women he has taken."

"At least I will not be sitting at home doing nothing while my best friend is being held against her will."

"We will handle this," he declared.

"How?" she asked.

"I will go to Hayley's as you suggested. I will tell him the same story except you will not be involved."

"It will not be as effective," responded Lavinia. "He will be watching you, but he would never suspect an empty-headed bit of muslin would be searching his estate for missing women. You can keep him busy while I snoop."

"It's far too dangerous," said Drew, although his protest was not as strong as before.

"Drew, you will be there and I will be close by,"

pointed out Robert. "Even Ranson will be in attendance and you know we can count on him."

Lavinia did not like Robert's reference to Lord Weston; however, she said nothing for she did not want to discourage Drew from agreeing to her plan.

"Lady Fitzhugh is in agreement with this?" Drew asked.

"She helped plan it," said Lavinia.

"And your father?"

"Aunt Hope is going to talk with him today. She is going to request that I join her on a visit to one of her old friends. She will also suggest he return to the country and that I stay with her for the remainder of the Season. I believe he will readily agree, for you know he's been ill and only came to London for my benefit. I'm certain he will jump at the chance to return."

"How soon would you depart?" asked Robert.

"We have not yet decided . . ." began Drew.

Robert turned to Drew, his face a mix of anger and frustration. "You know we have no other plan. Do you want to sit idly by while Hayley ships Jessica to the Continent? Well, I do not and I will accept any assistance to ensure that it does not happen."

Drew's shoulders slumped in defeat. He was torn between the woman he loved and exposing Lady Lavinia to danger. He realized that her threat to continue without him was not an empty one and decided that she would be safer if he were with her. He still did not like the idea, but there was nothing to do but go along with it. He would not consider Ranson's reaction until he was faced with it.

"I will agree," he said, "but only because I know you would carry on even if I refused to be a part of it."

"Good," replied Lavinia. "Aunt Hope will arrive later this morning to talk to Father, and I will advise you as soon as we know when we will leave. I will give you directions to the inn. Robert, you must not allow yourself to be seen or recognized by any of Hayley's guests."

Robert nodded his agreement. "I'll arrive earlier than you so there will be no question as to whether we traveled together."

"Splendid," approved Lavinia. "Drew, Aunt Hope will arrange that at the very least her room is between ours, so that in case news of this ever gets out, we can prove that our being at the same inn was merely coincidence and that propriety was observed."

"One thing you haven't mentioned," said Drew.

"And what is that?" she asked.

"You haven't mentioned Ranson. You're aware he'll be there and if he is not forewarned his reaction could well ruin the whole thing."

"I am going to attempt a disguise which I hope will keep him from recognizing me."

"Impossible," said Drew.

Lavinia smiled. "We'll see," was all she replied.

They spoke a little longer before they completed working out details of the plan.

"Then it's only left to pack and leave once Father has gone," said Lavinia, when everything had been reviewed. "I will send you word when that has occurred."

"I hope none of us regrets this," said Drew, as they were leaving.

"We will only have regrets if we do nothing, for I'm certain Jessica is counting on us," said Lavinia.

Lavinia was awaiting word from her aunt, who had gone upstairs to visit Lavinia's father, when the butler announced Mr. Black. The Bow Street Runner entered the room with a confident stride.

"You appear optimistic, Mr. Black. Can I assume you have learned more about Miss Norville?"

"You may," he answered, "but I don't believe it is what you want to hear."

Lavinia thought of Hayley selling women into slavery and could not imagine Mr. Black would apprise her of anything worse than that. "Perhaps not, but I must know if I am to help her."

"I questioned many people and finally discovered who it was that Miss Norville left with the last night she was seen."

Lavinia's heart beat faster. "And that was?"

"A Mr. Thomas Carter. It seems Mr. Carter went outside to hire a hackney and told Miss Norville to wait a few minutes then to follow him."

Lavinia could hardly sit still. If she believed all indications, they pointed to Thomas being the cause of both Jeanette's and Jessica's disappearances.

"Now, I have someone who swore they saw Mr. Carter and Miss Norville entering Lord Hayley's home the next day. A few minutes later, Mr. Carter exited and rode away without Miss Norville."

Lavinia's hands tightened on the arms of her chair. "Are your resources reliable?" she asked.

Harry Black had received the information from another Bow Street Runner who had been hired by the Home Office to watch Lord Hayley and his activities; however, he could not reveal that to Lady Lavinia.

"They are extremely reliable, but I cannot divulge the source at this time."

"I understand," she replied, pondering the news she had just received. She felt certain now that Thomas did not see Jessica off to some mythical friend in York, but put her in Lord Hayley's hands, just as he had Jeanette.

"Did your source know what Hayley and Carter did the remainder of the day?"

"Hayley was at home until after dinner. Then he went to one of his establishments where he remained until

early the next morning. Carter had arrived there before
Hayley and gambled nearly the whole night. My source
said he was flashing plenty of blunt but lost most of it."

The money had to be what Carter had received for
Jeanette. She had no doubt that he would have also col-
lected a sum for Jessica. Lavinia wondered how much
he charged for his wife. The thought sickened her.

"You have done well, Mr. Black. If I need anything
further, I will contact you."

"Thank you, my lady. I'm glad you're pleased."

Harry Black bowed and left Lavinia alone in the
drawing room, mulling over the danger in which Jessica
and the other women were involved. She was still sitting
in the same position when Lady Fitzhugh entered.

"I have been successful; your father leaves for the
country in the morning," she exclaimed, before she observed Lavinia's expression. "What has happened?"

"Oh, Aunt Hope, I'm afraid the worst has been confirmed." She went on to relate her conversation with
Harry Black, unable to hold back the tears that rose to
her eyes.

"Child, you must keep up hope," advised Lady
Fitzhugh. "We must believe that if Hayley has Jessica
and this other girl, that they are both being held at his
country estate until after the house party. It is only good
business—and Hayley prides himself on being a good
businessman—to wait until he has all the women together to transport them to the coast altogether."

"You make them sound like animals."

"It is harsh, but that is exactly how Hayley views
them. They are a cash crop for him and he does not
regard their humanity at all. But we must not allow that
to deter us. Know that he will treat them well because
if he does not they will bring little or nothing at all. So
don't think that they are being starved or beaten. They
may be locked up, but their basic needs will be met."

"That is little comfort," said Lavinia, still sniffling.

"It must do for the time being," said Lady Fitzhugh, patting her niece's shoulder. "Now no more tears. We both need a clear head to put our plan into action."

Lavinia dried her eyes and sat up straighter in her chair. "I am ready," she stated resolutely. "We cannot rid society of Lord Hayley and Thomas Carter soon enough for me."

ELEVEN

The inn was still as well-kept as Lady Fitzhugh and Lady Lavinia remembered. The building was of substantial size. A large dining room was separated from the drinking room by a hallway which ran down the middle of the building to the kitchen at the back. The innkeeper had learned long ago it was better to keep the travelers who didn't drink apart from the regulars who only visited the tavern to partake of the fine ale which was served.

Just inside the front door was a staircase that led to rooms upstairs. An addition had been added to the building since the ladies had last taken shelter under its roof. It was along this passage that they were led to the newer rooms and when they entered, they were well pleased with what they saw.

The rooms were larger than most and had windows that offered a view of the countryside. The linens appeared fresh and the beds comfortable. An armoire stood in each room and there was a small table and chair near the window, while two chairs flanked the empty fireplace. All in all, they were quite happy with their accommodations.

"We will freshen up and then go downstairs for tea," said Lady Fitzhugh. "I believe I saw Drew and Robert in the tavern. I will make certain they observe us entering the dining room, although they probably noticed us arrive. It will be natural that we strike up a conversation."

"Are you certain you haven't served as a spy before?" teased Lavinia.

"I would do much better than some," replied her aunt, while removing her hat.

A few moments later they made their way downstairs to the dining room and ordered tea. It was only a short time before Drew and Robert entered, each with a tankard of ale in their hands.

"Lady Fitzhugh, what a pleasant surprise," said Robert. "Are you on your way to Town?"

"I am going to visit an old friend," she replied pleasantly. "The trip is not agreeing with me so I decided to stop here for a few days."

"It is a pleasant place," he agreed.

"Indeed it is. They have made considerable improvements since I last visited here. You remember my niece, Lady Lavinia, don't you?"

"How could I forget?" he responded gallantly, bowing to Lavinia. "And, of course, I believe you are well acquainted with Andrew, Lord Stanford."

"I am old friends to both of the ladies," Drew said in greeting.

"Sit down and take tea with us," insisted Lady Fitzhugh. "Or perhaps you would rather drink your ale. But, at least have some of these delicious Portugal cakes."

"Don't mind if we do," said Drew, pulling out a chair and seating himself at the table. "Your company will liven up an otherwise dull day."

"Gammon!" replied Lavinia. "You were probably enjoying yourself far more in the tavern."

"Not so," said Robert.

Lavinia glanced around the dining room. Only one other table was occupied and it was at the other end of the room. "We should get started immediately," she said, in an undertone to Drew.

"Have already done so," he said, appearing satisfied with himself.

"What do you mean?" demanded Lavinia. "You have not done anything foolish, have you?"

"Don't get upset, Lavinia," urged Robert. "Drew has merely made an initial overture."

"Happened to ride by Hayley's this morning. Dropped in to pay my respects. Everything went just as we had planned. When he heard we were here he apologized for not having room for us. I told him you were a bit shy and he invited us to join the party whenever possible. He mentioned the gambling that went on, of course, and I expressed some interest in it."

"Good. When should we go?" Lavinia asked.

"Well, you must at least change," said Lady Fitzhugh. "You certainly cannot go to Hayley's house party dressed as you are now."

Lavinia looked down at her modest blue carriage dress and smiled. "You're right. I don't look like a high flyer," she admitted.

"Must decide what to tell Ranson when we see him," said Drew. "Will be like a bear with a sore ear once he knows you're there."

"I will avoid him as long as possible," Lavinia replied. "However, when he does recognize me, I will tell him the truth. After all, he is not responsible for me or my actions and has no say in the matter. He can continue enjoying the house party and ignore me completely."

"As if he would," said Drew.

"Well, he must!" insisted Lavinia, with some force. "I will not allow him to direct my life."

"Let him know immediately that I am with you," advised Lady Fitzhugh. "That should take some wind out of his sails. Now let us go upstairs and get you changed or else we could sit here the rest of the day and argue what is to be done with Weston.

"Drew, there is a flight of stairs at the end of the hallway which leads outside. Give us a few minutes, then meet Lavinia there with the coach," she directed.

Lavinia reached the bottom of the stairs and hesitated a moment, wondering how Drew would react when he saw her. She could not believe it herself when she had looked into the mirror. Her gown was much more daring than those she usually wore and she had tugged at the neckline before her aunt pulled her hand away, warning her to leave well enough alone.

Lavinia's cheeks were heavy with rouge, her lashes and brows blackened, while bright red lip salve made a mockery of her innocence. While that was outside of enough, there was one final touch that Aunt Hope pulled from a hatbox with a flourish. A wig. A very blond, very curly wig.

She wore it now and Lavinia felt as if she balanced an overlarge bird's nest on her head. She peered through the black veil that her aunt had added in hope of forestalling Lord Weston's discovery of her true identity, and prayed she would learn news of Jessica at Lord Hayley's.

Lavinia straightened her shoulders and reached for the door handle. Every minute she wasted was another minute that Jessica was suffering. She pushed open the door and stepped outside, where Drew awaited with the coach.

"Good Lud. Is that you, Lavinia?" he asked.

Lavinia giggled. His expression of disbelief confirmed that her disguise was a good one. "It is," she said. "Do I look the part?"

"You have captured it to perfection," he assured her.

"We must go while I still have the courage."

"You do not need to do this," said Drew.

"I must do something," she insisted as she had before. He nodded and handed her into the coach.

"There is something I must tell you," he said as the coach drew away from the inn. "You don't need to worry about seeing Ranson this afternoon. Unless he has changed his plans, he is at the races with some of the other men."

"How did you come about this news?" asked Lavinia.

"I spoke at length with Hayley when I visited with him earlier in the day. He mentioned the different activities that were available and told me that my good friend Weston would return in time for dinner this evening."

"Is his . . . Is Miss Morris at the estate?"

"I don't know, but surely you aren't going to approach her if she is. She would know nothing about Jessica."

"I do not know what I'm going to do," Lavinia confessed. "I've never searched for anyone before, particularly at a house party such as this one."

"Be careful, Lavinia. From all I know, Hayley's outward congeniality conceals a violent man who would do anything to protect himself. If he feels you're endangering his livelihood, your position in the *ton* will do nothing to save you."

Lavinia subdued the shudder that threatened to shred her self-confidence. "I will do everything I can to blend in. You must remind Hayley that I'm extremely shy and that you hope coming to his house party will help me become more comfortable with others. You can tell the same thing to Lord Weston," she suggested.

"Ranson knows me too well," said Drew. "Convincing him that I brought a new ladybird to Hayley's house party is going to be nearly impossible. Telling him you are too shy to speak to him is too much to ask him to believe. He will be suspicious as soon as he sees me and the only thing I can do is to say I am here to help him."

"But he will suspect me as well."

"Will tell him you were the only woman I could find at such short notice and that you are not . . . that is, you are a bit nonsensical."

"I feel doom hanging over my head," said Lavinia.

"You insisted on pursuing this," Drew reminded her. "Doing the best I can with an extremely difficult situation."

Lavinia laid a comforting hand on his arm. "I know you are and I am grateful for your assistance. I only hope we can find Jessica."

"So do I," agreed Drew, as the coach turned into the drive leading to Hayley's house.

Hayley's country estate was not at all what Lavinia expected. The drive was smooth and led them through a park that fell away from both sides in long stretches of green carpets of grass. Trees and bushes were growing in attractive groupings and Lavinia could see the glint of sunshine on the water of an ornamental lake in the distance. They crossed a stone bridge that arched over a stream and continued toward the large brick house that stood solidly in front of them. It was not covered with ivy or crumbling into dust. The windows gleamed and the building itself had not one vine twining up its sides. The coach rolled to a stop in front of the house and they were immediately met by one of Hayley's stable boys dressed in a smart blue and gold uniform.

Hayley did things in style, thought Lavinia, even though he is hanging on to the fringes of society. Accepting Drew's hand, she stepped out of the coach and they approached the house. Before Drew could lift the shiny brass knocker, the door was opened by a black-clad butler, and just behind him stood Lord Hayley.

"Stanford! Good to see you again so soon," he boomed, in a hearty voice of greeting. "And I see you brought your lady friend this time."

"Yes, this is uh . . . this is Rose," said Drew.

"Welcome," said Hayley. "I understand you are a little shy, but you have my assurances that you will feel quite comfortable here in a trice."

"Thank you, my lord," said Lavinia, keeping her head bowed and dropping a quick curtsy.

"Let me show you around, so you will be familiar with the house and you will be able to meet whoever is here. If you return for dinner tonight, the others who are out at the moment will be here."

Lavinia breathed a sigh of relief that she had passed the first test. If Hayley had thought it odd she was wearing a veil and did not look up, she supposed he had attributed it to her shyness.

She and Drew followed Hayley while he gave them a quick tour of his house, introducing them to various gentlemen and their mistresses as they progressed. After it was over, Drew accompanied Hayley to the gambling room while Lavinia settled in the drawing room in a chair near Stephanie Morris. She needed to consider her next step in attempting to locate Jessica and decided to spend a few minutes with Lord Weston's latest demirep.

She felt a familiar surge of what she would not allow herself to call jealousy rise in her chest. As she quickly studied the woman, she saw that she wore a green gown, which reminded Lavinia of the scene she had had with Lord Weston in the park. She was not jealous of her, she insisted silently. All she wanted was to find Jessica and return home safe and sound.

"You are with Lord Stanford," said Stephanie, before Lavinia could speak. "He is such a lovely gentleman."

"You know Drew?" asked Lavinia.

"He is a great friend of Lord Weston, whom I accompanied here for the house party," imparted Stephanie.

"I haven't met Lord Weston, but Drew has mentioned him. Is he here today?"

"No, he went to the races and won't return until just before supper. If you are here this evening, though, you will be able to meet him."

Since Stephanie seemed amenable, Lavinia decided she would see whether she could learn anything from her. "This is quite a large estate," she said.

"Overwhelming for me," agreed Stephanie.

"Lord Hayley showed us around the house a bit when we first arrived, is there much more to be seen?"

"I suppose you saw all of the downstairs. There are numerous suites and bedrooms on the upper floor and then the servants' rooms are just below the attic. At least, that's what I'm told. I've had no desire to look above the next floor myself."

"Do you know whether there is a dower house on the estate?"

"No, but again, I have not inquired. There very well could be a dozen and I doubt whether I would know. Why do you ask?"

"Just curious," Lavinia replied. "I am always amazed at how grand some people live while others are barely getting along."

"I know what you mean," said Stephanie. "I was in a dire situation myself until Lord Weston came along."

Lavinia could not help herself. "And he saved you?"

"Oh, yes," replied Stephanie, her eyes glowing. "If it had not been for him, I would have been on the streets—or worse."

Lavinia could not believe the woman felt that she had been rescued by Lord Weston and owed him the total devotion she saw in her eyes. "I assume there was a price in return for his largesse," she remarked.

"Nothing that I was unwilling to do," replied Stephanie. "But then I suppose you feel the same about Lord Stanford."

"Somewhat," said Lavinia, "but he is secretly in love with a woman he can't have. Her name is Jessica Carter. Have you heard of her?"

"No, but I had not been in Town long before we came here, so I had no time to become familiar with any of the gossip."

Lavinia was disappointed, even though it was ridiculous to think that Jessica's name would be mentioned if she were being held captive here at the estate. She must be more realistic if she hoped to find out whether her friend was here.

"I believe I will take a slower look around; would you care to accompany me?"

Stephanie appeared pleased with the invitation. "I would be happy to," she said. "I have been sitting here all morning and would welcome a walk."

"Discover anything?" asked Drew, once they were on their way back to the inn.

"Not a thing." Lavinia turned to him, a scowl on her face. "I will never learn anything like this," she complained. "I must think of something else."

"Spent nearly the whole afternoon around Hayley and didn't detect anything unusual either."

Lavinia was silent for a moment. "The servants," she finally said. "If we are to uncover anything it will come from the servants. If the women are here, they must be fed and housed. It follows that there are servants who do the cooking and cleaning. They are the weakest link. I know that Hayley has been very careful in hiring them, but they cannot be perfect. What do you think?" Lavinia looked at Drew, hoping he would agree with her.

"Possible," responded Drew. "But how do we go about watching and listening to them. Too late to get a new person hired on and don't think they would speak freely in front of us."

"Don't be too sure about that," said Lavinia. "They may not talk in front of a peer of the realm, but a courtesan is an altogether different matter. I cannot believe that they would pay any more attention to a bit of muslin than they would a spot on the wall. Servants have their own rank and a Cyprian would not even be on the bottom of the ladder."

"What will you do?" asked Drew.

"I will see how close I can get to the servants without arousing suspicion. I will need to be there at mealtime," murmured Lavinia, deep in thought. "Then I'll be able to see whether they deliver food to anyplace other than the dining room."

"Can't do it tonight. Promised Hayley we'd be there for supper."

"How am I to get past Lord Weston if we must have drinks before dinner with him?"

"Know the exact time supper will be served. Told Hayley we would be there, but might be late. Thought we would arrive just when everyone is being seated. Will probably be too far away from Ranson during supper for him to see you clearly."

"That doesn't sound like a very precise plan to me," said Lavinia.

"Best I could do at the time," replied Drew.

"Just like my new name?"

"Best I could do at the time," repeated Drew, with a mischievous smile.

"I don't mean to complain about either," she apologized. "It seems I thought of everything but a name. Why did you choose Rose?"

"Your perfume," he answered.

"Well, thank you for being so quick. We will do whatever we can to make our arrival time work out. I know that Lord Weston is going to discover me eventually; I only hope I can determine where Jessica is being kept before that happens."

"You must rest once we get back to the inn," said Drew. "Tonight may prove to be a long one."

"You are certainly going to look the part," said Lady Fitzhugh, as she helped Lavinia dress that evening. In order to reduce the chances of being found out, the two ladies had traveled without a maid, choosing to rely upon the inn's maid for whatever services they should need. Thus they were alone and were able to speak freely.

"I could never have done this without you," said Lavinia.

"Well, perhaps not as well," conceded her aunt. "What are your plans for this evening?"

"I don't really have any," answered Lavinia. "I cannot spy on the servants while I am at dinner and I looked over the house today. I even made my way upstairs, but found no place to hide women."

"We never thought they'd be in the house itself," Aunt Hope reminded her.

"I know." Lavinia sighed. "I was just wishing I could find an indication she was there."

"Don't feel guilty about coming up empty-handed," advised Lady Fitzhugh. "If Hayley has been doing this for some time, he's going to be hard to catch. Be patient and, by all means, be cautious. He is a dangerous man who will stop at nothing to assure his own safety."

"He wouldn't do anything to me with everyone around," scoffed Lavinia.

"If he wanted you out of the way, you would be gone before anyone would know it. And, just like the others, you would never be seen again."

"You're scaring me," said Lavinia.

"I meant to. That is the only way you'll survive this game and I don't want to admit to your father that I've lost you." She gave Lavinia a hug and stepped away from her. "I think you'll do," she said, running an appraising eye over her niece.

Lavinia rose and stood in front of the cheval mirror, where she could view her entire ensemble. Her gown was a shade of purple that would cause royalty to think twice about ever wearing the color again. The *décolletage* was so low that Lavinia immediately covered it with her hand.

"You're spoiling the effect," said her aunt, pulling her hand away.

"I cannot wear something so scandalous," she objected.

"That is exactly the idea. I will speculate that there will be many others lower."

"I have seen them in the theaters in London, and I would not wager against you," Lavinia agreed. "But it is far different when I am wearing such a gown myself."

"You wanted to fit in," her aunt reminded her.

Lavinia studied her reflection again. Her blond wig was smoothed into a more reasonable fashion than earlier in the day; however, the cosmetics on her face seemed even more garish than they had that afternoon. Before she left, she would again attach a tiny veil that would tickle the end of her nose and which she hoped would cover some of the rouge and blackened lashes.

"Surely Lord Weston will not recognize me if I keep

my distance," she murmured, turning first one way, then another.

"That will take some doing with Drew being there. You know Weston will want to talk to him and he will of course be curious about the woman he brought."

"I will discuss it with Drew," she said, pulling on her gloves and picking up her cashmere shawl.

"I wish you good luck," said her aunt, opening the door and peering out into the hall before stepping back.

"I'm afraid I'm going to need it," Lavinia confirmed.

Lavinia and Drew arrived at Hayley's just as everyone was sitting down to supper. The dining room contained a long main table with four smaller tables set up around the room to accommodate the overflow of guests. The china and crystal glasses, the silver cutlery, the embroidered serviettes were all of excellent quality, and Lavinia assumed that dinner would be one of the best she had ever consumed; that is, if she could get a bite past the lump in her throat.

They were the last to enter and found themselves at one of the smaller tables. Lavinia drew a breath of relief, for she had seen Weston and Stephanie seated near Hayley at the head of the main table.

Lavinia was not wrong about the quality and quantity of dinner. The dinner began with both duck and chestnut soups. Next came poached fish with fruit, then beef à la royale with the holes in the beef stuffed with bacon, parsley, and chopped oyster; potatoes and celery hearts had been cooked in the rich gravy which accompanied it. Leg of mutton was served, along with cornish hens with rice stuffing, venison in currant sauce, and a chicken mousse comprised of an excellent Cheshire cheese and rich cream. The vegetables were too numerous to mention, but included stuffed artichokes and asparagus in cream.

Eyes were glazing over by the time the cakes and puddings, pies and tarts were offered. Lavinia only hoped that Jessica and the other women were dining as well.

As soon as dinner was over, the women retired to refresh themselves, leaving the men to blow a cloud over their brandy.

"I couldn't believe my ears when Hayley said you called," said Ranson, claiming a seat next to Drew. "What the devil brought you here?"

"Thought I'd see what the attraction was," Drew replied.

"If you're a rake, you're in the right place," said Ranson. "And you have a woman with you. I didn't recognize her from across the room."

"That is Rose. She's shy and a little odd, but I find her good company."

"You must introduce us when we return to the drawing room," said Ranson.

"Had any luck?" asked Drew.

Ranson glanced around the room. "Can you ride with me in the morning? I don't feel safe talking here." His voice was urgent, but he spoke quietly, with a pleasant smile on his face.

"Before breakfast?" asked Drew

"The best time to be certain to be alone," he agreed. "Everyone else will still be abed."

The two men followed the others into the drawing room where the women had congregated. Stephanie walked forward to meet them, linking her arm with Ranson's and smiling up at him.

"You were gone an extraordinary length of time, my lord."

Ranson leaned over and whispered in her ear, "And you are learning your role extraordinarily quickly," he teased.

"Perhaps I should be an actress," she shot back, with an answering smile.

He straightened. "Look who has joined our party," he said, indicating Drew.

"It is good to see you, my lord,"

"Pleasure," said Drew, looking around the room. "Seen Rose?"

"Yes, I did and she left a message for you. It seems she developed a megrim and returned to the inn. She said she would send the coach back for you, but that you should stay and enjoy yourself."

"Sounds as if Rose is a very understanding lady," said Ranson, "but I had hoped to have met her myself."

"Tomorrow will be soon enough," said Drew.

There was still a light showing in Lady Fitzhugh's room when Drew returned that evening. He tapped on the door, hoping to find both Lady Fitzhugh and Lady Lavinia still awake.

Lady Fitzhugh opened the door. "Drew, we thought you might stop in to tell us what had happened. Come in," she invited.

Lady Fitzhugh and Lavinia were sitting in front of the fireplace and he drew up the chair from the desk and joined the two women.

"I'm sorry I didn't think to have something for you to drink," said Lady Fitzhugh.

Drew made a face. "No need to apologize. Have had too much already, but needed to appear that I was enjoying myself."

"Did you learn anything?" asked Lavinia.

"Not a thing," replied Drew. "But may do so in the morning. Am going riding with Ranson before breakfast. He might have discovered something."

"Did you tell him you were searching for Jessica?" asked Lavinia.

"No. Told him I'm just here to enjoy myself. Don't know whether he completely believes me or not. Think I should tell him I came to back him up."

"That might make him less suspicious of Lavinia," agreed Lady Fitzhugh.

"Tomorrow, I'm going to attempt to take notice of the servants," said Lavinia. "We have been discussing ways of doing so. There's a lovely herb garden outside the back entrance of the house. I have suddenly become very interested in herbs and will make this a favorite place to sit and perhaps sketch the plants. From that position I will be able to see when any of the servants leave the house and whether they are carrying anything.

"I suppose I could also ask Cook about some of her recipes. That would put me where I could keep an eye on almost everyone."

"The cook may not like talking to such a brazen hussy as you," teased Lady Fitzhugh.

"Then I shall tell her I will ask Lord Hayley to approve of it. I'm certain she won't risk his wrath."

"Must be careful," warned Drew. "Hayley hasn't avoided trouble all these years by being a cork-brained country bumpkin."

"I won't underestimate him," said Lavinia. "But I must do all I can to find Jessica. There is something you can do for me."

"Need only ask."

"While you and Lord Weston are riding in the morning, keep your eye out for any buildings on Hayley's estate. There could be a dower house, or a hunting box, or even an empty tenant farmer's house. Anyplace where he could hide women."

"Will make a point of it," promised Drew, rising to his feet. "Must catch a few hours sleep before morning."

He said his good night and left the women still sitting across from one another.

"We should also get some rest," said Lady Fitzhugh, without moving so much as a finger.

"Yes, we should," agreed Lavinia, "but I am almost afraid to go to sleep. I know that I'll dream of either Hayley or Lord Weston and I don't know which will haunt me most."

TWELVE

The morning looked as if it had been newly minted expressly for the two men to enjoy their ride. It was all rich verdant and early morning sunshine, with birds chirping and the smell of a fresh day.

"Can't imagine Hayley in a place like this," said Drew. "Think of him in dark, smoke-filled rooms and green baize tables instead of daylight and grass."

"But this is where he grew up," Ranson pointed out. "I suppose at one time he was an ordinary boy."

"Found out anything about him yet?" asked Drew.

Ranson looked around. They were riding down the middle of a great meadow. The only hiding place was an expanse of trees at the far edge, too far away to be a threat to their privacy.

"I didn't mean to cut you off last night, but I don't trust anything said in the house to be private," Ranson explained

"Best to think that way."

"It is a bit off-putting attempting to search," said Ranson. "Everywhere I turn I run into either Hayley or one of his men. He's been at this long enough not to leave anything to chance. I have, however, seen a few tenant farms and I believe a hunting box, but I haven't been able to get close enough to determine whether they're empty.

"There is a building behind the stables that is highly

suspect. I believe that could be the center of his counterfeiting operation. It seems likely that he would want that as close as possible."

"How do you mean to go on?"

"I don't know," Ranson admitted. "There's only so much one man can do."

"Have two now," said Drew.

"Thank you, my friend. I can always count on you. Regardless, even two men are not enough in some situations, and I believe this is one. I haven't been able to put a number to Hayley's men, but there are too many for us to overcome. The best thing seems to be to pinpoint the locations I feel he is using and then contact the Home Office with my suspicions. They can send enough men to raid the place."

"And the women?" asked Drew.

"That's another thing altogether," said Ranson, a frown furrowing his forehead. "I am uneasy leaving the women here—if they are here—and hoping the Home Office arrives in time to save them. I don't believe Hayley will keep them here for any length of time. As soon as the house party is over, I suspect he will be moving them."

"Won't allow that," said Drew. "Believe more strongly than ever that he has Jessica."

Ranson looked at him sharply. "Have you heard something more?"

"No, but have heard neither hide nor hair about Jessica since she disappeared with Carter. Have found no friends in York, nor any private coach that might have carried her there."

"It does look dark," agreed Ranson. "That's the real reason you're here, isn't it? You think Jessica's being held here."

"Only place left to look. One other thing. Robert's with me."

"Dash it! Drew. How long do you think you can keep his presence from Hayley?"

"Couldn't be helped," said Drew. "He was coming with or without me. Best I could do was convince him to wait at the inn while I approached Hayley. Don't believe he suspects me of anything. Since you and I are close friends, he probably thinks I don't want to be left out."

"Your story will most likely be accepted, but Robert showing up will most certainly alert him that something is going on."

"Robert promised he would stay out of sight at the inn. Hayley and his men should be too occupied to visit there."

"I hope you're right," said Ranson, "or we could all end up with more on our plate than we bargained for."

The two men rode in silence for a few minutes, each following his own thoughts.

"Did you find out anything else after I left London?" Ranson asked.

Drew shook his head. "Nothing at all. Robert has a Bow Street Runner working on Jessica's disappearance in case he didn't turn her over to Hayley, but I doubt he will find anything. That's why we came here; nothing more we could do in Town."

"Did you see Lavinia before you left?" asked Ranson.

"She's the same," said Drew, dodging his question.

"Still angry with me, I suppose," grumbled Ranson.

"If she only knew what you were doing."

"I can't take the chance," said Ranson. "Besides, if she said the wrong thing to the wrong person, she could end up in Hayley's hands as well. I'd put nothing against the man when it comes to protecting himself. Thank God, she's safe in Town."

"Any plans?" asked Drew, anxious to change the subject.

"I need to get closer to some of the buildings I've noticed. When we return, I'm going to have Cook pack a basket and Stephanie and I are going on a picnic."

"Near some of the buildings, I presume."

"As near as I can get without arousing suspicion. But no one should think anything is amiss if a man strolls into the woods with his mistress."

"Wish you success," said Drew.

"Will I see you later today?" asked Ranson.

"Will be at supper for certain," replied Drew. "Perhaps earlier. Depends upon . . . er . . . Rose."

"I look forward to meeting her," said Ranson.

"Nothing between us. She's only doing this as a favor so I can attend the house party," explained Drew.

"You didn't say anything . . ."

"No. No. Just that I was curious about what went on. She revealed she was, too, so we joined forces."

"She must be an exceptional woman."

"I think you would admire her, if you got to know her," replied Drew with a smug smile.

"I doubt whether we will have time for any long discussions while we are here, but perhaps when this is all over and we return to Town."

"Heard something interesting last night," said Drew. "Woman at the supper table with us mentioned Carter. Thinks he's charming and wanted to know why he wasn't here. Gentleman—Lord Blevins, I believe—said Carter was delayed, but would no doubt be here later. Never misses, according to Blevins."

"So Carter will be here," murmured Ranson. "Did he say when?"

"Didn't know. Just seemed certain he would be."

"Wonder what will happen when he sees us?"

"Shouldn't suspect you of anything. Doesn't know you were well acquainted with Jessica. However, he knows Jessica and I were once more than friends."

"Good, then perhaps he will focus his attention on you, which will allow me more freedom to move about."

"Best get back," said Drew. "You need to make plans for a picnic."

"And, Drew, thanks for coming. I feel better with another set of friendly eyes to rely upon."

Drew nodded, wondering whether Ranson would thank him if he knew Lavinia hid beneath Rose's blond wig.

"Good. We can go to lunch at Hayley's without fearing we will meet Lord Weston," said Lavinia when Drew told her Ranson and Stephanie were planning a picnic that afternoon.

"Asked Ranson about other buildings on the estate. Said there were some tenant farms and a hunting box. Didn't mention a dowager's house, but feel certain an estate that size would have one."

"Perhaps we'll find out this afternoon," said Lavinia, feeling more hopeful.

By early afternoon Lavinia's hopefulness had faded. She had spent time with the other women without learning anything new. She had taken up a spot in the herb garden, where she could watch the back of the house, but saw nothing more than the usual activities.

Drew had gone shooting with some of the men. He intended to see whether any of them would drop hints about ridding themselves of their mistresses and, at the same time, see if he could spy a house where Jessica might be kept captive.

Lavinia's skin prickled when she thought of Jessica being held by Hayley. She prayed her friend would be safe until they could find her. However, that didn't seem likely today.

It was early evening. Lavinia and Drew had returned to the inn to change for supper and were now on their way back to Hayley's estate.

"Neither of us learned anything useful today," complained Lavinia.

"Knew it wouldn't be easy," said Drew.

"I know," agreed Lavinia, "but I can't stand to think of Jessica in danger."

"Understand how you feel."

"Oh, Drew, I'm so sorry. You are as worried as I am and here I'm thinking only of myself."

"We'll find her. Will never stop till we do," he promised.

The coach rolled to a stop in front of the house, and they stepped down for another evening with one of the worst thatch-gallows in England. They had only been in the drawing room a short time when Ranson entered with Stephanie on his arm. The woman wore the magnificent necklace of emeralds and Lavinia felt anger well inside of her once again when she saw the jewels.

She wanted to confront Ranson and tell him what she thought of a man who would leave the search for Jessica so that he and his current mistress could attend a party. Jessica had always argued that Ranson would do nothing so despicable as to drive her sister from England. Lavinia only wished Jessica could know how he was behaving; perhaps she would believe the worst of him now.

Lavinia was not to be granted any time to gather her thoughts, for Ranson led Stephanie directly to them.

"I believe that everyone has met except for the two of us," he said to Lavinia.

"This is Rose," said Drew, briefly.

"I am pleased to meet you," said Ranson.

Lavinia kept her gaze directed to the floor, allowing the ever-present veil to cover as much of her face as possible. "And I you, my lord," she replied in a faint voice.

"Have you been in London long?" he asked.

"No, my lord."

Ranson was puzzled by Rose's behavior. Most light-skirts would be doing everything they could to attract his attention, despite being with someone else. It was no detriment to Drew or any other man; it was merely the way the game was played. The woman could find herself out on the street the next day and might need to call on the goodwill of another gentleman.

Rose caused a familiar stirring in his mind. Had he seen her somewhere before? If so, he could not recall the place. Something, though, continued to tug at his memory all the way through supper. Even after he and Stephanie were again seated at the main table near Hayley, and Drew and Rose were at one of the side tables, his gaze was drawn to her several times during the meal.

Drew attributed the veil she wore to shyness. Ranson thought that perhaps she intended to exude a sense of intrigue. Or perhaps she was a gentle woman who had fallen on bad times, as had Stephanie, and did not want to reveal her identity. Whatever the reason for the veil, it kept him from plainly seeing her face and determining whether he was acquainted with her.

Hayley claimed his attention and for the rest of supper he had no time to study Drew's new friend. He vowed to return to the puzzle after dinner.

"I think he suspects something," murmured Lavinia to Drew.

"What makes you think so?"

"He keeps glancing over at us. I had hoped my disguise would pass muster with him."

"Done the best you could," said Drew. "Ranson is awake on every suit. Difficult to fool him."

"I am going to avoid him as much as possible. Whenever you are able, continue to stress that I am not as outgoing as most of the women here."

"Won't work forever."

"Then I will think of something else," said Lavinia, not to be put off by Lord Weston when her friend's life was at stake.

Ranson was unable to further his acquaintance with Rose that evening. Hayley seemed to have personally taken it upon himself to see that his guest enjoy every minute of the night's entertainment. Drew joined them for a time in the gambling room before searching out Rose and returning to the inn.

"Did you learn anything?" asked Robert the next morning at the breakfast table.

"Nothing," said Lavinia, stabbing at her buttered eggs with her fork.

Robert looked at Drew, who shook his head, indicating he had no better luck than Lavinia.

"I'm certain the women—if they are at the estate— are not anywhere in the house," said Lavinia. "We've discovered some buildings where they might be held."

"I will search them," said Robert, tossing aside his serviette and pushing back from the table.

"You must not," begged Lavinia, reaching out to him. "We will do it in the course of our normal activities. It is the only way to ensure Jessica's safety if she is there.

Once Lord Hayley knows we are on to him, he will most probably spirit her away."

"I can't just sit and do nothing," complained Robert.

"Exactly what you must do," said Drew.

Robert buried his face in his hands. "I know. I know," he intoned. "It's just so devilishly difficult."

Lavinia's expression softened and she put her hand on Robert's arm, pulling his hand away from his face. "Look at me," she said, drawing his attention. "There is no need to be in such a taking. Both Drew and I will do all that can be done to find Jessica. Please believe that."

Robert offered her a weak smile. "I do believe you."

"Robert, we must keep one another company today," spoke up Lady Fitzhugh. "I understand there are some interesting ruins nearby. I know you do not feel like sightseeing, but humor me; it will give you something to do rather than sit here and worry."

"I'll put myself in your hands," he replied, straightening in his chair. He retrieved his serviette and made an attempt to continue with his breakfast.

"What is the plan for today?" asked Lady Fitzhugh.

"I'm taking my sketching materials so that I will have an excuse for wandering around the grounds," said Lavinia.

"Shooting or fishing, most likely," said Drew.

"Then you must get on with it," declared Lady Fitzhugh. "I don't want to alarm anyone, but there is little time left before the house party is over and Hayley will make his move."

"You need not remind me, Aunt Hope, for I have been counting each minute that Jessica is missing."

Lavinia walked softly down the hall toward the kitchen in Hayley's house. She halted just outside the door and bent to untie her slipper. If anyone came upon her she would have the perfect excuse.

The men who were leaving the house had already gone, and the others were scattered over the house and grounds indulging in various pursuits, while some were still abed sleeping off the effects of their liquor consumption from the night before. Of course, few of the women would show their faces below stairs before luncheon.

Lavinia listened to the local gossip and general complaints of the staff before the conversation yielded anything of interest.

"I tell you I'm tired a carryin' all this ever' day," said one of the kitchen helpers.

"Won't be long now till it'll be over," said the cook.

"I'll have one of the footmen assist you today," said the butler, who sounded as if he were having a second breakfast.

"Don't see no reason why somebody cain't cook over there," said the cook's assistant. "Be a lot easier on ever' body."

"Lord Hayley expects full secrecy from everyone on this," offered the butler. "If there were fires for cooking then someone would notice and start asking questions. You're getting paid well to keep your tongue between your teeth. I wouldn't start complaining if I were you or you might not live to spend it."

Silence fell over the kitchen at his blunt speaking. Lavinia could hear the people going about their business of chopping and mixing and stirring. Suddenly a figure appeared in the doorway.

"May I help you, madam?" asked the butler.

Lavinia dangled her slipper from her fingers. "I'm afraid I've broken the ribbon on my slipper," she said.

"Regrettable," he replied shortly. "If you will wait in the small salon, I'll send a maid to you with another ribbon."

"Why, thank you. You're too kind," she gushed.

She had found them! thought Lavinia, wanting to laugh out loud with elation. They were here on the estate. All she had to do was to follow the servants when they delivered food. Suddenly she frowned. It would appear too suspicious if she attempted to follow them now. The butler might believe a broken ribbon once, but if he found her lurking around the kitchen again she would be hard put to convince him she was not up to something.

She would take her sketch pad and find a place in the herb garden at the back of the house before luncheon. From there she could observe the servants as they delivered the meal. Perhaps she might even be able to follow them part of the way.

A knock sounded at the door and Lavinia welcomed the maid with a smile, all the while planning how she could successfully locate where Jessica was hidden.

"I have some news," whispered Lavinia to Drew once he returned from shooting.

Drew took her by the arm and walked with her to the French doors in the drawing room where they stood looking out on the park.

"Must be careful in the house," he warned her.

"I'm sorry, but I'm so excited I had forgotten."

"Hope you have something solid," he said, "for I've discovered nothing."

"I think I've found them," she disclosed in a barely audible voice.

"What!"

"I don't mean I've seen them, but I know they're here and how to locate them."

"Show you the view," said Drew, nodding toward the terrace outside the French doors. He opened the door and they walked across the terrace to the balustrade.

"Tell me what you know," he demanded.

She did not take offense at his urgency. Glancing back toward the drawing room, she told him what she had overheard that morning.

"They must be close by," she summed up.

"Still must find the location," he said, staring out across the green expanse of the park.

Tugging at his arm to get his attention, she said, "I can do it. I know I can. They will not take the women their meal until the guests have been served. As soon as lunch is over, I shall go to the herb garden with my sketch pad. I can at least see in which direction they go."

"Dangerous," remarked Drew. "Must promise you will only find their direction or else you may end up with them."

"You could find us," said Lavinia, still filled with joy at the belief that she would soon have her friend safe. "But I promise to take great care."

"You're going to miss luncheon," came Ranson's voice from behind them.

"Startled us," said Drew, turning toward his friend.

"My apologies, Miss Rose, I didn't mean to."

"Think nothing of it," she said, raising her handkerchief to her mouth so her voice would be slightly muffled.

"I still believe we have met before. I am good with faces and will remember sooner or later," he warned.

"Mentioned luncheon," said Drew, drawing attention away from Lavinia.

"I did, and I must find Stephanie." He nodded to both and strolled back into the drawing room.

"I thought he had found us out," said Lavinia, placing her hand over her pounding heart.

"Must be careful if we are to carry this off," said Drew.

"We will carry it off," stated Lavinia, a determined angle to her chin. "Remember, after luncheon make whatever excuse you need to cover my absence."

"You are exceedingly quiet," remarked Stephanie as they sat at the luncheon table.

"It is Drew's lady friend. There is something about her that puzzles me."

"She is a very friendly lady," said Stephanie.

"She has not shown that side of herself to me."

"I believe she is more reserved with gentlemen," observed Stephanie.

"She seems so familiar to me," mused Ranson. If only she would do away with that veil, he thought. If he could only see her eyes he was certain he would recognize her. When the veil had moved in the breeze when they were on the terrace, he had caught a glimpse of her nose, and the sense of familiarity struck him anew.

He glanced across the room again to where Rose and Drew were sitting. She sat straight in her chair, handling her utensils delicately. Drew made a comment and she smiled at him. Ranson froze in place, then his knife clattered to the table, drawing stares from those seated around him.

"My apologies," he said, recovering quickly. "Too much shooting this morning." His remark drew smiles and the others returned to their conversations, leaving him with his discovery.

The smile had revealed something more than merely familiar to him. He had dreamed about it every night. He had thought of nothing but placing a kiss at the dimple next to the corner of Lady Lavinia's lips; the very dimple which had appeared when Rose smiled a moment earlier.

There was no chance his fork would fall again, for he gripped it until his knuckles turned white. Dammit! He should have known something was wrong. Now that he thought of it, Drew had never kept a woman secret from him, yet he had not heard of Rose until she showed up on his arm two days ago. What a fool he had been!

He should have known Lady Lavinia would insist upon doing something to help her friend. But her being here meant she had put all the pieces together. It also meant that Drew and Robert were in it with her.

Ranson felt the earth move beneath his feet. There were too many people involved for Hayley to remain in the dark much longer. And once he found out, they would all be in extreme danger. The question was whether to continue at the party as merely another man enjoying some time with his mistress or to proceed to search for proof against Hayley. He would need to think further on it. At the moment, he must concentrate on the problem Lady Lavinia presented.

As soon as luncheon was over, Ranson glanced around the room to locate Lady Lavinia, only to find her gone. Drew was just leaving the room and Ranson hurried after him, catching up with him in the hall.

"Where is she?" he asked, without preamble.

"Who?" replied Drew.

"Don't play with me," said Ranson. "We have been friends too long. Where is La . . . Rose?"

Drew looked around to make sure that there was no one near them. "Found out, did you?"

"I don't know what took me so long," said Ranson, a disgusted expression appearing on his face. "There was something familiar about her from the moment we first met, but the wig and veil did an excellent job of obscuring her features."

"Capital disguise," agreed Drew.

"What were you thinking of, bringing her here?" demanded Ranson.

"Could not stop her. Same as Robert; she was coming with or without me. Only thing to do was try to protect her as best I could."

"I can well imagine her stubbornness on the subject," said Ranson. "I suppose I should thank you for keeping her in sight."

"No need," replied Drew. "Should know Lady Fitzhugh is at the inn with Robert."

"Good Lord! Did you bring the entire population of London?"

"Not enough rooms."

"This is no time for levity," growled Ranson. "It's the devil's own mess and we must get Lady Lavinia away from here before she is discovered."

"Unlikely she will be," said Drew. "Disguise is good and don't believe anyone here has ever met her."

"If Hayley finds her snooping around—and don't tell me she isn't snooping—that will be the end of her."

"She promised to be careful," said Drew.

"Ha! And you believed her?"

"Could only urge her to do so. Doesn't know the full story about why you are here. Assumes you are merely enjoying yourself with Stephanie. Doesn't think much of it, I can tell you."

"I can imagine. How did she find out about this?" asked Ranson.

"Robert and I were discussing Jessica's disappearance. He was desperate and spoke of the rumors about Hayley and women. Mentioned Carter had been seen with him numerous times. Robert voiced his opinion that Carter had delivered Jessica to Hayley."

"And Lady Lavinia overheard," finished Ranson.

Drew nodded. "Seems she has made it a habit."

"Well, we must find her and get her away from the house as quickly as possible."

"Don't think she'll go," speculated Drew.

"We'll see about that. Now where is she?"

"No idea."

"Then help me look for her. If you find her, bring her to the drawing room. Tell her not to make a spectacle of herself or we're all done for."

"Will do my best," said Drew.

Ranson stood for a moment after Drew strolled into the drawing room. Earlier in the day, Lady Lavinia had been carrying her drawing materials. He wondered whether she had used that as an excuse to search outside. He went through the front door and stood looking around the park. Although he could spy a few deer at the edge of the woods, he did not see one single human being. Turning on his heel, he returned to the front hall and followed it to the back of the house. He glanced into the kitchen where the staff was busy working. Stepping through the back door, he observed a flash of movement in the herb garden and made his way along the flat-stoned path that led there.

As he expected, Lady Lavinia was seated on a bench with her sketch pad in hand. "You have a talent for drawing, Miss Rose?"

Lavinia started, looking up at him and then quickly back at her pad. "Only to amuse myself, my lord. I am not an expert by any means."

"I'm surprised. In my experience, most women in your profession rarely exhibit an interest in drawing."

"My profession, my lord? While I admit how I make my living is not acceptable for many, it is better than starving. And if men such as yourself made more legitimate positions available for females, perhaps you would not be looking down at me now."

Lady Lavinia was a regular firebrand, thought Ranson, containing a smile. "I meant no disrespect," he said. "Tell me how you came to know Drew."

"I met him one evening," she replied briefly.

"I cannot see how we missed one another since Drew and I are together much of the time."

"You must ask him that," said Lavinia, keeping her gaze on her sketch pad so that her veil would cover as much of her face as possible.

"You are a very attractive woman," said Ranson, moving closer and seating himself beside her.

Lavinia moved away from him as far as possible, but he merely followed her.

"My lord, you are pressing me," she said, teetering on the edge of the bench.

"Not nearly as much as I intend to," he murmured. Suddenly his arm was around her and his lips were near her cheek, his breath causing the veil to flutter lightly.

"My lord!" she exclaimed, attempting to avoid his grasp. "I would be obliged if you would release me."

"This is definitely the wrong place to pretend to play the innocent with me," he said, holding her tightly.

"But Viscount Stanford," she objected. "He is your best friend."

"Exactly," Ranson replied, seemingly pleased that she had brought up the subject. "Drew and I have been friends since we were in leading strings and we have always shared everything."

Lavinia gasped. Her mind going blank with what he was suggesting. "Certainly you do not . . ."

"Come now, my dear, don't pretend you are shocked. You should be well acquainted with the ways of men— unless you are new to your profession—and that I do not believe."

Ranson stood and pulled her up with him. Her drawing materials fell to the ground as she quickly put her hands on his chest, pushing at him.

"I like a woman who does not give in easily. It makes the victory only sweeter." He bent down and touched his lips to the lobe of her ear, then to the sensitive area just below it.

He was moving far too rapidly for Lavinia's shocked mind to keep up. She had been prepared to face an angry Lord Weston who had discovered her identity, but she had never expected him to attempt to seduce her.

His lips continued their exploration and Lavinia grew numb as he pulled her closer. His mouth settled over hers and all logic deserted her. She could do nothing more than lean in to his strength and give in to the overwhelming emotion that engulfed her.

"We can go to my room," he murmured. "Drew and Stephanie are playing cards and will never know we're gone."

Lavinia's hands slid around his neck and she rested her head against his broad chest.

Ranson chuckled. "I see you're willing." His hands moved over the light muslin of her gown, tracing the delicious curves of her body as if anticipating what lay before them.

What was she doing? thought Lavinia, attempting to pull away from him. "This is outside of enough. I cannot do anything of the sort," she objected.

"Of course, you can," said Ranson. "If it will ease your mind, I'll advise Drew what is happening on our way upstairs."

"You will do what?" She squealed, aghast at his words. "What you are suggesting, sir, is beyond all reason."

"Come now, Rose, acting the innocent can only be taken so far before it becomes deadly dull. I admire you, and if Drew is willing to share, I see no reason to put aside our pleasure."

"You are no more than an animal," she hissed, struggling to escape his hold on her.

"Your protests are beginning to bore me," he said.

"Then leave me alone and find someone who doesn't."

"Everyone is involved in something at the time," he said. "That is why I thought it opportune when I discovered you here in the garden."

"Well, you are wrong, for I have no desire to make our acquaintance any more than what it is."

Movement behind Lord Weston caught Lavinia's eye. Two of the women who worked in the kitchen and a footman were leaving the house, their arms full. They placed their parcels in the back of a pony cart that was waiting nearby and drove off.

They are taking food to the women, thought Lavinia, and here she was being held captive by Lord Weston's lechery. "Let me go," she demanded, watching the pony cart over his shoulder.

"Why should I? You certainly don't have a better offer."

The pony cart disappeared from view and anger blurred Lavinia's reason. "You think I should swoon at the honor you are bestowing on me? Why you think so well of yourself, I don't know. You are nothing more than a man, and a poor example of one at that."

"Why, my lady, and I thought I had made an excellent impression on you."

"Excellent? I don't see how you could think that. Why . . ." The import of Lord Weston's words finally penetrated her blaze of anger. Had his address been sarcasm, or had he discovered her true identity? It did not take long for an answer.

"Indeed, my lady," he continued, his scalding words pouring over her. "We have waltzed and ridden together.

I have even kissed you before and you did not object overmuch."

Lavinia pulled away and he let her go. "How did you know?" she asked dully.

"I will admit you have an excellent disguise. The wig and veil, the rouge, all made it nearly impossible to detect your true identity. However, there was one thing you forgot and that was that delicious dimple at the corner of your lips."

Lavinia reached up and touched the offending dimple. Such a small thing to cause her plan to fail. "Now that you know, what are you going to do?"

"I am going to do nothing at all," he said pleasantly. "However, you and Drew will make your excuses to Hayley. Then you will collect Lady Fitzhugh and Robert at the inn and return to Town."

Lavinia stood for a moment, taking in his orders. She had been completely devastated when she realized he had recognized her; however, now that the initial shock had passed she found herself resenting his high-handedness. He had no right whatsoever to order her around. He was not her father, nor husband, nor guardian; he was merely a slight acquaintance. Of course, she had stolen three mistresses from him, but that did not indicate any intimacy at all.

The blood boiled in her veins as Lord Weston stood before her smug in his masculinity. "I am sorry you found me out, my lord, but that does not change my intent at all. As for you ordering me about, you have no authority whatsoever to do so. I am free to do what I want and I choose to be here."

"And your father agrees, I suppose," he said.

"That is between me and my father," she replied.

"Then it does not matter whether I talk with him or not."

"I do not think you would like to remove yourself

from the house party in order to speak with my father over such an incident. To begin with, you do not know him at all. Surely, you can imagine what he would think of a complete stranger coming to him with tales of my conduct. And if you should be so ill-advised to do such a thing, you would need to find him. He could be in London, or at any of several places in the country. They are far enough apart that the house party would long be over and forgotten by the time you located him."

Ranson knew she was right. He was merely threatening in order to get her to do his bidding; however, it looked as if his plan was not working. He must do something to keep her out of danger. Drew would have kept her from coming if he had been able, so he could not turn to his friend for help. It was up to him to think of something and his mind was empty of suggestions. Perhaps he should try a part of the truth.

"Lady Lavinia," he began.

"Don't you think you should continue to call me Rose in case someone is nearby?"

He closed his eyes and prayed for patience. "Rose, it is dangerous here, particularly for women."

"I am not a child, my lord. I have heard the rumors that Lord Hayley sells women into slavery and I am aware of the danger that surrounds him. However, that makes it all the more crucial that we find Jessica as soon as possible if she is in his hands. I am assuming that he will do away with the women soon after the house party and that leaves us but a day or two at the most."

Ranson could not fault her reasoning since it was the same conclusion he had come to. "Even if you are right and Jessica is being held here on the estate, there is nothing you can do about it."

"I realize I cannot fight Lord Hayley and his men

hand to hand; however, I can find out where she is, then ask for help in freeing her."

"And if you are caught before you are able to call for help?"

Lavinia's chin thrust upward with determination. "Then I will at least know that I did all that I could for my friend."

Lavinia observed the pony cart return, leaving the servants at the back of the house before traveling on to the stable. They had not been gone long so they had not gone far, she determined. Perhaps she could trace their path. The cart would certainly leave some sort of track that could be seen.

"I wish you would listen to me," said Ranson.

"I am listening, my lord, but it has not changed my mind."

Ranson leaned down and picked up her drawing materials. "Here," he said, handing them to her, "allow me to escort you back to Drew."

"No, thank you, my lord. I came out to rid my mind of worries for a moment and I intend to do so. Although, I believe I will find another scene to sketch since this one has lost its appeal."

Ranson could do nothing but watch as she strolled away from the house and into the park.

THIRTEEN

It took all of Lavinia's willpower not to look over her shoulder to see whether Lord Weston was watching her. It did not matter if he was, she decided, for he would not know that she was following the track the pony cart had made on its mysterious trip.

She walked well away from the flattened grass in case someone was watching and might wonder why she was taking the same course as the cart had. She stopped several times, pretending to sketch something that had caught her eye, then glanced around to see whether anyone was following her.

Evidently, Lord Weston had given up on her for the moment for he was no longer in the herb garden, and neither Lord Hayley nor any of his people were in sight, seeming to pay her no mind at all. As Lavinia approached the woods, she dropped all pretense of drawing and made her way quickly along what was little more than a footpath. The thickness of the woods soaked up the sunlight before it reached the ground and an eerie darkness closed around her. There was hardly any sound as she continued through the wilderness and she shivered as a chill ran through her. If anyone believed evil existed in its own right, then this is where it would reside. Before she realized it, a house loomed before her. She quickly ducked into the bushes beside the path.

The house was a sizable one to be hidden away as it

was. The trees and underbrush had been allowed to grow at will for what looked to be years, and vines climbed the walls, nearly swallowing the house. Lavinia assumed this was previously the dowager's house. Once Hayley had begun his trade in women it would have proven to be invaluable as a safe place for Hayley to hide the women he kidnapped and sold.

Except for the one narrow path, the woods were thick and dark on all sides. Lavinia doubted anyone would attempt to make their way through it with the sunny, green meadows of the park to enjoy. And without the scent of fires and cooking to draw attention, the house was nearly indistinguishable from the woods.

Now that she had found what she thought was the hiding place for the women, Lavinia wondered how she could get close enough to be certain. At that moment the door opened and Lavinia crouched even lower in the bushes. A large, rough-looking man holding a pistol stepped out and glanced around. Moving farther away, he motioned and two women came through the door, with another man following close behind

Lavinia did not recognize either of the women, but studied them carefully as they turned and walked away from the house, the two men—pistols held ready in their hands—attending them. They were allowed to stay outside for perhaps a half hour before the men herded them back to the front door. They waited while the women went inside and two others came out. Again, Lavinia did not recognize the women, but attempted to commit their features to memory in case she was required to describe them.

As before, the women returned to the house and the men waited as another woman came to the door. Lavinia's breath caught in her throat. It was Jessica. She was thin and wan-looking, but she was able to walk around, breathing deeply, as if she could not get enough of the fresh air.

It took all of Lavinia's strength not to call out and run to her side, but she knew it would do neither of them any good. She waited until Jessica entered the house before slipping quietly away. She made her way back along the path, almost too excited to think straight. She would first advise Robert; he was Jessica's brother and should decide how to go about rescuing her.

She encountered Drew walking toward her as she came out of the woods and hurried to meet him. "You are right on time," she said when she reached him.

"Ranson told me you came this way. Sorry he found out. Couldn't be helped."

"You're not to blame," she said. "I suppose I'm lucky he didn't see through my disguise at our first meeting. But that is of no consequence now." Excitement made her eyes sparkle even beneath the veil that nearly obscured them. "We must return to the inn immediately. Tell Lord Hayley I need to rest before the ball tonight."

Her enthusiasm infected Drew, and without question, he hastened to call for the coach and to make his excuses to Hayley. They were on their way to the inn in a very short time.

"Have you found something out?" asked Drew as they rode away from the estate.

"I have, but I want to wait until Robert and Aunt Hope are present to reveal what it is."

A short time later they sought the privacy of Lady Fitzhugh's room at the inn. "Don't dawdle," commanded Aunt Hope, once they were seated. "Out with what you have to say."

"Yes, Lavinia," said Robert, his face pale with tension. "Tell us what you have found."

Lavinia looked around at the small group of people who had followed her into what most would say was a birdbrained plan. "I have found Jessica," she announced baldly.

A shocked silence followed her disclosure. Robert dropped his head into his hands, while Lady Fitzhugh raised her handkerchief to her mouth. Only Drew remained outwardly unperturbed.

"Is she all right?" Robert asked, raising his head and staring at her thorough red-rimmed eyes.

"She appears to be unharmed," said Lavinia, reaching out to touch his arm. "She is thinner, but that is to be expected, I suppose. However, she walked around outside for some time without showing any sign of injury."

Lavinia then commenced from when she followed the cart tracks and told them all she had seen.

"We must go to her immediately," said Robert, rising from his chair.

"Not so fast," said Drew. "Must make plans."

"Why? We know where she is and Hayley should not give us any trouble once he realizes we have found him out."

"Hayley will do anything to save himself," said Drew. "If we are not careful, we may all end up laid in the dust."

A sharp knock sounded at the door before it swung open to reveal Lord Weston. "I surmised I would find you all gathered together." He walked in, closing the door behind him. "Robert. Lady Fitzhugh. I have already spoken to Drew, but I thought both of you had better sense than to allow Lady Lavinia to put her life in jeopardy."

Lady Fitzhugh made a very unladylike sound. "Do not come on to me in such a manner. I was a friend of your mother's and have watched you being bathed. So do not attempt to browbeat me or I will tell everyone the whereabouts of your birthmark."

Ranson's face flushed. "Pardon, my lady. I did not

mean to insult you, but finding Lady Lavinia at a Cyprians' house party was more than enough to leave me disgruntled."

"I'm certain it did, but there is a good reason for everything."

Unable to keep silent any longer, Robert burst in. "She has found Jessica," he said, looking more alive than he had since his sister had disappeared.

"What!" exclaimed Ranson, pinning his gaze on Lavinia. "Where did you see her? Are you certain it is Jessica?"

"I know Jessica when I see her," said Lavinia, his inane question putting her on her high ropes. She once again recited how she had found the house where the women were being kept.

"That is such a thick woods no one ever goes there," said Ranson. "And if there are no fires allowed in the house then it is highly unlikely anyone would suspect it was there. You knew about this when we spoke, didn't you?"

"I had been watching the servants and saw them leave the house after you found me in the garden. I was going to follow them then, but you spoiled my plan," she complained.

"You should have told me."

"Why, so you could tell me I am all about in the head? You had no faith that I could find Jessica so why should I have faith in you?"

Ranson ignored her questions since he had no answers. "We must be careful," he said to Robert. "One wrong move and we could lose her, or worse. Hayley is not going to leave any witnesses to his crimes."

"We must get her out of that house," insisted Robert.

"And we will," confirmed Ranson, "but we must wait until tomorrow."

"Why? For God's sake?" questioned Robert. "I cannot bear to think of her being held a moment longer than necessary."

"I realize it is difficult for you, but Hayley will not harm Jessica. We must plan how to rescue her and the other women without harm coming to any of them. In the meantime, we must continue as if nothing were amiss. Which means," he continued, looking first at Drew then at Lavinia, "that you will attend the ball tonight just as you had planned."

"I cannot be under the same roof with that man again now that I know for certain he has Jessica," said Lavinia.

"If you care for Jessica as you say you do, then you will be there tonight," said Ranson. "If Hayley suspects anything out of the ordinary, he may spirit the women away to where we may never find them."

"If you truly believe that, then I will go," Lavinia replied.

Ranson nodded his approval. "Drew, Robert, walk with me downstairs. There are some items we must discuss."

"Then discuss them here where we may all be privy to them. I believe I have proven my right to be involved in Jessica's rescue."

"You have indeed," agreed Ranson. "But what I have to say concerns more than Jessica and I am not at liberty to share it with everyone."

Once the three men had walked out of the inn, Ranson turned to them and spoke in a low tone. "I am going to send a message to the Home Office telling them what we have discovered and asking for support. I will arrange a meeting place for early in the morning. Then, I will take my usual ride and meet with them to explain our plan."

"And what is that?" asked Robert.

"I have found where Hayley is counterfeiting and some of the men will be instructed to go there in order to raid the building. Others will enter the house itself and secure everyone there. The rest will hide themselves in the woods around the house where the women are kept. When we arrive, we will lead the men to rescue the ladies.

"What we don't want to do is to move too fast. Remember, if this party is like the others, there will be men leaving alone when they arrived with their mistresses. I want those men identified. We'll rendezvous in a concealed place. I'll give you specifics tonight," said Ranson to Drew.

"I only hope we will not be too late," said Robert.

"As long as you don't do anything foolish, the plan will work and Jessica will remain unharmed. I know it's going to be difficult, but you must remain patient for one more night. Do either of you have any questions?"

"What about Stephanie?" asked Drew.

"I will make certain that she is safe," replied Ranson, as they reached the horse he had left tethered outside the inn. He swung into the saddle. "I have been gone too long. I don't want to give Hayley the slightest reason to become suspicious. Drew, I will see you tonight. Robert, keep a cool head until tomorrow." He turned his animal and rode away, leaving the two men to stand staring after him.

"Well, he is gone," said Lavinia, moving away from the window overlooking the yard below. "I wonder what he is up to?"

"You may trust that it is something important," said Lady Fitzhugh. "I never believed that Ranson came to Hayley's country estate for mere pleasure. I believe he's playing a deeper game than that."

"I wonder whether we will ever know?"

"Possibly, when everything is done and over with,"

replied Lady Fitzhugh. "Now let us look over your gown for this evening. Your disguise will be much easier tonight since you can do away with your veil and wear a mask."

"Thank goodness. I don't believe I'll ever wear a veil again."

"Except on your wedding day," said her aunt.

"And that may never come," she replied sharply.

That evening Lavinia dressed in a gown of sapphire blue, with a low-cut neckline and tiny puffed sleeves. The gown was heavily decorated with silver embroidery and pearls. Pearls were looped through the curls of her blond wig, while a silver mask covered most of her face.

She did not look forward to the evening. It seemed dreadfully coldhearted to be going to a ball while Jessica and the other women languished in the house in the dark woods. Drew had reminded her several times on the drive to Hayley's house that they must continue as if nothing were amiss if she wished Jessica to escape unharmed.

"I will do it if you say it is necessary," she had told him. "But my heart will not be in it."

"Understand," he said, his voice more gloomy than she had ever heard.

"Oh, Drew, I'm sorry. I'm such a selfish person. I know that we both love Jessica and that this is as bad for you as it is for me."

"No need for apology," he replied, patting her hand. "Everything will come right."

"I pray it will," she said, as the coach rolled to a stop at Hayley's house.

* * *

"You are looking charming this evening," said Ranson, when Lavinia and Drew arrived at the ball.

"Don't suppose you mean me," joked Drew.

"Indeed not," agreed Ranson. "I was directing my remark to Miss Rose."

"Thank you, my lord," replied Lavinia, executing a slight curtsy.

Lavinia glanced around the ballroom and was relieved to see that most of the women's gowns were even more revealing than the one she wore. "I must admit this is a unique experience," she said, fluttering an ivory fan to cool her flushed face.

"One I hope you will not experience again," Ranson murmured, so that only she could hear his words. "Remember, we need only get through this last night and then we will all be safe. Do not act out of the ordinary in any sense."

It took all of Lavinia's willpower to restrain her anger. "My lord, you insult me. I believe I will be able to keep my wits about me for a few hours."

"No offense was intended," Ranson replied quickly. "It is a bothersome habit I have of reminding everyone what needs to be done."

"Then you should restrain yourself when you are around me. I have no need to be treated like a child."

"We will do just fine," said Drew.

"I know you will," said Ranson, as a couple strolled by and nodded. "There's a buffet set up in the dining room. And the ballroom is just behind the drawing room where the orchestra is playing if you feel the need to dance." He turned again to Lavinia. "I hope you will do me the honor at least once this evening."

"Of course, my lord," she answered, irritated that he knew she could not refuse him.

"Then I must return to Stephanie. I cannot ignore her

too long or Hayley might wonder about the depth of our commitment."

Lavinia did not like the flash of annoyance she felt when Lord Weston mentioned Stephanie's name and chided herself for responding so. It meant nothing, she told herself; nothing at all.

Lavinia danced with Drew several times during the evening before they went into the supper room. The tables were crowded with dishes to tempt even the most discriminating taste, along with complementary wines.

Although Drew brought her a plate, Lavinia was too much on pins and needles to do any more than push the food around on her plate to make it seem she was eating.

After supper, the two of them strolled through the house, looking in on the gambling room where Lord Weston was playing hazard with Stephanie at his side.

The night passed more swiftly than Lavinia had thought possible. It was nearly time for them to leave when Ranson came to claim his dance.

"It seems we have done this before," he teased, as he led her onto the floor.

"I suppose one woman tends to fade into another once you have danced with so many," she replied with a smile.

"You wound me, Miss Rose," he replied, as they matched their steps to a waltz.

"Not as much as I would like, my lord," she said, maintaining a pleasant smile on her face.

He bent his head next to hers and she thought he intended to kiss her again. "You must believe that I would never intentionally insult you," he murmured in a low voice. "When all this is over, there is much I need to explain."

"Is it possible?"

"I believe it to be," he replied, then straightened

again. "We should not seem on too friendly terms or Drew will be forced to act the jealous protector."

"You need not worry, my lord. He is a very mild man and I do not expect anyone would believe he would object to your teasing."

"He is very well thought of by everyone," Ranson agreed. "I wish there were some way for him to find happiness with Lady Jessica."

"I have faith that they will be together someday," replied Lavinia.

"And what of yourself? Is there someone special you've met since you've been in London?"

"The compliments and conversations have all seemed the same to me. I would like to meet someone with more independence of mind; one who is not afraid to swerve from what is the current thing."

"Such as our experience at Lady Swearington's?" he asked, a devilish glint in his eyes.

"I wish you would stop bringing that up at our every meeting," she spat out.

"I believe you are exaggerating, my lady. Perhaps you often dream of it and confuse it with our conversations."

Lavinia knew he was teasing her, yet she could feel her cheeks turn hot and could not keep herself from responding. "I certainly do not dream of you," she said in a low voice.

He drew her close. "But I dream of you," he murmured.

Lord Weston's voice poured over her like honey, causing her to lose all the animosity she had built up toward him. However, before she could gather her wits to reply, the music came to an end.

"The dance always seems too short when you are in my arms," he said, as the orchestra finished playing and people began leaving the dance floor. He led her back to where Drew was conversing with Stephanie and the two couples bid one another good night.

"Seemed to go well," said Drew, on their way back to the inn. "Hayley issued me an invitation to the next house party."

"As if there will be another," remarked Lavinia.

"Did not think I should impart that information to him."

Lavinia glanced at him and gave a short laugh. "You have a unique sense of humor," she said.

The coach was nearing the inn before she spoke again. "Do you think tomorrow will go well?" She wanted his reassurance that Jessica would be returned safely.

"If all goes as planned," replied Drew. "Don't see why it shouldn't. Ranson is excellent at working things out."

"I pray that he has done so this time."

Lavinia barely slept the remainder of the night. Robert and Drew left before sunup to position themselves at the appropriate place, while Lady Fitzhugh kept vigil with Lavinia as they waited for news from the Hayley estate.

It was nearly noon before a cloud of dust heralded the arrival of several coaches escorted by outriders. Lavinia and Lady Fitzhugh arrived in the courtyard just as Robert leaped out of the first coach and reached up to lift Jessica to the ground.

The women exchanged hugs as tears coursed down their faces.

"I am fine," replied Jessica to their repeated questions of her health. "I assume Hayley took good care of us so that we would bring a good price. The other women— where are they?"

"Don't fret over them," said Robert. "We have rooms for them here at the inn and they will be treated well." He turned to Lavinia. "You might be interested to know that Jeanette Norville was one of them."

So Harry Black was right about Jeanette, thought Lavinia. She would see that he received a bonus for his work. "What of the women who were left this time?" asked Lavinia.

"We found four women who had been drugged and were still in their rooms. They will also be cared for until they are ready to be on their own."

"I must talk to them," murmured Lavinia.

"We both shall," said Lady Fitzhugh. "If they accept our invitation, we will find them suitable housing until there is room at Hope House."

"Hope House?" queried Robert.

"I will explain later," said Jessica. "For now, I want to enjoy my freedom."

"There is something you should know," said Robert, his face solemn. "It's about Thomas."

Jessica turned pale, her eyes wide. "Is he here?" she asked, her voice quivering. "I cannot see him. I will not go back to him. No one can force me to do that."

Robert took her hands. "Please, Jessica. There's no need to be concerned about Thomas, for he will never bother you again. He came to the estate this morning just as we were beginning to move against Hayley. There were two women with him whom he evidently meant to sell to Hayley. When he saw what was happening, he leaped out of his coach and before we knew it, he had attacked our men."

Robert paused and Lavinia was certain that they all knew what his next words would be. "I'm sorry, Jessica, but he was killed. Our men attempted to take him without harm, but he would not allow it. He fought like a madman and severely injured two of the men before . . . before . . ." His voice trailed off.

Jessica was silent while the news of her husband's death became a reality. "I cannot cry now," she said. "Perhaps later when I am able to consider everything. But Thomas was not a kind husband; not even a loving one. He married me for my family name and my money, not for love of my person. Lately, he had become cruel and hateful, and you can see what happened to me when he found out I was of no use to him. He sold me as a slave to the most despicable of men. I will not say I'm glad that he is dead, but I am relieved." Then she burst into tears.

"I shall take her upstairs and sit with her," said Lady Fitzhugh, putting her arm around Jessica and leading her through the door while Robert watched with anxious eyes.

"Aunt Hope will take good care of her," said Lavinia. "She has made many women's nightmares disappear with her wise words."

The frown on Robert's brow seemed to smooth out a little and he turned to Lavinia. "Ranson's plans worked out to perfection. He was in the heat of the battle and came away without a scratch."

Lavinia had wondered about Lord Weston, but could not make herself ask. She had comforted herself that they would have been advised immediately if he had been wounded.

"What of Drew?" asked Lavinia. "I assume he is safe or you would have told me by now."

Robert nodded. "He was right at Ranson's heels. The two of them make a forbidding pair. I intend to always be on their side." He smiled, rubbing a weary hand over his face. "He came through it unscathed, as did Ranson. We had minor injuries among the men who were here to help us, but nothing serious. Hayley and his people are on their way back to London under heavy guard. They will get what they deserve," he said grimly. "Drew and Ranson are returning to Town with the prisoners. They need to report what has happened to the Home Office as soon as possible."

"The Home Office?" asked Lavinia.

"Yes. It seems they have been investigating Hayley for some time now; however, they lacked hard evidence to move against him." Robert stopped short of revealing that Ranson had been asked to step in. He would leave it up to his friend to make whatever explanation was necessary to Lavinia.

"I suppose there is nothing left to do but to return to London and resume our usual activities," she said.

"That sounds like an excellent idea to me," replied Robert. He held out his arm to her. "Shall we go inside and partake of a victory luncheon."

"I should be pleased, my lord."

Nothing had changed in London. The same people were attending the same routs, balls and soirees, with what seemed to be the same *on-dits* making the rounds. News of Hayley's downfall was being circulated, but all the details had not leaked out and Lavinia and Jessica's parts in the scandal were safe from public knowledge.

Lavinia had seen Drew, but Lord Weston was playing least in sight. Drew explained that he was busy with the Home Office, explaining what had occurred at Hayley's estate. He followed Robert's example and did not mention Ranson's official part in the investigation.

Lavinia attempted to convince herself that she did not care about Lord Weston's absence. He was not bound to seek her out and she, needless to say, would never request that he call on her. Her business with him was nearly over and she would be happy when it was complete. She needed only to somehow finish her revenge on him and then she would be done.

It was two days later before Ranson presented himself at Lady Fitzhugh's home. His face was solemn when he stood in front of Lavinia in the drawing room.

"I hope you suffered no ill effects from your experience," he said stiffly.

"I am quite well, my lord. It appears that you also came through the fray with no injuries."

"I was luckier than some," he said.

"Would you care to sit down?" she said, sitting on the settee and waving her hand in invitation toward a chair nearby.

A silence fell once they were seated and Lavinia made no effort to break it. Lord Weston finally cleared his throat and leaned toward her.

"Lady Lavinia, there are rumors circulating about what happened at Hayley's."

"And you are surprised at that?" she asked.

"Not at all, but it came to mind that somehow your part in it could become known."

"I don't see how that could happen," she said.

"Stranger things have occurred. If what you have done makes the circuit of *on-dits* in the *ton,* we both know that you will be ruined."

"What! Because I chose to help rescue my friend, I will no longer be welcome in anyone's drawing room?"

"No. It will be because you chose to appear as a demirep at Hayley's house party," he replied bluntly.

"My aunt was with me, as were Drew and Robert. How can anyone fault that?" she asked.

"You may rest assured that once it is known, they certainly will," he contended. "But there is one way that it can be avoided. I have come here today to ask you to marry me. Once you are my wife, no one would dare whisper such a rumor."

A jumble of emotions filled Lavinia. For a moment, sheer joy dominated, until she realized that this was not what she should be feeling. Lord Weston was her enemy. He had insulted her sister and caused her to leave her home. She reminded herself that she should feel nothing but contempt for the man.

"You . . . you . . . How could you even think that I would consider marriage to you? You are a user of women and I would never put myself in such a position as to be your wife."

It was Ranson's time to turn red with anger. Rising to his feet, he said, "You may ask anyone. I have never treated any woman less than she should be. And I have certainly never misused you in any way."

"A man does not need to sell women as Hayley did in order to mistreat them. Your way is much more subtle. And I have firsthand knowledge of your insensitivity."

"I have no idea what you are talking about," he said, an expression of bewilderment on his face.

"I suppose you have no recollection of my sister."

"I don't believe I've had the pleasure," he replied.

"Her name is Barbara," Lavinia said.

Ranson appeared baffled. "I do not know anyone by the name of Barbara."

"That proves how little my sister meant to you. I realize that you have known many women in your life, but you met my sister at her come-out some four years ago. You led her on until she found herself in love with you and then you tossed her aside like a used handkerchief. It is that callousness that ruined my sister's life and forced her to flee the country of her birth to seek asylum on the Continent with our aunt."

"It cannot be," he blustered. "If I have met your sister, I am sorry to say I do not remember her and I cannot think of any reason why I would offend her in

such a manner. You must have mistaken me for someone
else."

"There is no mistake, my lord. I have heard it with
my own ears and have letters which state your cruel
actions."

"Then your sister must be mistaken," he insisted. "I
give you leave to inquire among my friends as to how
I conduct myself. My father taught me to treat every
woman with respect and I have always done so. You
cannot find anyone who will say differently."

"Save my sister," she answered sharply. "And perhaps
your mistresses."

"You know nothing of my mistresses," he said stiffly.
"And it is not fitting that we discuss the subject."

"I know more than you think," she said, a sly smile
curling her lips and causing her dimple to deepen. "Have
you forgotten Stephanie and I became acquainted at the
house party? She is a very lovely person."

"There is something you need to know before we talk
of Stephanie."

"I cannot imagine what that would be."

"We were never what you think we were."

His comment was too vague for her understanding.
"What do you mean?" she asked, a frown marring her
forehead.

"Pardon me for speaking so bluntly, but Stephanie
was my mistress in name only. There was never anything
more than friendship between us."

Lavinia was silent a moment, then began laughing.
At first low, then increasing in volume until tears formed
in her eyes and rolled down her cheeks. "My lord," she
gasped. "You must truly think I am a green girl if you
expect me to believe that. I know the woman; she would
tempt any man. Then there are the emeralds. I doubt
whether you give such expensive gifts to mere friends."

Ranson was rigid with anger. "If you do not believe

me then there is no reason to continue this conversation."

Lavinia felt disappointed that he had given in so easily. After all the years of holding a grudge against the man she wanted more of a reaction from him. She knew of one sure way to get it and this might be the last time she would have the opportunity to tell him face-to-face.

"Now it is my turn, my lord. There is something *you* need to know."

"I can't imagine what you could have to say to me that would be of any interest," he replied.

"I believe you had three mistresses before Stephanie who disappeared."

"You have been listening to gossip," he accused her.

"I have more than gossip to rely upon," she replied smugly. "You see I have met each of them."

Ranson was clearly dismayed. "You did not."

"Oh, but I did. They were Joylene, Lilly, and Felicity," she said, holding up her hand and counting them off on her fingers one at a time.

"You could have learned that from some of the *on-dits*," he charged.

"I could have," she agreed, "but I didn't. I learned that and much more from them as I was convincing them to leave you."

Ranson was at a loss for words. He did not want to believe what she claimed, but she was compelling enough to persuade him that she spoke the truth. He had always known there was something more behind the disappearances of his mistresses than mere dissatisfaction with him as a protector. However, with the Hayley business coming right on the heels of the women vanishing, he had not had the time to pursue the causes for their leaving.

"Why did you do it?" he asked, his voice dull and his face solemn.

"For revenge," she spat out. "You had taken my sister from me and . . ."

"I told you, I did nothing of the sort," he protested.

". . . and I was not going to allow you to get away with it. I spent the time until my come-out planning what I would do and when I arrived in London, I began my campaign."

Ranson could not believe that this woman whom he had held in his arms could have—at the same time— been plotting his social downfall. "How could you have met them?"

"I cannot tell you specifics, but be assured that women have ways of their own to circumvent the hold men have over every bit of their lives. I was able to meet with the women and explain they could have a different way of life—a respectable life that did not rely upon the whims of a gentleman. They chose to take me up on the offer. It was really exceedingly easy to win them over."

"Then they are well?" he asked.

"Of course," Lavinia answered. "I'm surprised that you care enough to ask."

"Lady Lavinia, no matter what your sister told you, or what you have heard from my mistresses or from the *ton,* I have been deeply concerned over the fate of the women. I was ready to launch a search for them once I returned to London, but now I need not do that for I know that you will take good care of them. If for nothing more than to make a fool of me."

"I hope you feel the fool," she said, nearly snarling as she released the anger that had built up over the years. "It is too much to ask for with your title and fortune, but I hope that not another woman will even look at you, let alone become your mistress or wife."

"I believe it will be some time before I desire the company of either," he replied sarcastically. "You realize that if I put this story around about you that there would not be a single man brave enough to make you an offer."

Lavinia had not given the repercussions of her actions a single thought, but she would not allow him to see that.

"And your father," he went on, "of course, knows all about your little game. Consider how entertaining it will be for us to get together and discuss over a glass of brandy his daughter's harmless diversions."

"You wouldn't dare," she objected, livid with anger. "He has been ill."

"He will be well one day and I am in no hurry. Delay will only give me more time to anticipate and savor the moment of denouement."

Ranson was well satisfied with the expression on her face. Evidently, she had thought no further than getting her revenge on him for some imaginary offense her sister had suffered at his hands, a sister that he did not even remember ever having met.

Lavinia could not believe she had allowed herself to get into such a fix. Her father would probably lock her in her room until her hair was gray if he learned what she had been up to. Well, she would at least have the satisfaction of saving three women and getting her revenge on Lord Weston. She would never allow him to know he had scored a hit.

"Do what you must," she told him, attempting to appear as unconcerned as possible. "I merely wanted you to know that everyone is not fooled by your genial façade."

"You do not know what damage you have done; what trouble you have caused me beyond losing a mistress."

"That is gratifying to know," she replied.

"You are wrong, Lady Lavinia. Your actions could have caused us to have lost Jessica, and at the very least made her rescue more difficult than it should have been."

"What do you mean?"

"You know all the *on-dits*. I leave it for you to discover. In the meantime, I bid you good-bye—and I do mean good-bye. If we happen to meet in the future, do not take it amiss if I ignore you." He turned sharply on his heel and stalked out of the room.

A few moments later, Lady Fitzhugh entered and found Lavinia still staring at the door. "Weston was here?" she asked.

"He was," Lavinia replied shortly.

"I assume it did not go well."

"If you consider that he bid me a final good-bye and threatened to ignore me if ever we met again not going well, then it did not."

"What in heaven's name caused him to do that?" asked Lady Fitzhugh.

"I told him I had stolen three of his mistresses," said Lavinia.

"We had best sit down," replied Lady Fitzhugh, with a sigh. "I don't believe you have advised me of everything you have been up to while in Town."

"There are a few things," agreed Lavinia.

FOURTEEN

Lavinia was still feeling down-pinned a few days later when she received a tremendous surprise. Her sister, Barbara, came knocking on Lady Fitzhugh's door. After the hugs and tears were over, Lavinia led her to the settee in the living room, where they sat side by side.

Barbara and Lavinia had been close and had shared confidences during their childhood. It had been painful when Barbara had left suddenly for the Continent with little more than a hasty good-bye.

"Tell me, how did you get here? Why did you decide to return? You must tell me everything," Lavinia demanded.

Barbara laughed at her younger sister's impatience. "We will have plenty of time to talk," she said, "for I intend to make it a long visit. In fact, I will be living here in England from now on."

"Oh, Barbara, I'm so happy," said Lavinia, once again hugging her sister and dissolving into tears.

"You are becoming a watering pot," accused Barbara, handing Lavinia a handkerchief to wipe away her tears. "Before I explain let me tell you that I stopped in the country and father is doing much better."

"I am so glad," said Lavinia. "I knew that the Town air was not good for him."

"He plans on coming back for the Little Season, but

he insisted I journey to Town to visit you and enjoy the remainder of the Season."

"I am so happy you did," said Lavinia, reaching out for her sister's hand.

"And I have a tremendous surprise," continued Barbara, a huge smile brightening her face. "I am married!"

Lavinia was speechless for a moment. "But . . . who?"

"Lord Adam Thornton. A wonderful man who happened to also be visiting the Continent. It was love at first sight," said Barbara. "From the moment we met I knew that we were destined to be together." She blushed like a green girl instead of a grown woman.

Lavinia was bewildered. "When you left, you vowed you would never marry."

"Did I?" asked Barbara, a baffled expression on her face. "It must have been a temporary phase, for I did not hesitate when Adam offered for me."

"Don't you remember crying and telling me that Lord Weston was forcing you out of the country? That he had insulted and embarrassed you to the point where you could never return?"

"You must have misunderstood," said Barbara, "for I am here, am I not?"

"I am not making this up," insisted Lavinia. "You even threatened to throw yourself off the bridge before facing him again. Soon thereafter, you left England to stay with Aunt Charity."

"And I am so glad I did or I would have never met Adam," replied Barbara. "But I remember Lord Weston now that you remind me. I was but a green girl at my come-out and he was such a handsome, dashing young man." Barbara closed her eyes as if attempting to visualize what had happened, then continued. "We met several times during the Season; we danced and I believe he even took me in to dinner once. He was on every mother's list as a husband for her daughter and he escaped all of them."

"Including you," stated Lavinia.

Barbara chuckled. "Including me," she agreed. "I was prone to dramatics at that point in my life and I suppose I overreacted when he did not fall head over heels for me."

"You told me you hoped Lord Weston would suffer as much as you did. In fact, you insisted you would not return until he had."

"I should have been on stage," replied Barbara, clearly amused at her youthful folly. "I hope you did not take me seriously."

"Of course I did. You were my sister and Lord Weston had driven you from our home."

"Oh, Lavinia, I never meant for you to think that. I suppose it might be partially true that I left because at the time I did think I had made a fool of myself over Lord Weston. However, he was not the main reason. I had always wanted to visit Aunt Charity and it was an excellent opportunity. I recognized early on that I was not suited for coming to London for the Season merely to find a husband. It seemed such a cold way to begin a lifetime of living together. I think I used Lord Weston as an excuse to leave. He did nothing more or less than many other young men. I had merely focused my attention on him because he was the only man I admired, and when he did not return anything more than friendship, I allowed myself to become downcast. Aunt Charity's invitation came at that time and I accepted."

Lavinia could not believe her ears. After all the years of planning, the effort she had put into luring Lord Weston's mistresses from him, she now found that it had all been in vain.

"I'm sorry, Lavinia. I never meant to leave you thinking Lord Weston had driven me away. I hope it has not caused you any undue worry."

"I will admit I have thought more than once about it since you've been away," replied Lavinia wryly, vowing never to allow her sister to discover what she had done. "However, I'm too happy to have you back to complain."

The two sisters spent the rest of the day catching up on what had happened since they had last seen one another. Lavinia attempted to forget Lord Weston and her unjust treatment of him, however, he lingered in the back of her mind, nudging her now and again to remind her of the guilt she felt.

A sennight later Lavinia was still wrestling with what she had done. Further discussions with Barbara convinced her that it was a combination of Barbara's youthful histrionics and her youthful misunderstanding that had resulted in the theft of Lord Weston's mistresses.

But no matter how innocent the mistake, she had done the earl a great disservice and felt fortunate that the rumor of his involvement in his mistresses' disappearances had not spread or been taken seriously.

Lavinia had begun going out every evening with the explicit purpose of searching for Lord Weston. She had not exactly worked out what she would say to him if he would acknowledge her, but she felt driven to apologize for what she had done. Even though he might never forgive her, she must make the effort.

She was in her small sitting room mulling over what had happened since she had come to London when Jessica arrived, looking happier than Lavinia had ever seen her.

Jessica did not even greet Lavinia before she burst out, "He loves me!" She grabbed Lavinia's hands and pulled her to her feet, leading her in a dance around the room.

Both women collapsed on the settee, laughing. "I assume you mean Drew," said Lavinia, when she had regained her breath.

"No other," replied Jessica. "I never knew he was so romantic. He begged me to allow him to make up for all that I had suffered since my marriage. Just as if it were his fault that Thomas had behaved in such a horrible manner."

"Because he loves you," said Lavinia.

"Yes," agreed Jessica, with a dreamy expression on her face. "Of course, we will wait the appropriate time."

"It will pass before you know it," Lavinia assured her.

"I am certain you are right, but it seems like forever."

"I believe it best that you have some time to get over what you have suffered from Thomas."

"Perhaps you are right," said Jessica, considering her situation. "I want to get rid of everything Thomas touched."

"That means we have a great deal of shopping to do," replied Lavinia. "We will strip the shops bare."

The two women smiled at one another again. Their friendship had only deepened since Jessica's rescue from Hayley's estate.

"I don't believe I would have ever been found if it weren't for you," said Jessica, suddenly serious.

"That isn't true. There were many others who did more than I."

"You located where I was being held and without that I might now well be a slave to a stranger." She shuddered at the thought.

Lavinia placed her hand over Jessica's, giving her a comforting pat. "You would have been found before that happened. Drew, Lord Weston, and your brother were determined to find you. Now, don't dwell on it any longer."

Jessica had been resting at home, but Lavinia had visited her nearly every day and had told her about the argument with Lord Weston and also about the mistake she had made concerning Barbara and the earl. During the same visit, Lavinia put forth her plan to find Lord Weston and to apologize for what she had done.

"Have you seen Lord Weston yet?" Jessica asked.

"No. It seems he's playing least in sight. Not that I blame him," she said, pouting a bit. "But you would think when I am prepared to humiliate myself in front of him that he would make himself more readily available."

"Unless he has developed second sight, I doubt whether he knows you are searching for him to ask his pardon."

"You know I do not like the idea," mused Lavinia, "for I cannot immediately put aside all the ill feelings I have nurtured these past years, but I know that I must make amends with him."

"I hope you don't mean to put it to him in that manner," said Jessica, smiling at her friend's forthrightness.

"I will be decorous and solemn as befitting the occasion," replied Lavinia with a grimace. "I don't want you to think I am insincere in my feeling. It is just that I do not like to think of bowing to Lord Weston even when it is called for."

"Perhaps you will feel differently when I tell you what I have learned," said Jessica.

"Why do I feel that what you are going to say will not make me feel better about the whole thing?"

"Because you most likely will not, but I will say it anyway. You need to know before you confront Lord Weston."

Lavinia braced herself to hear the worse. "Go ahead,"

she instructed. "I am ready to hear whatever it is you are bursting to tell me."

"Before I begin, you must know that Drew told me this and I trust him implicitly."

"As do I," said Lavinia.

"Also, you must not mention where you heard this for I do not want Drew accused of gossiping about his best friend."

"Agreed. Now get on with it before I grow old and gray," Lavinia remarked crossly. "I'm sorry. It seems that all I do lately is apologize for my hasty words."

"I understand," said Jessica, "and I should not tease you, so I will hurry on with it. Drew confided that Lord Weston has been working for the Home Office through a request directly from the Prince Regent himself."

Lavinia silently groaned. She had felt certain that Jessica's news would cause her guilt to multiply.

"It seems that Lord Hayley had been under suspicion for some time for numerous violations of the law."

"You mean beyond kidnapping and selling women?" asked Lavinia.

"Oh my, yes," said Jessica. "There have been a large number of thefts here in Town this Season and he was suspected of being behind them. It seems a few days before each burglary, there would be a large event held which Lord Hayley would attend even though in many cases he wasn't invited. It was noted later that he was seen in parts of the house that were unusual for guests to be in. Then, a short time later the house would be robbed, mostly of jewels and other priceless objects."

"He was certainly an impudent man," Lavinia commented.

"There's even more," warned Jessica. "He had been running unlicensed public houses for years without being called to book for it and they found a counterfeiting operation hidden in an outbuilding on his estate."

"He evidently was a cunning man if he was able to avoid any substantial proof of how he made his living for so long," judged Lavinia.

"He was," agreed Jessica. "That is why the Home Office needed someone like Lord Weston to help reveal Lord Hayley's criminal exploits. They asked him to work his way into Lord Hayley's circle and attempt to prove his guilt."

"So that was why he was spending so much time at Lord Hayley's establishment," mused Lavinia.

"That is so," acknowledged Jessica. "He was to get an invitation to Lord Hayley's house party in order to explore the country estate. The rumor was that besides all his other crimes, Lord Hayley would buy and sell women."

"So we discovered," said Lavinia.

"But there is more to that also. Not only did he receive women from such people as Thomas, but the men who attended the house party would often leave their mistresses behind when the party was over. It seems that some needed the money Lord Hayley paid them, while others found it much easier to dispose of their mistresses in that manner once they tired of them."

"I cannot believe they could be so cruel," declared Lavinia.

"You may take it on good account that all I have told you is true."

"It isn't that I don't believe you, it is only that it's difficult to accept that humans can treat one another so abominably."

"I know. I doubt whether I would have believed it if it had been someone other than Drew relating the story."

"So everything that Lord Weston did was to help put a stop to Lord Hayley," said Lavinia.

"It would seem that way," acquiesced Lavinia. "Have you given a thought to his mistresses?"

"Of course I have. Perhaps I should not have concentrated on removing Lord Weston's mistresses, but I did them no harm. I have it on good account that they are doing well and will soon be ready to leave Hope House to begin their new lives. It is difficult for me to even consider apologizing for helping them escape, but I suppose I should do so," she conceded.

"There is another way in which to look at Lord Weston's mistresses. Drew said he was tiring of the idea of keeping a mistress; however, when he was asked to help with Lord Hayley, he realized he would need to have a mistress in order to attend the house party."

"Oh, no," groaned Lavinia, covering her face with her hands.

"I'm afraid so," said Jessica. "Each time he would acquire a woman's company in order to gain admittance to the party, she would disappear without a trace. The house party was drawing closer and he was becoming desperate, particularly when the rumors started flying and a great many women began avoiding him."

"If I had only known," moaned Lavinia.

"He could tell no one; he only confided in Drew because he urgently needed help to find someone to attend the party with him. He finally met Stephanie when she first came to Town. She accepted that the rumors were unsubstantiated. Then Lord Weston explained as much as he could as to why he needed a mistress as quickly as possible.

"Drew says she accepted his proposal and they began a campaign to convince Lord Hayley that they would like nothing more than to attend his house party. It took some doing but, as you know, an invitation was issued."

"And I know the rest," said Lavinia. "How could I have been so blind? My interference could have cost you your life."

"You helped save me," insisted Jessica.

"If my plan to keep Lord Weston without a mistres had worked, he would not have been there to help rescu you," replied Lavinia.

"Without you, our hiding place might never have bee discovered," countered Jessica. "Now I want to hear n more about it."

"You realize this makes it more important than eve for me to make things right with Lord Weston. And, dra it! The man is nowhere to be found."

"He has had to spend quite a bit of time with th Home Office advising them of what occurred with Lor Hayley. At least, that is what Drew tells me."

"Surely that is over by now," remarked Lavinia.

"I believe so; however, Drew says that Lord Westo has no desire to socialize these days."

"I can't blame him," concurred Lavinia, "but he mus go out sometimes."

"He . . . that is . . ." stammered Jessica.

"You are keeping something from me," accuse Lavinia. "What you are hiding cannot be any worse tha what you have already revealed, so tell me the rest."

"It is only that Lord Weston is understandably bitte over what occurred between the two of you. Drew say he spends his time at the clubs and gambling estab lishments where ladies do not go. Even at these place he usually ignores the women who hang on his arr looking for attention."

Lavinia felt a stab of jealousy picturing the earl sur rounded by women. "And what of Stephanie. Has h given her up already?"

"I don't know everything about what has happene to Stephanie," Jessica replied.

"Oh, no, not another vanishing mistress!" exclaime Lavinia.

"Not at all," said Jessica, laughing. "It seems tha Stephanie had come upon hard times. Her husband die

uddenly leaving her with hardly a shilling to her name,
o she came to London to make her way. She searched
or a position until her funds ran out, then turned to the
nly way left to make her living."

"If only I had known, I could have helped her," la-
nented Lavinia.

"Everything has turned out well for her," Jessica said.
'Lord Weston did not . . . Well, there was nothing be-
ween them but friendship. When they returned to Lon-
lon, he arranged something for her, but Drew would
iot tell me all about it for he had given his word to
Lord Weston. However, he assures me she is happy and
s going about building a new life."

"If Drew says it, it must be so."

"You still do not believe Lord Weston," asked Jessica.

"It is not that I don't trust him," Lavinia replied. "It
s just that I have doubted him for so long, it is a dif-
icult thing to put aside even though I know his word
an be depended upon. I believe that when I see him
lext everything will be straightened out."

"You might have a difficult time in doing that,"
varned Jessica. She leaned toward Lavinia. "I cannot
peak for Lord Weston, but from what I have learned
rom Drew, he held a deep admiration for you, far more
han for anyone Drew can remember."

"Do you think . . . do you think he might love me?"
Lavinia asked hesitantly.

"I do not know how he feels now, but before you
evealed what you had done to him, yes, I believe he
night have."

And she had thrown it all away, thought Lavinia. If
he could only go back with the knowledge she now
eld and do it all over again. But that was impossible,
o she would make do with what she had and perhaps
here would be a chance for her.

It was far too late to help her, but she realized that

she had come to love Lord Weston despite the ill feelin
she had held against him. It was beyond all reason, b
there it was. Perhaps somewhere deep inside she h
recognized him for an honorable man and had allow
her feelings to grow without acknowledging them. If s
had, then it was the only reasonable thing that she h
done since she had come to Town.

"Do you think Drew could help me meet Lo
Weston?"

"I don't know whether he would involve himself
Lord Weston's business, particularly since he is at da
gers drawn nearly all the time with everyone arou
him."

"I would not ask him to intercede, merely to help n
find him," explained Lavinia.

"I will see him later this afternoon and can inqui
however, I cannot promise anything."

"Your best is all that I can ask," said Lavinia, alrea
considering the words she would use when she met Lo
Weston again.

"Don't believe this is a good idea," said Drew.

"You worry far too much," replied Lavinia, allowi
him to help her from the coach.

It was nearly a sennight after Lavinia's discussic
with Jessica and her wish was on the verge of bei
fulfilled.

With Jessica's encouragement, Drew had agreed
help Lavinia meet Lord Weston.

"I do not want it to be a formal thing," Lavinia ha
insisted. "I want to meet him when he is unaware."

"Want to get me called out? Grass before breakfast
asked Drew.

"You know good and well that he would never
you harm," Lavinia had told him. "It's imperative th

I speak with him, Drew. You've described how he's been behaving since the Hayley affair has been settled. I believe that I can help him return to his old self again. After all, I was the one who put him up in the boughs; surely I can bring him down."

"Gently?" Drew had asked.

"As softly as possible," she affirmed.

Once he had agreed to help, Lavinia hatched her plan. She would meet Lord Weston in one of the establishments he now frequented. He would not suspect she would come to him in such a place and would more likely fall into her scheme far easier than arranging a meeting in a formal setting.

Lavinia hesitated as she stepped down from the coach. If all went well she would be face-to-face with Lord Weston in a few minutes.

"Sure you want to do this?" asked Drew, giving her a last chance to withdraw.

Lavinia almost stepped back into the coach. Her stomach swirled and where she was previously so confident in her persuasive powers, she now doubted that she could convince a starving man to eat, let alone win over Lord Weston.

However, she had come too far to back out. She must see this through no matter what the outcome. If she failed, she would at least know that she had tried her best.

"I am ready," she said, taking his arm and walking to the door of the large brick house.

It was dim inside and the air was full of smoke and liquor fumes. The rooms were crowded with men gambling while the women stood behind them watching the play, some running their hands over the men's shoulders, or leaning their hips against them. Occasionally, they would bend over and whisper in the man's ear, frequently eliciting a chuckle in return.

Other women roamed the room, moving from man to man attempting to arouse some interest in what they had to offer. Others stood near the bar, conversing with the men who were more interested in drinking than gambling.

Lavinia had often wondered what the inside of the gambling hells were like. Now she knew and she had already had her fill of them.

"Where is he?" she asked Drew.

"Take some time to find him," said Drew. "Sure he is here though."

"I believe I see him," she said, suddenly stopping, flicking open her fan and holding it in front of her face. "Over there, in the corner."

"Better eyes than I have," said Drew.

"I will wait here by the door. You have only to direct him to me. I will do the rest."

"Not so certain this is the right thing to do," grumbled Drew.

"I will see that he does not put any blame on you," she assured him.

"Do not move from this spot and do not speak to anyone," he warned her before walking away.

Only a few moments more, she thought, watching Drew approach Lord Weston. The two men spoke and Lord Weston looked her way. She held her fan a little higher, it wouldn't do for him to recognize her too soon.

"I didn't expect to see you here tonight," said Ranson as Drew appeared at his side.

"Brought someone to see you."

"Dammit, Drew, you know that I have no desire to socialize. That's why I'm here. No one will force a conversation on me and I do not even need to be courteous if it isn't my desire."

"Might enjoy this."

"I cannot think of one person I would enjoy seeing. Now go back and tell whoever it is that I'm too busy to talk."

"Can't do that, she's over by the door," he said, nodding in the direction of the other side of the room.

"She?" Ranson followed his direction and saw a woman standing by the door. In the dimness, he could only see that she had dark hair and was wearing a mask, holding a fan in front of her face. He could not distinguish the color of her gown, but it fit snugly over the curves of her body.

"Surely you did not bring me a candidate for my next mistress," he said. "You above all others know that I've had enough of women for a long time."

"Humor me. At least go and say hello. That is all I ask."

Ranson frowned at him. "If it were anyone else . . ." he began. "All right, all right. A few minutes then." He took a deep breath, straightened his shoulders as if going into battle, then began making his way across the crowded room.

"Have done all I can do," muttered Drew, drawing suspicious stares from the people near him.

Lavinia watched him approach. The nearer he drew, the closer she came to turning and running from the house. However, she mustered all her courage and held her place.

As Ranson approached, he noted that the woman's hair appeared to be either dark brown or black. He could not tell whether he knew her, for the upper half of her face was covered by a mask and she held a painted silk fan over the lower part. Her dress was a dark blue, with some sort of sparkling trim, which matched the mask she wore. In his preoccupation, he did not recognize the gown and mask as the one Lavinia had worn to the masked ball.

"Ma'am"—he gave a small bow—"my friend said you wished to speak to me."

"But not here," she replied. She took him by the arm; however, he did not move.

"I am doing this as a courtesy," he said coldly. "If you cannot say what you want here and now, then we have nothing to discuss."

A few people around them were staring and Lavinia was becoming agitated. She could not lose him now; it had taken her far too long to run him to ground.

"I would appreciate a few minutes of your time," she said, slowly lowering her fan and giving him a faint smile.

Even in the dimness of the room, Lavinia could see him visibly pale. "What are you doing here!" he whispered vehemently.

"I came to see you. Since you have stopped frequenting the *ton*'s events, I was forced to come here."

"I thought I made it perfectly clear the last time we spoke that I never wanted to see you again." His voice had risen and a few more people switched their attention to them.

"If you don't want to make a spectacle of yourself, you will accompany me outside. I only ask for a few minutes of your time, then you can return to this . . . this"—her gaze swept over the room—"to whatever you call this," she finished.

Ranson could see that she would not be moved unless he accompanied her. Taking her arm, he pulled her none too gently through the door and out into the hallway. Without saying another word, he continued to the door and through it into the London night. Once they reached